Félix Rocquain

The Revolutionary Spirit Preceding the French Revolution

Félix Rocquain

The Revolutionary Spirit Preceding the French Revolution

ISBN/EAN: 9783337227487

Printed in Europe, USA, Canada, Australia, Japan

Cover: Foto ©Andreas Hilbeck / pixelio.de

More available books at **www.hansebooks.com**

THE REVOLUTIONARY SPIRIT

PRECEDING

THE FRENCH REVOLUTION

BY

FÉLIX ROCQUAIN

CONDENSED AND TRANSLATED BY
J. D. HUNTING

WITH AN INTRODUCTORY NOTE BY PROFESSOR HUXLEY

LONDON
SWAN SONNENSCHEIN & CO.
PATERNOSTER SQUARE
1894

CONTENTS.

INTRODUCTION.

THE interval between the fall of the Bourbon despotism and the rise of that of Napoleon, during which the social and political foundations of old France were swept away, forms an epoch in the history of the modern world, the importance of which looms the larger the farther the stream of Time carries us away from it. Far-reaching as were the moral and political consequences of the great events of the sixteenth century, they begin to look small beside those of the later age; and even the speculative controversies of the Reformation dwindle down to mere theological squabbles in face of the issues tried at the great popular assize of the Revolution, when every authority, whether its pretensions were human or divine, was called upon to make them good before the tribunal of reason.

And, while the questions debated with so much rancour and fought over at the cost of so much bloodshed, between Papists and Protestants, are rapidly losing their interest, in view of the sense of the insecurity of the ground upon which both combatants take their stand, which is rapidly growing among thinking men; the grave political and social problems which press for solution, at the present day, are the same as those which offered themselves a hundred years ago.

In the Draft of a Constitution, which Robespierre drew up and presented to the Convention in 1793, I fail to discover any article which goes beyond the requirements of liberal politicians among ourselves, who would be shocked to

be considered extremists. Moreover, the *à priori* method
of the *Philosophes*, who, ignoring the conditions of scientific method, settled the most difficult problems of practical
politics by fine-drawn deductions from axiomatic assump-
tions about natural rights, is as much in favour at the end
of the nineteenth, as it was in the latter half of the eighteenth century.

Under these circumstances, it should be needless to com-
mend the scientific study of the phenomena of the revolutionary epoch to all thoughtful men. Histories of the
French Revolution abound; but too many of them are
elaborate pleadings for one or other of the parties concerned
in the struggle, not without an eye to the illustration and enforcement of the writer's own principles; or they are vivid
pictures drawn by literary artists, which may enable the
reader to see, but do not greatly help him to understand, the
Revolution. Most of us, however, can be trusted to bring a
goodly store of both partizanship and imagination to the
study of the past; what most lack is the scientific temper
which aims only at accuracy in matters of fact, and logical
impartiality in drawing conclusions therefrom.

Goethe has somewhere said that the most valuable result
of the study of history is the enthusiasm which it creates;
and it may be true that such is the best to be got out of
ordinary histories. But the enthusiasms thus begotten have so
often turned out to be mistaken; the "verdict of history"
has been so often upset on appeal; and experience drives
home to every man so strongly the extreme difficulty of
arriving at just judgments about the conduct of others, even
when he has ample means of knowing the circumstances,
that there is great room for historians who will renounce
the enthusiasm and verdict business and be content with

devoting their best efforts to the exposition of the bare cold-blooded truth.

I am disposed to think that the conception of the nature and the causes of the French Revolution, which is most widely prevalent among us (students of De Tocqueville and of Taine, of course, excepted), departs widely from this ideal standard. Its causes are popularly sought in the decay of religion and morality consequent upon the diffusion of the teachings of a handful of sceptical and levelling Philosophers; and its nature is defined as an outbreak of the covetous ferocity of the mob let loose, when the bonds of society had been destroyed by these same terrible *Philosophes*. Even the question, whether the Revolution was perhaps the result of a whole nation going mad, has not seemed inconsistent with the sanity of the querist. And yet, when the facts of history are fully and impartially set forth, the wonder is rather that sane men put up with the chaotic imbecility, the hideous injustices, the shameless scandals, of the *Ancien Régime*, in the earlier half of the century, many years before the political *Philosophes* wrote a line,—why the Revolution did not break out in 1754 or 1757, as it was on the brink of doing, instead of being delayed, by the patient endurance of the people, for another generation.

It can hardly be doubted that the Revolution of '89 owed many of its worst features to the violence of a populace degraded to the level of the beasts by the effect of the institutions under which they herded together and starved; and that the work of reconstruction which it attempted was to carry into practice the speculations of Mably and of Rousseau. But, just as little, does it seem open to question that, neither the writhings of the dregs of the populace in their misery, nor the speculative demonstrations of the

Philosophers, would have come to much, except for the revolutionary movement which had been going on ever since the beginning of the century. The deeper source of this lay in the just and profound griefs of at least 95 per cent. of the population, comprising all its most valuable elements, from the agricultural peasants to the merchants and the men of letters and science, against the system by which they were crushed, or annoyed, whichever way they turned. But the surface-current was impelled by the official defenders of the *Ancien Régime* themselves. It was the Court, the Church, the Parliaments, and, above all, the Jesuits, acting in the interests of the despotism of the Papacy, who, in the first half of the eighteenth century, effectually undermined all respect for authority, whether civil or religious, and justified the worst that was or could be said by the *Philosophes* later on.

These important truths appeared to me to be so clearly set forth and demonstrated in M. Rocquain's "L'Esprit revolutionaire avant la Revolution," when I fell in with the book some years ago, that I ventured to speak of its merits, forgetting at the time the commendation of the work by Mr. Lecky in the fifth volume of his "History of the Eighteenth Century in England," which it would have been much more to the purpose to quote.

However, I may congratulate myself on having done some service by suggesting the translation of M. Rocquain's work. The hint has been carried into effect; and the English version which has been prepared by Miss Hunting, with the author's sanction, though abridged, in deference to practical needs, appears to me to present a clear and adequate view of the scope and substance of the original.

T. H. HUXLEY.

AUTHOR'S PREFACE.

THE state of public opinion which gave rise to the French Revolution was not the outcome of the teachings of the Philosophers. The entire century prepared the catastrophe.

On the morrow of the death of Louis XIV., there were manifested signs of that feeling of opposition to the Church and Throne which, aimed as they were at the two strongest institutions of the old form of government, eventually brought about the ruin of both. This double opposition was caused by the attacks made by an intolerant autocrat upon the sacred rights of conscience. At the commencement of the Regency the general resentment was for a moment appeased, but it broke out again with renewed force when the Duc d'Orléans, who had at first appeared to discard the policy of the late King, made, in his turn, common cause with Rome. Thenceforward two parties were formed; the one included the Jesuits and the Superior Clergy, the other the entire Nation. During the Ministry of Cardinal Fleury this alliance between Royalty and the Holy See was strengthened, and all the methods of an arbitrary Government were employed to substitute Romish theories for the Gallican doctrines held by the majority of the people. Discontent seized upon the lower orders of the clergy, the magistracy, the *bourgeoisie*, and the people. From being religious the opposition became political. When, after the death of Cardinal Fleury, Louis XV. took hold of the reins of Government, it was hoped that things would take a different course. But the indolence of the Monarch permitted the Ultramontane party to regain its ascendancy, and the excessive zeal of the superior clergy stirred up the most stormy opposition.

As always happens, the opposition was increased by all kinds of extraneous grievances.

When the Philosophers came to set fire to the house, it already tottered on its base. These men did no more than unite in a Code of Doctrine the ideas that were fermenting in all minds. From the middle of the century the spirit of opposition had become the spirit of Revolution.

It is of this fermentation of public opinion, of this spirit of opposition deepening into a spirit of Revolution, and manifesting itself with increasing distinctness, that we have striven to indicate the origin and retrace the progress. The numerous brochures that appeared at this epoch, in particular those that attracted the attention of the Government and provoked severities, have been our first source of information. In the eighteenth century the pamphlet was the organ of public opinion. The Government defended itself against the pamphlet as in our day it defends itself against the newspaper. The Council of State, the Parliament, and sometimes the Grand Council or the *Châtelet* pronounced judgment, declaring these pamphlets suppressed, and this declaration involved the destruction of every copy of the incriminated work. Such a sentence was equivalent to a mark of infamy, and the common hangman was usually entrusted with the execution of it.

In the course of our researches we have sometimes made use of these writings themselves, and sometimes of the decrees which they called forth, and which were posted, cried, and sold in the streets, and nearly always included a statement of the objects of their promulgation. Those of the Parliament, especially, were accompanied by *réquisitoires*, in which the spirit of the condemned works were remarked upon, and the most offensive fragments thereof cited. Having, in the process of time, become very rare, these decrees form an important collection at the *Archives Nationales*. Until now, no one has made extracts from them. It must not be thought that all the decrees were inspired by the same spirit. On the contrary, while those of the Council of State faithfully reflected the ideas of the Government, those of the Parliament often opposed the theories of the reigning powers.

Together with the valuable and often unexpected information contained in these documents, we have also called to our aid the *Mémoires* of contemporaries, and have thus been enabled to connect the movement of public thought with that of public events, and to show facts giving birth to ideas and ideas to facts. Besides this, we have chronicled the discourses, threats, and murmurings that denoted the state of popular feeling. We have made mention of seditious writings, placarded furtively by night at street corners. We have recalled the uprisings and revolts, and revealed, in fact, not only the daring acts that sprang from philosophical doctrines, but the rising tide of human passion.

Whatever judgment may be passed upon our work, there will, at least, be found in it much information, now brought to light for the first time, that must form a useful adjunct to the history of public opinion in the eighteenth century.

Our design has been neither to defend a cause nor to sustain a thesis, but solely to relate what has been, and, in carefully reproducing the past, to leave to readers the task of making their own reflections upon the events which are here narrated.

FÉLIX ROCQUAIN.

THE REVOLUTIONARY SPIRIT

PRECEDING

THE FRENCH REVOLUTION.

CHAPTER I.

The Regency

(1715-1723.)

TOWARDS the end of his reign, Louis XIV. became friendly with
the Court of Rome, and submitted to the direction of the Jesuits,
who were its most ardent auxiliaries. By this conduct, he ran
counter to the inclinations of the majority of his subjects, for,
though repudiating Protestantism, France continued hostile to all
ultramontane pretensions. The Declaration of the Assembly of
the Clergy in 1682, which denied the authority of the Holy See
over temporal powers and proclaimed the Councils superior to the
Popes in matters of faith, represented the true sentiments of the
country. Under the influence of the opinions that dominated his
old age, Louis XIV. thought he was not doing enough for the
Church in maintaining by force a single form of religion throughout his realm. In imitation of Constantine and Theodosius—to
whom he liked to hear himself compared—he wished to preserve
the purity of the dogma and to govern consciences. The
Jansenists, attached to doctrines that Rome had condemned,
particularly attracted the severities of the Monarch.

Among the books forming the nourishment of pious souls was

A

one entitled *Moral Reflections on the New Testament*, by Father Quesnel, priest of the Oratory. This work, written in 1671, had edified the Church for forty years, without rousing the least contradiction. A new edition, published in 1699, was dedicated with permission to the Cardinal de Noailles, Archbishop of Paris. Clement XI. had eulogised the book, and Father La Chaise, Confessor to Louis XIV., had it always on his table, saying that, at whatever place he opened it, he found something to edify and instruct him. But the Jesuit Le Tellier, who had replaced La Chaise in the King's favour, denounced it as infected with Jansenism, and pressed the Monarch to ask the Pope for a Bull condemning its errors. The question of doctrine was, in reality, the most insignificant of the causes that led to this move on the part of the King's Confessor. The Jesuits had recently been compromised by certain Chinese affairs, and Le Tellier wished to re-establish the credit of his order by uniting it in a common cause with Rome. By procuring a Bull, which branded a large number of the propositions contained in Quesnel's book, he sought to obtain an acknowledgment of the infallibility of the school of Molina.[1] At the same time he struck at the Cardinal de Noailles, his Jansenist rival in the King's favour. Upon the suggestion of Le Tellier, many bishops censured the *Moral Reflections* in mandates which they distributed throughout Paris. Other prelates, not less easy to persuade, consented to sign letters, prepared by him, in which they implored the King to protect the Faith. Louis XIV., who had fallen, as age crept on, into a state of almost superstitious devoutness, and who had been

---

[1] It is superfluous to remind the reader of the differences which marked the doctrines of the Jesuit Molina and Jansenius (Bishop of Ypres). These distinctions were entirely forgotten during the course of the agitations about to be recounted. Suffice it to say that the designations—Moliniste, Jesuit, Ultramontane and Constitutionist, were employed indifferently in referring to the partisans of Rome and the *Constitution Unigenitus*, which will be spoken of hereafter ; while for their adversaries the titles Jansenist, Quesnellist or Gallican were impartially used. However, these distinctions escaped Bayle (author of *Dictionnaire historique et critique*), who declared that after having well examined this quarrel between Jansenism and Molinism, he found in it unanswerable arguments on both sides !

accustomed for some time to consider the Jansenists as "a republican party in the Church and State," requested a Bull of Clement XI., which he pledged himself, in advance, should be received throughout his kingdom.

Yielding to the desire of the Monarch, the Pope ordered a plan of a Constitution [1] to be sketched out. But Le Tellier extended the thread of his intrigues to Rome itself. A certain number of copies of the Bull, drawn up upon his information, had already been printed when it was submitted to the Pope by Cardinal Fabroni who, to some extent, dominated the Holy Father's mind. The authors of the Bull, having some difficulty in finding material for censure in Father Quesnel's book, represented that the harm contained in the *Moral Reflections*, was the more dangerous because difficult to perceive, "like an abscess that must be pierced in order to expel the matter." Clement XI. expressed his surprise and wished to make corrections. Fabroni flew into a passion, called the Pope "feeble" and "childish," upheld the document in its entirety, then, leaving him bewildered, hastened to post it in all the public places. The same day it was dispatched by a courier to Le Tellier, who prevailed upon the King to affix his assent to it, before it had been officially presented to him by the Nuncio. Such, according to the Duc de Saint Simon, and other contemporaries, was the origin of the notorious *Constitution Unigenitus*.

When the Bull became known to the public, the outcry was universal. The condemnation of texts of St. Paul, St. Augustin, and other Fathers quoted in the *Moral Reflections*, the Ultramontane maxims with which it was filled, and the suspicious part that the Jesuits had had in it, stirred up against that body the court, the city, and the provinces. Of the hundred and one propositions condemned, the ninety-first, in particular, was the object of the most heated comments. It ran thus: "*An unjust excommunication ought never to prevent us from doing our duty.*" In placing a stigma upon this tenet, virtue herself was outraged, a

---

[1] "An authoritative ordinance, regulation or enactment, especially one affecting ecclesiastical doctrine or discipline." Webster. (*Translator's Note.*)

blow was struck at the independence of kings, and the fidelity owed to sovereigns by their subjects was called into question. An assembly of bishops was convoked at Paris. Forty accepted the mandate; Cardinal Noailles and fourteen prelates repudiated it. Divisions took place in the episcopate and among the clergy and the religious societies. The laymen themselves took sides. Le Tellier did not budge. The opposing bishops were sent back to their dioceses, and the prelates, who had not been present at the assembly, were called upon by letters from the King to give their adherence. The Sorbonne, which had rejected the Bull by a majority of votes, received an order to register it. The same obedience was exacted of the Parliament. Vainly did the Proctor-General,[1] d'Aguesseau, address respectful remonstrances to the Monarch. The Parliament found itself forced to yield, and on February 14th, 1714, with the ordinary reservations of the rights of the Crown and the liberty of the Gallican Church, it registered the *Constitution*.

In the letters-patent, sent to Parliament with the text of the Bull, Louis XIV. ordered the suppression, not only of the *Moral Reflections*, but of all works published in its defence; and forbade, under a severe penalty, the production of any more in the future. But all his authority was powerless to restrain the effervescence he had excited. Interdictions, imprisonments, and exile could not subjugate excited consciences. Louis XIV. was greatly troubled by this opposition—the first he had experienced in the whole course of his reign—and, in his dying hours, he addressed the bishops, whose counsels, together with those of Le Tellier, had guided his conduct, and before God rendered them responsible for the state of agitation in which he left the Church.

"Louis XIV.," says Saint Simon, "was regretted only by the "valets of his household, by a few other persons, and by the chiefs "of the affair of the *Constitution*." The populace, but just delivered from the fatal war of the Spanish succession, ruined by

---

[1] Under the old *régime* the *Procureur-Général* combined the posts of Attorney-General and Chief Magistrate or President of the Parliament. He was next highest in office to the Chancellor. (*Translator's Note.*)

taxes, and exhausted by the universal distress, accused the Monarch of being the cause of their misfortunes.

The [1] Parliaments, whose voices he had stifled, could not forgive him for domineering over them, and trembled still with the shame of having been forced to legitimize princes born of his adulterous *amours.* Tired of a despotism that had subjected all things to itself, the nation thanked Heaven for a deliverance which seemed to promise it a peaceful future and, at least, a certain amount of liberty.

At the beginning of his regency, the Duc d'Orléans appeared to enter into the feelings of the country, and, in a measure, he exceeded his promises. He granted to the Parliament the right of remonstrance, and caused it to annul the testament of the late King, thus investing the magistrates [2] with an importance that avenged them of their past servitude. By his severe treatment of those who had enriched themselves with the spoils of the people, he identified himself with the popular grudge against the revenue farmers, and, in the face of the disorder in which he found the finances, he very nearly convoked the States-General. In the edict which excluded bastard princes from the succession to the throne, he declared that, in default of legitimate heirs, France alone had the right to award the crown ; he thus placed in opposition to the will of the sovereign, the rights of the people, which, he said, had been too long overlooked.

In religious matters the Regent appeared to be no less resolved to depart from the views held by his predecessor. He liberated all persons imprisoned for the cause of Jansenism, and nominated Cardinal de Noailles, whom Louis XIV. had disgraced, Presi-

[1] Parlements—the name then given to a certain number of superior courts of judicature in Paris and the capital towns of the various provinces, which constituted the highest court of appeal, and registered edicts and declarations of the kings. This last office enabled the members of these courts to take part occasionally in political affairs. But their functions were almost purely judiciary, and bore no trace of resemblance to those of the members of the English Parliament. (*Translator's Note.*)

[2] The members of the Parliaments were called councillors or magistrates. They will, throughout this translation, be referred to as magistrates ; the appellation of councillor being reserved for members of the *Châtelet* the king's and other superior councils. (*Translator's Note.*)

dent of the Council of Ecclesiastical Affairs. Le Tellier, pursued by public hatred, fled into exile. There was even talk of suppressing the Jesuits—a measure which would have touched popular feeling more nearly than the assembling of the States-General, for we have no evidence that any idea of its convocation had entered the public mind. But the talk resulted only in their being forbidden to enter the confessional and the pulpit. The Duc d'Orléans, going beyond the ideas of the Nation on yet another point, had some thoughts of recalling the Protestants, but he allowed the violent laws, passed against them in the former reign, to stand ; only ordering that they should not be carried out.

The question of religion was the one that, above all others, held the minds of men in suspense. Judging by the disposition shown by the Government, it was thought that all that had been done by the authority of the *Constitution* would not now be adhered to. The Jesuits took alarm. Twelve prelates wrote to the Pope, exhorting him to hold firm. In Paris and the provinces, pamphlets were circulated stating that the faith was imperilled, and condemning the adversaries of the Church as schismatics and heretics. The Archbishop of Arles declared that the opponents of the Bull were more culpable than was *Adam after eating the forbidden fruit.* In spite of laws which recognised in the representatives of the Holy See only ordinary ambassadors, and which forbade the passing of communications between them and the Episcopate, the bishops were called upon in brochures to join themselves to the Nuncio and act with him. The Jansenists raised their voices in their turn. It having been rumoured that Cardinal de Noailles had demanded from the Holy See the explanation of the Bull, the three hundred parish priests of the diocese of Paris, one hundred and thirty-two doctors of the Sorbonne,[1] and whole bodies of monks informed the Archbishop that whatever explanation of it might be given, they were resolved to repudiate it.

In the month of March, 1717, four bishops executed before

[1] The Sorbonne was one of the four constituent parts of the faculty of theology in the University of Paris, and the members of the college were either doctors of medicine or bachelors of theology. (*Translator's Note.*)

notaries a deed, founded on the declaration of the clergy in
1682, by which they appealed from the *Constitution* to a future
General Council. The Sorbonne registered this deed, and
a bailiff from the *Châtelet* [1] had the hardihood to go to Rome and
post a copy on the walls of St. Peter's. He even dared to enter
the Vatican and insinuate himself into the presence of the Pontiff,
whose slipper he kissed, and, whilst talking to him personally, he
served him with the document. From all ranks of the clergy
arose supporters of this protest. The Officiality (*i.e.*, doctor's
commons) of Paris was besieged by priests and ecclesiastics of the
second order coming to register their appeals. The Church of
France found herself, thenceforward, split into two factions, the
acceptants and the *refusants*. The *acceptants*, wrote Voltaire,
" were the hundred bishops who had adhered under Louis XIV.,
" together with the Jesuits and Capuchins; the *refusants* were
" fifteen bishops and the entire Nation."

The Duc d'Orléans resolved to address himself directly to the
Pope, and to solicit him, of his superior knowledge, to grant him
the means of pacifying public opinion. A Declaration of October
7th, 1717, informed France that negotiations for that purpose
had just been entered upon with the Court of Rome. By the
same Declaration, the Regent ordered all disputes upon the
matters that had created the divisions to cease during the course
of the proceedings at the Holy See, and interdicted the publication of books, pamphlets, or memorials, relating to the differences. This order proved equally displeasing to both Jansenists
and Jesuits, and on each side the talking and writing continued.
In a pamphlet, favourable to the Bull, the fact was recalled that
a sovereign of the Roman Empire—during its decline—had prescribed an analogous silence in respect to religious quarrels, and
that his edict had been nullified by the Council of the Lateran.
Later on the Bishop of Apt, who had dared to say in one of his
mandates, *that he was not of the same opinion as St. Paul*, published a statement entitled, *Appeal from the Minor King to the*

---

[1] *Le grand Châtelet* and *le petit Châtelet*, names of two civil and criminal
courts in Paris, now no longer existing. (*Translator's Note.*)

Major King on the Declaration of October 7th. The Parliament of Aix, to which the haughty Prelate was bold enough to address his brochure, noted that the title alone was an attack on the principle of monarchy, for it detracted from the power of the Regent and presupposed the possibility of interference with the office of the Crown, "which would be a weakness contrary to the essence of monarchial government." Both of these publications were burned by the public executioner.

Had the Regent pursued a different course, he would no doubt have been able to dominate the situation from the beginning. Before deciding upon approaching the Holy See, he had consulted a man of great intelligence—the Duc de Saint Simon. He led him one evening into his box at the opera and, during the entire performance, discussed with him the difficulties that the affair of the *Constitution* had raised. Misled by incorrect reports, the Duc d'Orléans had imagined that "a very large number were for the Bull, while the opposing party consisted of a mere handful." The Duc de Saint Simon showed him that "the main body of the court, clergy, society, and the people throughout the kingdom" were among the *refusants*, and that with the numbers, the character of this section ought to be taken into consideration. In it were found the most virtuous and most learned of the bishops, almost the entire company of the clergy of the second order, the parliaments, colleges, schools, universities; in a word, all whom the Nation counted the most enlightened and most worthy of consideration. Pointing out to him the effect already produced by the Bull, Saint Simon showed him how, in the first instance, its professed object was the condemning of a book, but that, at that moment, it had no less a design than to cause "all that was included in the *Constitution* to be received, signed, believed, and judged as an article of faith;" and that, in that way, the Court of Rome sought to rule France, as she already ruled Portugal, Spain, and Italy. Finally, he urged upon the Regent the necessity of encouraging the appeals, especially those of the parliaments, round which all France would assuredly rally, of intimidating the Nuncio, of addressing the Pope in firm, but respectful language, and speaking very plainly to the Jesuits ; in which case, the *Constitution*, with all its contrivances and annoyances, would fall to the ground. But, though gifted with brilliant qualities, the Regent lacked both audacity and firmness. As he said, he was less afraid to face powder and shot than a scheming parson. He feared the manœuvres of the bishops, he feared the Jesuits. A man, to whose shameful ascendancy he then submitted—the Abbé Dubois—increased, by his insinuations, the Regent's natural timidity.

Just what might have been expected came to pass concerning the negotiations entered upon with Rome. In abandoning to the Pope, that is to say, to the men who influenced him, the task of healing the divisions, Rome was left mistress of her own actions and encouraged in her effrontery.

In the month of August, 1718, the tribunal of the Holy Inquisition condemned all the appeals that had emanated from France, and, in particular, that of Cardinal de Noailles. Six months later, the Pope, in a violent letter addressed to all Catholics " of whatsoever state, degree, order, or condition," exacted, under pain of excommunication, a complete and unreserved obedience to the *Constitution*. This letter emboldened the Ultramontane party. Many bishops threatened those in their dioceses, who rebelled against the *Constitution*, with ecclesiastical penalties. The Parliaments of France—agreed upon the maintenance of the liberties of the Gallican Church—protested against this latest act of the Holy See. They accused the Court of Rome of placing itself above the Councils and of wishing to introduce, under cover of the Bull, that doctrine of Infallibility which it had endeavoured for centuries to establish, and which, for centuries, France had repulsed. The University of Paris which had, as yet, taken no ostensible part in the debates, mingled, in its turn, in the strife and appealed against both the *Constitution* and the last letter of the Pope. Cardinal de Noailles responded to the censure passed on him by causing his " Act of appeal " to be posted on all the churches of the capital. The confidence with which the first acts of the Regency had inspired the Jansenists began to be shaken.

The austerities practised on the Protestants in the provinces and even in Paris showed that, from that side also, the Government was departing from its first tendencies. If the Duc d'Orléans seemed to be belying his promises in religious matters, he was repudiating them no less in political affairs.

For a century the States-General had fallen into disuse. The right of remonstrance, which had been restored to the Parliament, constituted the sole guarantee of the country against arbitrary government. But in August, 1718, the Regent held a court where, in an edict registered "by express command of the King," he curtailed the Parliament's right of remonstrance and forbade its interference for the future in financial or administrative business. The following day the President and two judges were arrested and conducted into exile.

A parliamentary Decree of January 14th, 1719, directed against Jansenist and Jesuit brochures, showed the progress of the ideas of both parties. In one of these documents, it was affirmed that the Pope was "infallible in all doctrinal decisions," and it was, therefore, no less heretical to reject the Bull, than to "deny the incarnation of the Word and the divinity of Jesus Christ." Another upheld with equal spirit the supremacy of the Councils, and compared these assizes of the Universal Church to the States-General, which, said the author, "rejoice during the period of their assembly in all the rights of sovereignty." The Parliament condemned the first utterances as contrary to the liberty of the Gallican Church, and denounced the latter as a violation of the Royal authority. "In France we recognise no other sovereign "than the King," said Guillaume de Lamoignon in his speech, pronounced upon this occasion. "It is his prerogative to make "the laws: *what the King wills, the law wills.* The States-General "have only the rights of remonstrance and most humble supplica-"tion. The King defers to their complaints and prayers according "to the ruling of his prudence and his justice. If he were obliged "to accord them all their demands, he would cease to be a King." The thoughts of both Ultramontanes and Jansenists had, as is seen, gone far beyond Père Quesnel's book of devotion.

Following out his plan, the Duc d'Orléans commissioned the Cardinal de Noailles and certain bishops to unite in a "code of doctrine" such explanations of the Bull as should render it equally acceptable to both parties. With this end in view, he enjoined, by Declaration, a fresh silence of one year upon the disputed points. A few days after the Declaration appeared, the Bishop of Soissons addressed to the Regent a public letter, in which he said that, "The prescription of silence in regard to matters of faith had never been of use except to the enemies of faith." The Archbishop of Rheims, not content with hurling invectives at the little band of recalcitrant bishops, whom he compared to Luther, to the followers of Arius, Nestor, and Eutyches, nor with asking that the Church should treat them as pagans and publicans, also set himself against the conciliatory designs of the Regent, and maintained that all endeavours to effect an arrangement should be repulsed. He called upon the bishops to join in a rebellion against the Government, and urged them to refuse subsidies to the State, unless the Regent purchased their "free gift" by his complete adherence to the *Constitution*. The Parliament committed both letters to the flames. When informed of the judgment passed upon him, the Archbishop of Rheims had a Te Deum chanted, to return thanks to God for having been affronted by schismatics. Rome consoled him for the insult by nominating him a Cardinal. The Bishop of Soissons having retorted to the magistrates that the Church was superior to their Decrees, and that it was not for them to judge her, *even for the crime of high treason*, was ordered to pay ten thousand *livres* [1] as penalty. But the Regent did not insist upon his paying the fine, for fear, as he said, that he too might become a Cardinal.

At this juncture, Law [2] began to apply his celebrated scheme, and the fever of cupidity was suddenly substituted for that of religious discussion. It seized upon the people and the magis-

[1] *Livre*, formerly the monetary unit in France, and equivalent to the franc. (*Translator's Note.*)

[2] John Law, born in Edinburgh, 1681. By his persuasion the first public bank of circulation was established by the Regent in 1716. (*Translator's Note.*)

trates, upon princes and bishops. But this new and totally distinct agitation destroyed the last remnant of the Duc d'Orléans'
popularity. When, for the majority of those whom the system
had misled, the certainty of ruin succeeded to the *mirage*
of illusory riches, and even the lower classes found themselves
"hard hit," there was a general explosion of anger against the
Government. For the first time, since the death of Louis XIV.,
the people throughout Paris assumed a threatening attitude, and
a revolt was feared. The Parliament shared the public resentment, and proposed to put an end to the fatal Regency by an
authoritative stroke. The young King was to be seized, declared
to have attained his majority, then solemnly conducted to the
Louvre by all the magistrates in their red robes. The Duc
d'Orléans upset this audacious project by banishing the Parliament to Pontoise, and on the day he took this measure, he
deemed it necessary to line the streets of the capital with troops.
But the soldiers themselves were ready to rebel, and if, at that
critical moment, one of the princes of the blood royal had placed
himself at the head of the Parliament, he would have been in a
position to deal an authoritative stroke, perhaps even that of
taking possession of the Regency, for the people would undoubtedly
have followed him.

In spite of threats and tumult, there was no rebellion. Yet,
deep down in men's hearts, hatred was as strong and virulent as
ever. Then it was that those libels, pamphlets, and *phillipics* of
every sort multiplied. Notes containing the words, "*Kill the
tyrant, and do not be afraid of creating a disturbance,*" were
scattered about the streets, and the Princess Palatine received
many letters, threatening to assassinate her son. But the Regent,
who might have counted the fact of his having escaped at that
csisis among his *bonnes fortunes*, did not lose sight of his designs
in regard to the acceptance of the Bull.

On March 13th, 1720, thirty bishops present in Paris signed a
"Code of Doctrine" drawn up by Cardinal de Noailles. Fifty
other prelates, to whom couriers were dispatched, also gave their
signatures. Without further extending the number of ad-

herents, the Regent addressed a Declaration to the Parliament at Pontoise, which ordered the acceptance of the Bull by the entire kingdom, and quashed all the appeals made in reference to it.

On all sides protests were immediately raised. It was maintained that the public conscience could not be constrained by explanations which had not received the unanimous assent of the Episcopate, and upon which the advice of the whole of the second order of the clergy had been ignored. The University of Paris, the theological faculty, and a number of priests wrote to the Parliament, persisting in their opposition. The latter body, for its part, did not seem disposed to register the Declaration. The Bishop of Marseilles—an ardent *Constitutionist*—published a mandate, in which he announced that Heaven was affronted by the disobedience of the appellants, and attributed to them the presence of the plague which then desolated the region of *La Provence*. The Archbishop of Arles also imputed to them the visitation of grasshoppers that infested the country districts of his diocese. These attacks exasperated the Jansenists, without shaking their constancy. "Thus it was of old," they said; "the " pagans accused the Christians, who would not adore their idols, "of being the cause of every evil that attacked the Roman " Empire."

The Duc d'Orléans rashly hastened the *dénoûement*. He withdrew his Declaration from the hands of the Parliament and addressed it to the members of the Grand Council, who all but unanimously rejected it. All Paris applauded their firmness. The Regent, wholly taken aback, sought more effectual means. He repaired to a sitting of the Grand Council, followed by all the Princes of the blood royal, by six Marshals of France (those known to be Jesuits), and by several dukes and peers, and carried the vote. The method employed was doubly arbitrary, for the Grand Council had no right to effect this registration, and the princes, who had voted severally, ought, by reason of their relationship, to have counted only as one voice. For these reasons, the registration was regarded as null by the public, and the Pope refused to consider any, save that of the Parliament,

valid. The Regent was obliged, therefore, to send back the
Declaration to the Parliament. But in the interval
men's passions had become more heated. It was said
that the magistrates were determined to appeal from the
Bull to a future Council General and to make this appeal in the
name of the Nation. Cardinal de Noailles, repudiating the " Code
of Doctrine," of which he was the author, intended to go to
Pontoise at the head of his clergy, accompanied by deputies of the
Sorbonne and the University, to renew his appeal before the
assembled Parliament. The Duc d'Orléans, who had thought
himself sure of the Archbishop, treated him contemptuously.
" I have long been warned," he said, " that you are nothing but a nincompoop and stupid ass." Yielding to the
importunities of the Regent, but not to his insults, the Cardinal
de Noailles consented at last to publish a mandate, in which he
declared his adhesion to the Bull as interpreted by the "Code of
Doctrine." According to Barbier, the lawyer, this " very cun-
ningly-worded " mandate was nothing but "a verbal quibble upon
points of theology." The Parliament had been threatened with
transportation to Blois if it rejected the Declaration a second
time, and among the confidants of the Regent, there was talk of
suppressing it, and of instituting in its place two new assemblies
at Tours and Poitiers. Although the magistrates did nothing
at Pontoise, but " enjoy good living, amuse themselves and
take exercise," their situation wearied them. Their fears of an
aggravation of the conditions of their exile triumphed over principle,
and on December 4th, 1720, they registered the Declaration in
indefinite, equivocal terms, which meant about as much as if they
had not registered it at all. Their recall to Paris was their reward for their docility.

If, by its uncertainty, the language of the Parliament left the
door open for the renewal of the disputes, at least the terms of
the Declaration were sufficiently precise. It not only quashed all
former appeals, but forbade any fresh ones to be made, and ordered
a final silence in regard to the *Constitution.* In spite of these
injunctions, three of the bishops, who had appealed in 1717,

hurled forth mandates in which they confirmed their appeals. These mandates having been suppressed by a Decree of the Council, the prelates replied in a pamphlet, in which they protested against the Decree. Three months later, a letter appeared, signed by several bishops and addressed to Pope Innocent XIII., who had succeeded Clement XI. This letter compared the situation of the Church in France to that of the ancient Eastern Church, which was persecuted by princes and Arian bishops, and finally branded the *Constitution* as "a law full of iniquities and errors," such as *Pagan Rome would never have tolerated.*

The Government suppressed the letters as it had suppressed the mandates, but it could not prevent this double protest finding an echo in the public mind. A printed list of the names of two hundred new appellants was circulated in Paris. It was seized by the police. Another list followed containing four hundred names. The Prefect of the Police commanded the signatories to appear before him and represented to them that, in disobeying the Declaration of August 4th, they became rebels to the authority of the King. "The King," they replied, "is master of our goods and persons, not of our consciences." This time it was from the Jansenist quarter that the wind of rebellion blew. The Government displayed great severity. It flung forth orders of exile, and *lettres de cachet* flew hither and thither. The number of appellants only increased. To the lists of Paris succeeded the lists of the Provinces. There were soon some of these registers in every town in the kingdom. Like the early Christians, the Jansenists were ready to submit to any proofs in order to testify to the Truth. To the bishops, who complained of their audacity, the Government replied: "What do you expect us to do with men who speak only of the next world and are ready to forsake all they have in this one?" This movement had all the characteristics of a declared opposition, yet far from monarchial sentiments being shaken, affection for the young King seemed to be increased by the feeling of estrangement which the Regent inspired.

Louis XV. fell ill, and the Parisians exhibited marks of genuine consternation. The entire Nation was eager for news of him, and the report of his recovery gave rise to great rejoicings. The Duc d'Orléans went in a magnificent coach to hear the *Te Deum* sung upon this occasion at *Notre Dame*. When he entered the cathedral, the people within and without maintained a dead silence. After him the Maréchal de Villeroi, governor of the young King, presented himself, and for a quarter of an hour the air rang with enthusiastic acclamations. One saying at this crisis faithfully translated the sentiments of the crowd. It was the cry of the fishwomen : *Long live the King, but the Devil take the Regency.* Far from abating the embryo opposition, the acts of the Regent in every way promoted its growth. He inclined again to the Ultramontane party. Two letters, that Innocent XIII. had addressed to the King and the Regent against the Jansenists, were allowed to be published without first being approved by letters-patent or registered by the Parliament ; a novel mode of procedure in France, contrary to all rules, and one which laid the kingdom open to Romish influences. The cognizance of affairs relating to the Bull was taken from the Parliament in an underhand manner and delivered over to the jurisdiction of the Council of State. Under the name of the "Pope's Chamber," a commission, established at the Arsenal, was directed to restrain the publication of books contrary to the Holy See and the *Constitution*. Finally, in order the more effectually to repress all expressions of thought, the book-trade laws were revised. A regulation, containing a hundred and twenty-three articles, more minute than any which had appeared in the reign of Louis XIV., was drawn up. The strict execution of this, had it been effected, would have prevented anything being published without the permission of the reigning power.

Encouraged by these signs of favour, the Jesuits renewed an attempt that they had made without success in the preceding century. To the numerous colleges which were under their rule, they wished to join the faculties which would give them the right to confer degrees. At their secret solicitation, two new Universities at Dijon and Pau were about to be founded and delivered into their hands. But through the opposition of the

University of Paris, round which all the other Universities of France rallied, the project miscarried.

In politics, the Regent continued, by his arbitrary methods, to alienate public confidence. It is true that he allowed the Parliament to keep its right of remonstrance in financial and administrative affairs, in spite of the edict of 1718, which had taken it away, but in practice he paid no regard to it.

After at first displaying tendencies very different from those of the late King, the Regent, breaking his vows and deceiving the expectations of the people, returned openly to the paths traced by Louis XIV. He reverted to them in politics by his arbitrary acts and his disregard of rules; in religion, by concerting with the Jesuits and the Holy See. "Rome rules us more than ever," wrote a man, fitted by his intelligence and impartiality to judge of events; "our liberties are slipping away from us and *we are falling into Infallibility.*" No one then perceived the danger of the situation. Nevertheless the danger existed. Besides the religious opposition, which might at any time be increased by circumstances, and develop into political insubordination, the body of magistrates, chafing in its abasement, and the people, who began openly to discuss their princes, afforded easily combustible elements. Whilst the upper ranks of the clergy seemed ready to blow the fires of sedition, the *bourgeoisie* had not forgotten that there were cases in which, by the avowal of the Government, the rights of the Nation were superior to the will of kings. The Regent, by the revolting cynicism of his morals, had not only drawn upon himself personally the well-merited contempt of the people, but he had lessened the majesty of sovereignty. The nobility also had lost their prestige. Their cupidity, revealed by their shameless transactions in connexion with Law's scheme, their public debaucheries and the crimes, of which some nobles and even some princes had been guilty, caused the lawyer Marais to exclaim: "Never have the nobles of France been less noble than at this time!"

All these facts were equally the causes of disturbance, and likely, some day, to give rise to a feeling of decided antagonism to Royalty.   On the side of the Church the situation was still more ominous.   If the disputes in regard to the *Constitution* were prolonged, it was feared a schism might be caused and the Christian Faith itself shaken.   Already the Episcopate, by its ambitions and intrigues, had begun to alienate from itself all public esteem, and to share the discredit which had fallen upon the Jesuits.   Rome presented less the appearance of a venerable guardian of Christian doctrine than of a power jealous of extending its empire, even at the expense of honesty.   When Dubois, whose godlessness and immorality were notorious, received a Cardinal's hat as the price of his concurrence in the Declaration of August 4th, 1720, everyone was filled with indignation.   The Bishops of France dishonoured themselves no less in 1723 when they unanimously chose as President of their General Assembly, him whom Rome had dubbed a Cardinal and the Regent had just made Prime Minister.

Such acts could only develop the germs of unbelief, which had already begun to manifest themselves.

It was in the midst of these signs of a coming disruption in the Church and State that the majority of Louis XV. was officially proclaimed on February 22nd, 1723.

On August 10th of the same year, Dubois died, covered with honours, riches, and shame.   Four months later the Duc d'Orléans, who had succeeded him in the office of Prime Minister, expired, in his turn a victim to his own excesses.

CHAPTER II.

Ministry of the Duc de Bourbon and the First Half of the Fleury Ministry.

(1724-1733.)

In the same hour that the Duc d'Orléans died, the Duc de Bourbon begged of the King the office of Prime Minister. Though a mere man of pleasure, tied to the apron strings of the Marquise de Prie, and knowing nothing of the science of government, he obtained the place. Eighteen months later, placards posted in the Palais-Royal and other parts of Paris, demanded his dismissal.

The government of " M. le duc " followed more nearly than that of the Regent the lines laid down in the previous reign. The Jesuits were allowed to get the upper hand, and under their direction Louis XV. married Marie Leczinska, who owed to their patronage her nickname of *Unigenita.* A Declaration was issued against the Protestants which, had it been carried out to the letter, would have proved more severe than the Edict of 1685. Yet the Parliament registered it without comment. In religious matters, the thoughts of all men were entirely taken up with the Bull.

The prophecies of Saint Simon were rapidly fulfilled. Until 1724, the doctrine of Infallibility had been propounded only in letters and mandates. In that year an entire book appeared in which the absolute sovereignty of Pontiffs and their superiority to Councils was insisted upon. This publication asserted that bishops derived their authority from the Holy See and not from Jesus Christ, and, recalling the fact that the Saviour conferred upon St. Peter dominion over Heaven and earth, insinuated that the Popes had authority over kings. " This," said Gilbert de

Voisins, in denouncing the book before the Parliament, "is a "designed attack on our maxims, a work expressly directed against "the Gallican Church and against France."

The Jansenists, whom the Declaration of August 4th, 1720, had not succeeded in quieting, continued to write and print. One of their chiefs, the Bishop of Montpellier, published a memorial, of which the title alone, *Remonstrances with the King*, proclaimed the hardihood. Twice did the Council of State order the suppression of writings from the pen of this audacious bishop. In the following year the General Assembly of the clergy addressed to the King a letter, in which it upheld the *Constitution* as an article of Faith, and exhorted the Monarch to have recourse to severe measures to combat heresy. This letter was suppressed by the Parliament, but not by the Council of State. Whilst religious questions continued to agitate men's minds, there arose another cause of trouble. In the summer of 1725 bread became very dear. The bungling administration of "M. le duc," and perhaps, as was supposed, certain frauds in which the Marquise de Prie was concerned, were the chief causes of this state of affairs. Riots took place at Caen, Rouen, and Rennes. In Paris, a mob of eighteen hundred persons collected in the streets and committed acts of pillage. A cavalry charge dispersed the crowd and two of the ringleaders were hanged. This action put an end to the uproar but did not diminish the wrath of the populace. Notices insulting the Ministry and threatening to set fire to Paris kept up the ferment, and not until measures were taken to lower the price of bread was calm re-established.

One month before this outbreak a scene had taken place in the Parliament that left deeper marks of discontent. The Government wished to levy a tax of one-fiftieth on all incomes. This tax was equitable enough in itself, since it affected all classes of society, including the clergy, alike, but the country had not yet recovered from the panic of 1720, and money was still scarce. The Duc de Bourbon, anticipating resistance, resolved to impose the tax in a "Bed of Justice." Contrary to custom, he gave no preliminary notice of his intentions, and when the time came to vote, the entire body of magistrates refused to do so, saying that they could not vote on a subject of which they were ignorant. The Advocate-General, speaking in the name of the magistrates, told the King that they were ready to sacrifice their fortunes and their lives to his interests, but that it would be easier to make that sacrifice than to give their assent to edicts presented to them under such conditions. The King signified, through the Keeper of the Seals, that he *would* be obeyed, and the Decree was registered. In the same session another totally unexpected edict was imposed, in which all members of the Parliament who had not served for ten years were prohibited from speaking upon affairs of State. "You have to-day become the enemy of the entire kingdom," said the Prince de Conti to the Duc de Bourbon on the evening of the "Bed of Justice." The situation was rendered more serious by the authorisation, in the presence of the Sovereign, of the first arbitrary acts of which the Nation had had to complain since his majority. The Minister soon realised that he had gone too far, and, though he maintained the imposts, he repealed, six months later, the edicts that had affected the parliamentary suffrage.

The conduct of the Duc de Bourbon had inspired such aversion in the popular mind that, when a court intrigue turned him out of office, the people were with difficulty prevented from lighting bonfires. Fleury, Bishop of Frégus, who was over seventy years of age, and who had for a long time paved the way for his own elevation, replaced him. This Prelate's influence over the young King, whose tutor he had been, was complete. Shrewd, bland, and insinuating, simple in his manners, and apparently disinterested to the point of refusing the title of Prime Minister, Fleury was secretly possessed of the passion for power. For nearly seventeen years he exercised a dominion more absolute than that of either the Regent or the Duc de Bourbon. He was naturally fond of order, economical, and almost avaricious. Under his management the finances were placed on a sound basis, and only the wars that troubled the latter part of the reign threw them once more into a disorganised condition. His economic measures enabled him to revoke the income-tax, and the morals of the court, restrained by his surveillance, ceased to scandalise public opinion. Yet, in spite of these reforms, Fleury's administration proved fatal to France. Power remained too long in the hands of a man whose mind, as time went on, became enfeebled by age, and whose religious intolerance constituted the distinctive feature of his long ministry.

Behind the mask of the Duc de Bourbon, Fleury had been the real author of the Declaration against the Protestants, and, on coming into power, he found it necessary to gain the support of the Jesuits in order to keep his office. In 1725, the higher ranks of the clergy had protested against the income-tax, and in 1726, Fleury—who had been created a Cardinal on his accession to the Ministry—decided that the "goods" of the clergy, being dedicated to God, were placed above the traffic of men and ought never to be subject to taxation. Encouraged by this treatment, the bishops sought to put to proof the Cardinal's zeal for the *Constitution*. They solicited of Louis XV. a Declaration which should relieve them of the necessity of keeping silence in regard to the Bull. All the King's authority, they said, was needed to repress the licence provoked by pernicious writings, which affronted apostolic constitutions. Without altogether yielding to the desires of the bishops, the Minister showed plainly that he shared their sentiments. An aged priest of the Oratory—Father Soanem, Bishop of Senez—had published a pastoral instruction, in which he condemned the Bull and renewed a previous appeal to the Council General. Cardinal Fleury caused him to be tried by a provincial council, suspended from his functions, and shut up in an abbey. By this unaccustomed proceeding, he struck at a universally esteemed Prelate, who was a distinguished preacher, and a man of apostolic life, who gave all his substance to the poor. The President of the Assembly that condemned him was the disreputable Abbé Tencin, Archbishop of Embrun.

This act of severity renewed all the ardour of the disputes. Fifty parliamentary advocates signed an Opinion, in which they established the right of appeal to the future Council, and pronounced the decision of the Embrun Assembly to be null and void. The Minister, aided by Hérault, Lieutenant of Police, did all he could to prevent the publication of this document. Booksellers were forbidden, under pain of death, to print it. Yet it was found in the hands of all Paris. The superior clergy cried out that the advocates, being laymen, ought to be punished for setting themselves up as judges of the Faith, and Rome prohibited the reading of the *Opinion* under penalty of excommunication. The Government, however, thought it best to suppress it only by a Decree of Council.

This incident ended, another occurred, which caused no less sensation. It was rumoured that Cardinal de Noailles, desiring to end his life in the good graces of Pope and King, was about to adjure all his past conduct and profess unreserved adherence to the *Constitution*. The Jansenists tried to shame him out of this act of desertion. Bills were posted, offering 100,000 crowns reward for the Archbishop's lost honour. Protests addressed to him by numbers of the parish priests of his diocese were suppressed by orders of the State Council, and an appeal against the last of these orders was also denounced. In their denunciation, the Councillors of State asserted that this unusual step on the part of the clergy revealed the existence among them of "a spirit of independence and revolt," and implied that they had formed themselves into a kind of league, which was a violation of the laws of the State, and which showed that they pretended to have power to remonstrate with the Sovereign—a pretension contrary to all Church discipline and public order. Yielding to the importunity of the Minister, Cardinal de Noailles allowed a mandate to be extorted from him, in which he notified his entire submission to the Holy See, and accepted the *Constitution* "purely and simply." As the parish priests refused to read this mandate from their pulpits, it was posted on the doors of the churches. For fear of a disturbance, this operation was performed in the early morning. Officers of the police accompanied the bill-stickers, but the same night all the notices were either torn down or covered with mud. In October, 1728, the Jansenist opposition had made considerable progress. Excepting the court abbés and the bishops—of whom only eight still rebelled against the *Constitution*—the second order of the clergy, the majority of the *bourgeois* and professional classes, together with the people at large, were all ready to make war on the Jesuits. Women of all classes mingled in the strife, and became no less ardent partisans because they understood nothing about the real issue. Very few people indeed, even among the lawyers who had signed the Opinion, comprehended the doctrinal questions that formed the grounds of the disputes. But it was enough that the Bull served as a flag for the Ultramontanes, to rally against it the Jansenists, or, more properly speaking, the Gallicans, together with all the enemies of Rome, and the mal-contents of all classes who liked excitement or longed for novelty. From all time, opponents to acts of tyranny have been recruited in this fashion.

The mental situation facilitated the circulation of anonymous writings. The sale of the "Ecclesiastical News"—the gazette of the opposition,—which for many years defied the researches of the police, could only have been effected by this universal complicity. Cardinal de Fleury thought that a re-doubling of severities might stay the on-coming tide. He issued a Declaration on May 10th, 1728, by the terms of which every printer convicted of having printed "memorials, letters, the 'Ecclesiastical News,' or other works" relative to the disputes, and, notably, contrary to the Bulls received in the kingdom, would be condemned for the first offence to the pillory, and for subsequent offences to the galleys. Similar penalties were established against colporteurs, and authors were threatened with banishment for a term of years, or in perpetuity. From the first, the Minister personally saw to the carrying out of these laws. Yet his measures had no effect. In despite of the law, secret printing-presses were set going. If surveillance were feared at Paris, the work was carried on in the provinces; if in the provinces, the type was set up and impressions taken abroad. Ecclesiastical and secular corporations, as well as many private individuals, had their own printing-presses, which they worked in hiding.

Two pamphlets, that the Parliament committed to the flames in March, 1729, showed to what a state of passion both parties had worked themselves up. In one, no less a proposal was made than to revive against the Jansenists, the horrors of the Saint Bartholomew massacre. In the other, which was addressed to the plenipotentiaries who were then holding at Soissons a convocation in the interests of Europe, the Jesuits and their doctrines were denounced, and protection against them solicited from foreign powers. The last act of Cardinal de Noailles' life was to restore to the Jesuits the use of the pulpit and the confessional, of which they had been deprived since the beginning of the Regency.

The day on which his successor Vintimille—who was nicknamed *Ventremille* (thousand stomachs) on account of his immoderate enjoyment of the pleasures of the table—took possession of the Archbishopric, some one wrote on the door of his palace that Saint Antony (Cardinal Noailles' name was Antoine) was dead and had left his pig in his place.

The new Archbishop soon showed himself to be much attached to the *Constitution.* At a great dinner that he gave to the ecclesiastics of his chapter, he begged them to give him a proof of their zeal by accepting the Bull. Out of twenty-nine, twenty-five gave their adhesion. The clergy of his diocese, however, were not so docile and, before long, he had interdicted three hundred priests. The Government, for its part, had exiled a number of parish priests and others, who were opposed to the Bull. At the same time, a *lettre de cachet* deprived doctors of the Sorbonne of their rights to votes and emoluments, and, in that manner, the registry of the Bull was imposed upon the college, which went thenceforward by the name of the "carcass." New causes of trouble were thus stirred up, and one day the Archbishop was insulted in the streets.

A fresh act of the Court of Rome added to the excitement. Benedict XIII. changed the lesson in the breviary that related to Gregory VII. for one in which that Pope was praised for excommunicating an Emperor and releasing his subjects from their oaths of fidelity. In a prayer joined to this lesson, God was implored to give strength to the successors of Saint Gregory to follow so glorious an example. Through the instrumentality of the Ultramontane party, which had its headquarters in Paris, at the house of Madame de Tencin (who was no more respected than her brother, the Archbishop of Embrun), a printed leaflet of the lesson and prayer was circulated among the public. The Parliament ordered the suppression of this leaflet. It is impossible, said the King's advocate, to tolerate a writing which tends to shatter the inviolable and sacred principles of the attachment of subjects to their Sovereign. Rome replied by a letter insisting on the acceptance of the new legend by the entire Catholic Church, and overruling the decisions of all secular powers, *even Sovereigns*, who attempted to oppose it. The Parliament suppressed the letter. These exaggerated doctrines of Ultramontanism had their counter-strokes in the Jansenist camp. The same day that the Parliament pronounced itself against the Pontifical Brief, it committed to the flames a writing addressed to the Archbishop of Paris by the " faithful " of his diocese. In this letter it was asserted that there were circumstances " in which a pastor should obey his flock," that it was the duty of the faithful to defend the truth against the Pope and bishops, and that, if the Episcopate lapsed into error, it ought to be "*instructed, corrected, and judged by the people.*" It was no longer the spirit of mere opposition, but of revolution, that began to permeate the Church, and it only wanted a few years for this same spirit to be introduced into the State.

The recantation of Cardinal de Noailles, and the pressure brought to bear upon the Sorbonne, had been the preliminaries of a measure that Fleury was preparing to bring forward. On the 24th of March, 1730, he addressed a Declaration to the Parliament, which enjoined all the ecclesiastics of the kingdom to receive the *Constitution* "purely and simply," and he imposed the Decree in a " Bed of Justice " held by the King on April 3rd. But the presence of the Monarch himself could not restrain all demurs. One magistrate said aloud that the ninety-first article of the *Constitution* tended to snatch the sceptre from the King's hands. The next day, the Parliament assembled to deliberate upon what had taken place, but the King forbade them to consult either "directly or indirectly" upon the Declaration. The magistrates protested against the prohibition, and Abbé Pucelle boldly declared that the respect due to the Sovereign consisted sometimes in transgressing his orders. The King angrily threatened the magistrates, and there was talk of exiling the Parliament to Amboise. The Parliament yielded.

The public, no less than the magistrates, were startled by the Declaration. Placards were posted at the Tuileries bearing the inscription, "Long live the King! Perish the *Constitution* and those who uphold it!" A few months later, the Council of State condemned an Opinion of forty advocates in favour of those priests of various dioceses, who had appealed to the Parliament against the censures of their bishops. This Opinion affirmed the right of the clergy of the second order to prosecute their superiors before the magistrates. But it touched also on questions of a different nature. "The authors of the consultation"—so ran the decree of the Council—"do not fear to advance the principle that, *according* "*to the Constitution of the kingdom, the Parliaments are the Senate* "*of the nation,* while the King is called merely *chief* of the nation"— the sentences in italics are underlined in the original document. "All that concerns the administration of Justice is there referred to "the *nation* to that which is called its *sovereign tribunal,* to the "ordinances, *which have been established by its will* in the assem- "bled States. The authors of this Opinion speak too of .... the "jurisdiction, *sovereignly exercised by the Parliaments over all* "*members of the State,* as having the representative character of "the *public authority,* but do not leave it to be inferred that that "authority rests in the Prince as its source. They even propound "the general maxim that '*laws are real conventions between those* "*who govern and those who are governed;*' a maxim which would not "be approved even in a Republic, and which is absolutely intoler- "able in a Monarchy, since, in depriving the Sovereign of his most "august office, that of legislator, he is reduced to treating with "his subjects on terms of equality by form of contract, and is con- "sequently subject to receive the law from those to whom he ought

"to give it. Finally . . . . the authority of the Church is no more
"respected than that of the King, and the principles set forth tend
"to stir up the people to revolt against all authority."

Forced to disavow their seditious Opinion, under pain of being deprived of their offices, the advocates issued a memorial of twenty-five lines, in which they acknowledged France to be a monarchial State, with the sovereign power vested in the sole person of the King, but they declared anew that the Ministers of the Church were subject to the jurisdiction of the Parliament, by means of an appeal from the ecclesiastical to the civil courts. The Archbishop of Embrun attacked this statement and spoke of the Parliaments as the "chimerical tribunals of the nation." The advocates, he termed revolutionary, irreligious, blasphemous, disreputable, etc., etc. The Bishop of Laon, in a pastoral charge, wrote that the Faith was nearly extinguished and could only be revived by delivering up part of the temporal power to the bishops. The Archbishop of Paris, in his turn, launched an ordinance, in which he denounced the forty lawyers as heretics, and maintained that the bishops, by virtue of their divine appointment, had a *co-active power* independent of all secular authority. In the end, the Opinion was proscribed by Rome, and the Parliament ordered the ordinance of the Archbishop of Paris to be suppressed until further notice. Some months later he was authorised by the Government to distribute it, whereupon the forty advocates pretended that, by this act, the Ministry gave its sanction to the accusation of heresy that had been made against them, and abstained from pleading. All the members of their profession followed their example. The hearings at the Parliament, the *Châtelet*, and the Grand Council ceased simultaneously, and ten of the barristers with their president were exiled. As they took their departure from Paris, they were the recipients of a popular ovation. The imprudence of an abbé, who preached against the advocates, and eulogised the Archbishop at the door of the Grand Chamber, very nearly provoked a tumult. "It only requires one fool to destroy a city," wrote Marais, *àpropos* of this incident.

Some occurrences in a corner of Paris became, just then, a

fresh cause of disturbance.   A Jansenist deacon named Pâris, who, during his lifetime, had slept without sheets, eaten only vegetables and given all his goods to the poor, died in 1727, after having appealed and re-appealed to a Council General.   Around his tomb, miracles now took place.   Women were seized with convulsions, and paralytics were cured and walked.   To the people, this spectacle meant the condemnation by God not only of the Bull, but of Rome and the bishops.   The Ministry tried, without success, to stay the course of this popular religious ecstasy. Portraits of the blessed Pâris were sold in the streets and his life was printed.   All this was "bad luck" for the *Constitutionists.* At Rome a Decree of the Inquisition condemned the *Life of M. Pâris* to be burned by the public executioner.   When the news of this condemnation reached France, it augmented the excitement and multiplied the miracles.

At the time of the exile of the advocates, the Bishop of Laon had launched a most abusive mandate against the Parliament. The offended magistrates decided neither to suppress nor burn it, for the reason that *suppression did not suppress, and burning created Cardinals,* but they agreed to prosecute its writer before his peers.   The Minister, however, prevented this scandal, but threatened to seize the Prelate's property, and revoke the privilege granted to him, according to custom, of printing his pastoral charges.

In the meantime, the Parliament having addressed a remonstrance to the King on the subject of the last ordinance of the Archbishop of Paris, the Monarch replied that he would never permit any ecclesiastical interference with his authority, nor would he prevent his Parliament from using, in this respect, the power he had confided to it, for the upholding of the laws.   Upon this, the magistrates drew up the celebrated Decree of September 7th.   In this act, taken word for word from the ancient ordinances, they asserted that "the temporal power was independent "of all other power, that to it alone belonged the task of "coercing the subjects of the King, and that the Ministers of the "Church were accountable to the Parliament, under the authority

" of the Monarch, for the exercise of their jurisdiction." The same evening, the Archbishop of Paris and several other prelates hastened to Versailles to interview Cardinal Fleury ; and on the following day a Decree of Council appeared quashing that of the Parliament as drawn up "against the will of the King, and inter-" fering with the power to make laws and rule his subjects, which " belongs to His Majesty alone." Though neither the Decree of the Parliament nor that of the Council had been printed, manuscript copies were circulated among the public. No doubt there would have been a disturbance if, in conformity to the usages of the Courts, the Parliament had not just then gone into vacation. As a measure of precaution, however, the Ministry had a Decree cried in the streets, which threatened to treat as rebels all who revived disputes concerning the *Constitution.* But, in spite of this threat, nothing was talked of but the *two powers.* "One " might have thought," wrote a contemporary, "that *two collateral* " *powers* did actually direct the State." Archbishops and bishops still continued to publish mandates. Cardinal Fleury, desiring to put an end to the agitation, lent an ear to a proposal to organise a *Coup d'État* against the Jansenists. It was pro posed to arrest about fourteen hundred persons—gentlemen of the Court, priests, lawyers, and private individuals. There was also talk of removing the tomb of " Monsieur Páris," but the Lieutenant of Police represented to the Cardinal the danger of the latter proceeding, and the project was abandoned. Later on, however, with the assistance of the military, the cemetery was closed.

The hour arrived for the Parliament to resume its sessions. The day of the re-assembly of the magistrates, a *lettre de cachet,* forbidding them to deliberate upon the treatment by the Council of their Decree of September 7th, was dispatched to them by Fleury.

The magistrates, who suspected the contents of the letter, refused to hear it read, and as the President informed them that the communication of an order from the King ought to precede all other business, they sat opposite to each other for several

hours, with folded arms. The following day they determined to
read the letter as well as another that not only confirmed the first,
but ordered the Proctor-General to denounce any members who
committed acts of disobedience.   Upon this, Abbé Pucelle
cried out that if the King were at the Louvre, they ought, though
they had to break down barricades to reach him, to proceed to
the steps of his throne, and lay their complaints before him.
Some one remarking that the King was at Marly, it was decided,
by acclamation, to go to him.   Fifty magistrates journeyed, thereupon, to Marly.   They found no one to receive them but a groom
of the chamber, who ordered them, in the King's name, to go
back to Paris.   They resigned themselves to the situation and
retired.   Subsequently the first President was commissioned to go
to the King, and beg of him to permit the Parliament to address
their complaints to him.   Louis XV. replied that he *would* be
obeyed, and turned his back on the President.   The magistrates
then passed a resolution to the effect that they would lay their
representations before the King at a more opportune moment.
But the word "opportune" offended Cardinal Fleury, who took it
to mean "a time when he should be no more," and the Parliament
was commanded to appear at Versailles.   There it received a
reprimand, and after that, there were no more references made to
the Decree of September 7th.

But tranquillity was not yet restored.   A fresh mandate of the
Archbishop of Paris condemned the "Ecclesiastical News," and
twenty-one priests refused to read the mandate from their pulpits
because in it the Bull was declared to be universally received by
the clergy.   One newly-appointed priest was about to read it
before two thousand people, but, as soon as he drew the paper
from his pocket, his congregation rose in a body and rushed from
the church.   The King sent an order to the Parliament to take
no cognizance of ecclesiastical affairs without first ascertaining
his intentions.   This time the magistrates could not contain
themselves, and decided unanimously to resign their seats "sooner
than be so disgraced."   The King commanded the attendance of
several of them at Compiègne, and there gave them decided evi-

dences of his displeasure. As the first President was about to speak, he ejaculated, "Hold your tongue!" and when Abbé Pucelle advanced, holding in his hand a written deposition of the complaints of the Parliament, he said to the Secretary of State, "Tear up that paper!" The same day Pucelle was exiled. When these affronts became known, the greatest consternation prevailed in Paris. The Parliament, using the right which the laws of the kingdom conferred upon it, declared that the mandate of the Archbishop offended against the constitution of the realm and prohibited its circulation. For fear that the Decree might be cancelled, as that of September 7th had been, the magistrates had it printed during a sitting. The Government quashed the Decree and four members of the Parliament were exiled. Upon this all the magistrates, save those of the Grand Chamber, tendered their resignations. One hundred and fifty magistrates quitted the *Palais de Justice* two by two. An enormous crowd collected and cried out: "These are true Romans, and the Fathers of their Country!" This move both surprised and embarrassed the Ministry, and the magistrates were given to understand that the King had resolved to degrade them from their nobility, to confiscate their seats and banish them thirty leagues from the royal domains. At these threats, those who had yielded to the force of example, rather than followed their own inclinations, talked of an arrangement. The Government met them half way. Advances were made on both sides, and the Parliament resumed its functions. Everyone felt, however, that this truce meant only a suspension of hostilities.

Following on to the re-installation of the magistrates, a brochure appeared treating of the *Origin and Authority of the Parliament*, and especially of the annulling by the King's Council of parliamentary Decrees. "When there is a question to be con-"sidered that affects the interests of the people," wrote the author of the pamphlet, "it ought not to be decided upon by the King's "Council. The King can contract with his people only in the "midst of his Parliament, which institution is as old as the Crown "itself, and the representative of the entire kingdom. The King's

" Council is a species of jurisdiction established in despite of the
" fundamental laws of the Monarchy. It has no public character,
" and when it quashes or invalidates the decrees of the Parliament,
" it commits an act of usurpation. The presence or absence of the
" King at his Council is a matter of little consequence ; it is not
" his business to destroy the laws ; the *rôle* of a sovereign is to
" maintain them. In doing so he fulfils his coronation oath and
" carries out the contract made with his people. As he cannot
" make laws without the concurrence of his Parliament, he ought
" to put up with the refusals and remonstrances of that body.
" Magistrates, who abandon their rights of resistance before
" Royalty, abuse their trusts and become criminals."

The Parliament destroyed this pamphlet by a Decree. Its
impartiality in so doing reflected the greatest credit on that
assembly, for the magistrates must at heart have been in favour of a
brochure that not only defended their rights, but obviously tended
to give them the status of an assembly of representatives of the
Nation. Not only the rights, but the very existence of the Parliament was now threatened. Not daring to demolish it entirely,
Cardinal Fleury tried to lessen its power. On August 18th, 1732,
he sent a Declaration to the magistrates, in which he changed its
order and usages, limited its action and deprived it in part of its
right of remonstrance. It was on this occasion that a Chief Justice
remarked to the Keeper of the Seals, that by this means the fire
would be stirred up afresh. "There is no question of extinguishing
" the fire," replied the latter, "but of sustaining the royal authority,
" which is all but played out." Many times did the Parliament
implore the King to withdraw the Declaration ; the Ministry, emboldened by the coming vacation, appeared resolute. On September 3rd, the Declaration was registered in a "Bed of Justice,"
which all the magistrates were required to attend. On their
return to Paris, they issued a Decree proclaiming the "Bed of
Justice" null and void. The result was that thirty-nine of them
were seized "in a single haul." But they were no sooner banished
than the Minister began to fear the consequences. In the month

of November—the usual time for the re-assembling of the Parliament—the letters of exile were revoked, the magistrates recalled, and the Declaration itself withdrawn. Such a weak act, after the previous rigorous measures, did not tend to raise the fallen *prestige* of the Government.

Jansenist passions had been intensely excited, and the recall of the magistrates did not appease them. Cardinal Fleury was personally attacked in an exhaustive libel. The second order of the clergy clamoured for the right to be heard on matters of Faith, and works were published asserting it to be the prerogative of sovereigns to interfere in the administration of the Church. The Bishop of Montpelier prophesied *an imminent revolution,* which would set up a new Church as successor to the " present betrayed and dishonoured one."

The Ultramontane party was not less excited. Its members declared openly that they had no more to hope for from either Government or Prince. In Sorbonne theses the powers ecclesiastical were exalted above all temporal authorities.

In the face of this tumult, Fleury was anxious and irresolute, and the King, who was, it is true, only twenty-four years of age, allowed all the cares of Government to devolve upon him. The demand of the bishops for a National Council, in which the Bull should be proclaimed an Article of Faith, only added to the general confusion.

The grave events that were just then taking place in Europe stopped the latter project. France was on the point of being involved in a war. Wise men hoped that this conjunction of circumstances would create a salutary diversion. " Though war " is a scourge," wrote one of these in the month of July, 1733, " we "shall be indebted to it for the peace of the kingdom."

Yet it is to this period that Lacretelle, for want of documents that have latterly become accessible, refers, when he writes in his *History of France in the 18th Century* : "This period shows us France unshaken ; it is one of those happy intervals that history praises by its silence !"

CHAPTER III.

Second Half of the Fleury Ministry.

(1733-1743.)

THE Jansenist opposition, which had, under the Regency, been confined to the domain of religion, was transferred at length to political ground. The King's authority counted for very little with either Jansenists or Jesuits. Yet their disobedience did less to imperil the power of the crown, than the inconsequent and alternately weak and severe actions of the Minister. Not that the principle of Monarchy was called into question, but disputes were rife concerning the rights of the Monarch. Royalty laid claim to its privileges in a series of Decrees of Council, and though, in the sphere of politics, war had not actually broken out, both sides were arming for the fight.

From the religious point of view, the situation was much more serious than it had been ten years before. Detestation of Rome and the Jesuits, distrust of the upper clergy, and the inclination of the laity to exalt themselves into judges of the Faith, formed the salient features of the revolutionary mental condition of the age. Men called out that Faith was extinct, and the Church about to perish, or become the prey of an imminent revolution. Signs of dissolution were indeed manifesting themselves in the very heart of Catholicism. With two parties claiming—each one to the exclusion of the other—the possession of the Truth, it was no wonder that doubt and scepticism assailed men's minds.

The gravity of the situation not being universally appreciated, the religious quarrels were made subjects of ridicule. Comic songs, directed against both Jansenists and Jesuits, were heard on all sides. This spirit of raillery, doubt, and schism fertilised the germs of unbelief. For the first time, the term "irreligious" was applied to the century. The introduction of political discontent into this religious ferment induced the development of those philosophical doctrines which were destined, later on, to exercise so great an influence. These doctrines had neither name nor flag, but they had begun to permeate public opinion, and had their adepts in the "Men of Letters," who ranged themselves in their battle against despotism upon the Jansenist side and attacked religious questions first. But whilst the Jansenists engaged in the fight in the cause of Faith, the *litterateurs* entered it in the name of Reason. Early in 1734, these budding *doctrinaires* announced their existence in a work that the Parliament condemned to be burned, as "calculated to introduce a dangerous libertinism into religious and social life." This work was the *Philosophical Letters*. Then, for the first time, the name of Voltaire was inscribed in a parliamentary edict, though, three years before, his *History of Charles XII.* had been seized, and his tragedy *Zaire* had but just been proscribed on account of one or two truths contained in the preface. About the same time, Montesquieu was on the point of being dismissed from the Academy because Cardinal Fleury considered his *Persian Letters* to be wanting in respect for the Government and for Religion. In 1735, Voltaire noted the birth of the philosophical movement, to which he was so soon to give a lasting impulse. "Everyone," he wrote, "is beginning to study geometry and physics, and to "dabble in reasoning. Sentiment, imagination, and the graces of "life are banished. No one, who lived in the time of Louis XIV., "would recognise the French, but would fancy that the Germans "had conquered our country." The fever of argumentation, that for twenty years had been promoted by the religious disputes, no doubt contributed to this change. But Voltaire complained that the philosophic quiet of the life he led was disturbed by the "Holy Inquisition." "Since I am forbidden to write," he said, "I will leave the Jansenists and Jesuits to damn each other, and "the Parliament and Council to wear themselves out in formulating "decrees, and be myself contented to *think* freely." But on the

occasion of the appearance of his *Philosophical Letters,* his house
was searched and he was obliged to quit Paris. Notwithstanding
the "Holy Inquisition" of which Voltaire complained, no action
on the part of the philosophers indicated a declared opposition.
During the whole of the second half of the Fleury ministry, they
only occasionally attracted the attention of the Government.
The Jansenists and Ultramontanes alone seemed capable of exciting
any great amount of interest.

The war that had been foreseen in July, 1733, broke out in the
following October. Austria had declared herself against the
election of Stanislas Leczinska to the Polish throne, and Louis
XV. took up the cudgels on behalf of his wife's relative. Apart
from the short skirmishes with Spain under the Regency, this was
the first time, since the reign of Louis XIV., that French troops
had marched beyond their own frontiers. The novelty of the
event, and the opportunity afforded for the gratification of the
bellicose spirit of the Nation, caused the outbreak of the war to
be welcomed with a burst of enthusiasm. Yet there were some
persons who commented upon the fact that, after so many years
of peace, it was found necessary to increase the taxes to meet the
expenses of the war, and the Jansenists objected to support
Stanislas, who was known to be an ardent *Constitutionist.* In
place of the constitutionary quarrels, the popular songs had for
themes the War and the Generals of the army. Public attention
was thus diverted from religious questions. Yet, all the time, the
clergy continued their disputes, and the Jansenist Bishop of
Montpelier again called attention to the miracles. Though the
public had been driven from the cemetery in which the remains
of M. Pâris were interred, the women who had been there seized
with convulsions still gave way, in the presence of enormous
crowds, to transports of ecstasy, in which they became entirely
insensible to pain. These marvellous performances gave rise to
the formation of various religious sects, who abandoned themselves to all kinds of fanatical follies, which did an infinity of
harm, not only to Jansenism, but to Religion itself. "If in our
"day," remarked a contemporary, "individuals are seized with these

"transports, one can no longer wonder how, in former times, the
"different cults arose. Politics were subsequently mixed up in
"them, and thus they became imperceptibly established faiths."
It was not long before such reflections as these were introduced
into philosophical writings. Religion was discredited on the one
hand by Jansenist extravagance, and on the other by the violent
recriminations of the Ultramontane party. In spite of the prescribed silence regarding the *two Powers* and the *Constitution*, a
"letter to His Majesty from the archbishops and bishops" maintained that the silence ordered in regard to the Bull and the *two
Powers* laid no obligations upon the ministers of the Church ; since
"except when it was expressly stipulated to the contrary, the
"*bishops were never subservient to the requirements of an edict.*" The
letter stated also that, in conforming to that silence, the bishops
would have displayed a culpable indulgence for heresy, for though
tolerance might be a part of all other religions, it could never be
an attribute of Catholicism, which, being alone in the possession of
the truth, *must reject all heresy with horror.*

Since the beginning of the war with Austria, the Minister, who
did not wish to have the inconvenience of internal struggles added
to the anxiety of a war in foreign parts, was forced to hold the
balance between the two parties. This fact was signified in a
Decree of Council promulgated in 1736, which condemned a mandate of the Bishop of Laon, together with a letter of the Bishop of
Montpelier, and in which it was stated that the King was resolved to
use all his authority to repress, without distinction, the efforts of
those who attempted to disturb the public peace This impartiality, however, was more apparent than real. The Lieutenant of
Police, acting upon his instructions, burned all Jansenist brochures
and punished the printers by putting them in the pillory. But
suppression by Decree of Council was the worst fate reserved for
the letters, mandates, and instructions emanating from the other
side. Above all things, the Government tried to prevent parliamentary interference, and to retain the sole cognizance of all
matters relating to ecclesiastical disputes.

In 1737 the war with Austria came to an end. As long as it

had lasted, the public had concerned itself but little with the *Constitution.* One occurrence, however, served to re-attract attention to it.

A man clothed in a long cloak penetrated into a room at Versailles, where Louis XV. was dining, and remained in silence, standing upon one side, until the King had finished his repast. Then he threw himself at his feet and presented him with a book, which he begged the Monarch, in the name of the Truth, which had for so long been hidden from him, to read. The King accepted the book, and was about to open it, when a gentleman-in-waiting snatched it from his hand, exclaiming that it might be poisoned. The man proved to be a member of the Parliament and an infatuated Jansenist partisan. He was immediately seized and taken to the Bastille. The book contained an account of the miracles of the blessed Páris and a long epistle addressed to the King, in which the author attacked Rome and the Jesuits, and denounced the King's Ministers, who, he said, deceived his Majesty in regard to the needs of Religion and the true interests of the Crown. While admitting the absurdity of the step taken by this magistrate, the Parliament protested against the rigorous punishment to which he was subjected, and stated that it was the privilege of all its members to be tried by their colleagues. The Government paid no heed to their representations. From the Bastille, the offender was transferred to a fortress one hundred and fifty leagues distant from Paris, where he remained until his death in 1754. In this unfortunate man the Jansenists recognised a martyr for their cause. He had no sooner been incarcerated in the Bastille than the *Hôtel Dieu* [1] was burned to the ground, and many inmates perished. A month later, a fresh conflagration destroyed the *Chambre des Comptes.* [2] The Jansenists, when accused of having caused these catastrophes, attributed them to the vengeance of Heaven. In spite of the defections caused by the growing scepticism of the age, the Jansenists still reckoned among their numbers two-thirds of the population of Paris.

[1] Chief Hospital of Paris. *(Translator's Note.)*
[2] Treasury Court. *(Translator's Note.)*

In 1738, the increasing age and weakness of Fleury led people
to talk of his death as an event of the near future. Young
courtiers tried to persuade the King to get rid of his old tutor.
But the Minister, whose passion for power increased with his age,
employed the same methods to keep his office that he had once
used to obtain it. He became a more rigid adherent than ever of
Jesuitism, and, emerging suddenly from his apparent neutrality,
quashed a Decree of the Parliament that suppressed the papal
Bull canonising Vincent de Paul. The magistrates' opposition
did not arise from any lack of veneration for the memory of
Vincent de Paul, but from the fact that the author of the Bull
alluded to Rome as the absolute authority in matters of faith.
Fleury quashed also a Decree promulgated by the Parliament
against some theses of the Sorbonne, in which the liberties of the
Gallican Church were attacked. About this time, too, he changed
the *personnel* of the Grand Council, in order that all its members
might be of his way of thinking, and letters-patent ordered the
submission of all matters connected with the Jesuits to the jurisdiction of that body. Later on, it transpired that the Minister
proposed to transfer all ecclesiastical appeals to the Grand
Council. "This," wrote d'Argenson, "was not only robbing the
"parliamentary crown of its choicest gems, but it was substi-
"tuting Ultramontanism for those vaunted Gallican liberties that
"had been called the palladium of France." For a long time the
bishops had been planning this authoritative stroke, and they believed now that their fondest hopes were realised. In the meantime they experienced another satisfaction.

The appeal, which, in 1718, the University had preferred
against the *Constitution*, was still inscribed in its registers
Fleury resolved to expunge it. Some of the members at once
announced their resolve to maintain their appeal. "We thought
"formerly," they wrote, "that the *Constitution* was detestable and
"attacked the very core of religion; we think so still." In May
1739, the ministerial design was consummated. The appeal was
erased from the register, and the *Constitution* accepted without
restriction or reserve. Eighty-four members of the University

publicly protested against this acceptance and were deprived of their degrees. The Rector and thirty-four of the best professors were turned out of their chairs. It was by such inconsiderate acts as these that the Government itself made converts to philosophical ideas.

At the same time that this blow was dealt at the University, all the priests of the parish of St. Roch, who were suspected of Jansenism, were suddenly removed. For the same reason, the Superiors of the order of the Calvary, in Paris, Poitiers and other towns were also suspended, and the order of the Oratory, which continued faithful to the memory of Father Quesnel, was threatened with suppression. Though these, and other still more violent measures were persisted in, the members of the Jansenist party increased visibly. Two reasons contributed to the growing rigour of the treatment of those opposed to Ultramontanism. The despised and detested Archbishop of Embrun had been created a Cardinal and was spoken of as the successor to Fleury, while the latter looked forward to assuming papal dignities, and sought to ensure his election as Pope by redoubling his severities against the Jansenists. In his eagerness to reach the utmost limit of power, he bethought himself of enlisting Voltaire in his service, and requested him to write a book against Jansenism. Voltaire consented, and began a series of letters, which would doubtless have borne the same relation to Jansenism that those of Pascal do to Jesuitism. But after commencing the work, he realised that he was committing a dishonourable act and threw his manuscript in the fire.

All this time aggravated instances of the refusal of the last sacrament and the rite of Christian burial to all who died appealing against the Bull were continually occurring.

In May, 1740, Fleury was disappointed in his hopes concerning the papal chair, and the zeal of the Ministry suddenly flagged. As the conduct of the Government no longer greatly irritated the Jansenist party, excited passions were calmed. At this moment two events of considerable gravity turned the attention of the public from the religious quarrels. Throughout the reign the

Cardinal's cheese-paring economies had kept the finances in fairly good order. But his increasing age rendered it impossible for him to exercise such strict surveillance as formerly, and in the wake of a disorganised finance, famine stalked through the land. Since the year 1739, in Tours, Maine, Angoumois, Haut Poitou, Périgord, and other provinces, men had been "dying off like flies" after having been reduced to eat grass with the sheep. In 1740, d'Argenson wrote that in two years, distress and hunger had caused more deaths than had all the wars of Louis XIV. On the 18th of September, as the King passed through the Faubourg St. Victor to go to call on the Cardinal at Ivry, the crowds in the streets cried: " *Misère, Misère*, give us bread," and cursed the old Cardinal. Men, quite beside themselves with want, threatened openly to burn the offices of the Comptroller-General of Finance.

Just at this time, when wheat was being brought, at great expense, from Poland, Naples, and Sicily, France was threatened with a war with England, and set about strengthening her navy, which had been long neglected. Though money was scarce, the taxes were raised. These circumstances produced general dissatisfaction, and people wondered that the King did not dismiss the Cardinal, who was in universal disfavour. But Fleury had carefully fostered in his young pupil an indolence and timidity that incapacitated him from reigning. Whilst want and hunger depopulated his kingdom, Louis XV. amused himself with hunting-parties and *fêtes*, or whiled away his time at Madame de Mailly's side. His apparent indifference to public calamities furnished the opponents of the Government with fresh grounds of complaint. Even in foreign countries, his apathy was commented upon.

The dreaded war broke out at last, but not on the side it had been expected. In October, 1740, Charles V. died. Immediately the entire court party cried out that the opportunity must be taken to destroy the power of the great Austrian Empire. It was resolved to support the Elector of Bavaria as a candidate for the throne, and the following year, the French armies crossed the

Rhine. This step was a final blow to the finances. Money was scarcer than ever and bankruptcies were frequent. The taxes were again raised, and a Declaration of August, 1741, levied a further impost of one-tenth on all incomes.

The campaign was, at first, successful. Before a single battle was fought, all Germany joined its voice to that of France, and in January, 1742, the Elector of Bavaria was crowned Emperor. But cruel reverses followed. The Minister had entered upon the war with uncertain allies, and without any distinct plan or careful forethought. His narrow and jealous despotism had deprived France of all her generals, and the result was, that the French armies were destroyed both in Bavaria and Bohemia.

No great battle was fought, and such feeble successes as the armies did obtain were due entirely to Comte Maurice de Saxe, who was an alien by birth and education.

But even the misfortunes of his armies did not rouse Louis XV. from his inertia. In spite of the hatred that Fleury inspired, his activity, which resisted all the inroads of age, won for him a certain amount of admiration. For the King nothing but contempt was felt. His morals became more and more irregular. Other favourites succeeded Madame de Mailly. Indeed, from that time forward a certain dignity was attached to the post of King's mistress. Public morality reflected this bad example. Licentious writings multiplied to such an extent that a Decree of Council— the first of its kind—was directed against all books offending against good morals.

Cardinal Fleury was becoming gradually more and more enfeebled. Some months before his death, however, he gave the Ultramontane party a last proof of his favour. In 1742, the Parliament had condemned a publication, in which it was stated that a minister of the Church could not allow enemies of the *Constitution* to approach the Lord's Table, without being guilty of the body and blood of Jesus Christ. The Government quashed the ruling of the Parliament, declaring it to be an encroachment upon the spiritual domain. In reality the Minister wanted to show respect for the bishops, who, in 1740, had handed over to the Government a gratuity of over three millions, and had just voted another of twelve millions. At the same time, Cardinal de Tencin, whom Fleury had designated as his successor was nominated Minister of State.

The Jansenists, who hated De Tencin even more than they hated Fleury, were filled with indignation and dismay, and declared loudly that Religion had received her death blow.

CHAPTER IV.

Government of Louis XV.

(1743-1751.)

On the 22nd of January, 1743, Cardinal Fleury breathed his last. Dearth and war were his sole legacies to his country, for he left her without a King and devoid of funds, generals, and ministers.

All hopes were centred in Louis XV. For three years the Parliament had held its peace, waiting for the new *régime*. The Nation flattered itself that its Sovereign, delivered from the tutelage in which he had been kept so long, would repair the disorders he had been unable to prevent. "The Cardinal is dead! Long live the King!" was the cry in Paris on the day that Fleury died.

It seemed indeed as if Louis XV. were going to respond to his country's hopes. "Gentlemen," he said, to the Secretaries of State, who brought him the news of Fleury's death, "behold in me the Prime Minister!"

Cardinal de Fleury had made some attempts to effect a peace, but his efforts had been unavailing. Louis XV. had Austria, England, Holland, and Savoy arrayed against him. In face of this coalition, he was constrained to augment his forces, and France soon had 300,000 men under arms. An ordinance of the King commanded the raising in Paris alone of 30,000 troops. This ruthless sacrifice of human lives, together with the news of a reverse, experienced by the French at Dettingen, gave rise to general expressions of discontent. Complaints were publicly made of the incapacity of the generals, the negligence of the ministers, and the heartlessness of the King. In view of, the perils that menaced the State from without and within, Madame de Tencin remarked : "Unless the hand of God intervenes, the State must be overturned ;" and in July, 1743, d'Argenson wrote : "*Revolution is certain* in this State." In 1733, a Revolution had been presaged in the Church ; now, ten years later, one was prognosticated in the State.

Renewed levies of troops and taxes increased the public anxiety. Whilst irresponsible ministers played "double or quits " with the destinies of the kingdom, Louis XV. issued letters-patent, conferring on Madame de la Tournelle the duchy of Châteauroux. The publicity given to these letters drew down upon the Monarch the most offensive criticisms. But when the King, emerging from his long and culpable inertia, started in May, 1744, to place himself at the head of his armies, the discontent abated. The activity and courage, which he so unexpectedly displayed, caused a sudden alteration in the public disposition towards him, and the deepest sympathy was excited by the news of his serious illness at Metz. The posting-places of the messengers were besieged for news, and his convalescence celebrated by every sign of spontaneous rejoicing. By an unhoped-for piece of luck, the successes of Maurice de Saxe—lately made Marshal of France— caused the incapacity of the rest of the generals to be forgotten. The victory of Fontenoy, which paved the way for the conquest of Flanders, and at which Louis XV. and the Dauphin were present, added to the Monarch's *prestige*. The Parliament sent a deputation to meet and compliment him on his return to the frontier, and Voltaire celebrated the victorious King in a poem, of which five editions were printed in ten days.

It seemed, at last, as if the new reign, so ardently longed for by both Nation and Parliament, had begun. The Cardinal de Tencin had been deceived in his hope of being made Prime Minister, and the King had confided the department of foreign affairs to the Marquis d'Argenson, a declared partisan of tolerance. For some years, no Decrees of Council or Parliament had been pronounced against writings concerning the Bull, and the complete silence, so often contended for since 1715, was at last obtained.

But these happy changes were of short duration. Louis XV., by recalling the Duchess of Châteauroux, from whom he had been publicly separated before the war, detracted from the *prestige* he had just won. The Duchess dying suddenly, to her succeeded another favourite—Madame d'Étoilles, who, as Madame de Pompadour, was destined soon to reign as actual sovereign. Thenceforward, the public antagonism to the Government revived. In spite of continued military successes in Flanders and Brabant, the Nation clamoured for peace. The glories of the victories were obscured by the evils of prolonged warfare.

The quarrels between Jansenists and Jesuits, though interrupted, had not been appeased, and Catholicism found herself face to face with a powerful foe. The philosophic spirit, which had been gradually developing since 1734, was about to demonstrate its actual power. In July, 1746, the Parliament consigned to the flames Voltaire's *Natural History of the Soul*, in which the spiritualistic theory, that disconnects mind from matter, was combatted, and Diderot's *Philosophic Thoughts*, which placed all religions on an equality, and concluded by renouncing every one of them. In 1747 the *Constitution* cropped up again. The Bishop of Amiens charged the priests of his diocese to refuse sacraments to all opponents of the Bull, and the Parliament suppressed his mandate. Emboldened by this act, an anonymous writer in the *Ecclesiastical News* attacked the *Constitution*, saying that, "God had permitted Satan to prevail." The Upper Chamber condemned this article to be burned, and, in his harangue, the Advocate-General declared that the *Constitution*, being a law of the Church and State, could not be attacked without an infringement of the respect due to the *two Powers.* The magistrates, who had no part in this action of the Upper Chamber, passed a Decree correcting the assertions of the Advocate-General, and maintaining the reservations that the Parliament had always made in regard to the *Constitution.* The King commanded the attendance of several of the magistrates at Versailles, and expressed to them his disapproval of their last Decree. "I have "broken and annulled it by an order of my Council," he said, "and

"I forbid you to make any representations to me on the subject."
The Parliament did not attempt to remonstrate with the Monarch,
but this humiliation created in the magistrates a profound
feeling of resentment.

In 1747, war broke out again. During the six years it lasted,
the incessant levying of troops and taxes brought the distress in
the provinces to a climax. Country districts were depopulated,
commerce destroyed, and agriculture abandoned. In Languedoc
and Guyenne, the dearth occasioned more serious riots than those
that had occurred in the latter part of the Fleury ministry. The
resumption of hostilities necessitating the opening up of new
resources, the taxes were again raised, and loans obtained by
means of lotteries. But money was not required for the armies
alone. Building and re-building were going on simultaneously at
Fontainebleau, Choisy, and La Muette. The days of Cardinal de
Fleury's cheese-paring economies were passed! Pleasure dominated the court circle more absolutely than ever. Madame de
Pompadour had introduced the fashion of private theatricals, and
the courtiers were constantly occupied in dancing ballets and
learning parts. These expenses and frivolities, in the midst of
the universal distress, excited the wrath of the populace. To
d'Argenson—whose wisdom had been the cause of his recent dismissal from the Ministry—there occurred the presentiment of a
coming change in the political order of France. " In view of the
"slight esteem in which Royalty is held," he wrote, in December,
1747, " will any one dare to take any steps towards the introduc-
"tion of a Republican Government? I can detect no fitness for it
"among the people ; as to the nobility and the tribunals, so long
"accustomed to servitude, it is far from their thoughts. Yet *these*
"*ideas are coming*, and new customs make their way rapidly
"with the French."

By a remarkable coincidence, d'Argenson uttered these words
only a few months before Montesquieu published his *Spirit of
Laws*, which drew a parallel between the monarchial and republican
systems. The definition given in it of a Monarchy as a form of government, in which "one alone governs but by fixed laws," was an in-

direct criticism on the established system, which was devoid of all rule and principle. Simultaneously with this book by Montesquieu, there appeared another, entitled *Morals (Les Mœurs)*, which proved to be the most aggressive work that the philosophical spirit had yet inspired. "The proposition of this book," said the Advocate-General d'Ormesson, " is to set up Natural Religion on the ruins of " all outward forms of worship. The precepts and ceremonies of the " ancient law are censured in common with the rites and sacra-" ments of the new. It is insisted upon that, in matters of faith, " man has hitherto been the dupe of ignorance and imposture, and " the sport of political intrigue. Reason is exalted as the sovereign "judge of Religion. Humility, mortification, penance, celibacy, " the indissolubility of marriage, and all Christian virtues, are " decried by the author, who endeavours, before all, to deny the "consequences of sin and the eternity of punishment in another life. " He even censures the penalty which human justice attaches to " the crimes of theft and homicide." [1] The Parliament consigned the book to the flames ; but this action only promoted its popularity. All men and women, who prided themselves on their intelligence, desired to read it. The sensation it produced testified not only to the disapproval felt in certain quarters of the severe acts of the Government, but also to the growing favour with which public opinion regarded the doctrines of Philosophy.

In May, 1748, the news reached Paris that, in consequence of the Congress, held at Aix-la-Chapelle, the preliminaries for peace had been arranged. This intelligence was received at first with delight. But when it became known that France was not to retain any of the towns she had conquered, and, moreover, that she was to receive absolutely no recompense for all her sacrifices, the people were filled with indignation at the conduct of the Government in allowing the blood and money of the country to be thus cruelly wasted. The Government sought in vain to gain the good opinion of the public by organising a *fête* to celebrate the peace. The Ministry even suppressed some taxes, and thus showed plainly that it feared a popular demonstration. But the Nation desired

[1] Death was the penalty of both crimes. *(Translator's Note.)*

D

something more than this. The King had promised to abolish, at the conclusion of the war, the income-tax of the one-tenth. Now that peace was proclaimed, the people, acting upon their own judgment, refused to pay this tax. Letters were printed and pushed under the doors of houses, calling upon everyone to join in the refusal. The Ministry asked the Parliament to commit these "seditious writings" to the flames. The magistrates, who were themselves opposed to the tax, refused. The Parliaments of Aix, Pau, Bordeaux, and Toulouse went a step further and forbade the tax-payers to tender and the collectors to exact payment of the one-tenth, under penalty of corporal punishment. In the face of this agitation, the Government felt bound by its promises, and without yielding entirely, endeavoured to pursue a medium course. An Edict, reducing the one-tenth to a twentieth, was submitted to the Parliament. The magistrates rejected it. Louis XV. intimated that he *would* be obeyed, and the Parliament submitted. To rid themselves of all responsibility, the magistrates inscribed on their registers that they conformed at "the express desire of the King." But the public desired the abolition and not the reduction of the tax, and continued to complain. Men's minds were in such an acrimonious condition that whatever the Government did was taken in bad part. The peace, the taxes, the King's expenses, his pleasures, and his mistresses were all shocking and revolting.

The ferment had not subsided when a fresh cause of trouble arose. The new Archbishop of Paris, Christophe de Beamont, had begun to issue *lettres de cachet* against the clergy of his diocese—sometimes to banish them from their parishes, and sometimes to interdict them in the performance of their duties. In the end he ordered that all persons should be deprived of the Holy Communion, who could not present a "ticket of confession," signed by a priest, who adhered to the *Constitution*. Coffin, the former Rector of the University, and a devoted Jansenist, was the first to experience the effects of this order. When upon his deathbed, his parish priest refused to administer the Sacrament to him, and he expired without receiving it. Over four thousand people of all classes went to his funeral and, by their action in so doing, protested against the rigorous measures of the Archbishop. A nephew of the deceased—a lawyer of the *Châtelet*—made an appeal to the Parliament, founded upon the Opinions of nearly sixty barristers. The King arrogated the cognizance of the matter to himself, and a Decree of Council suppressed the Opinions of the advocates. This Decree, which seemed to accord the bishops full licence to play havoc with the constitution of the Church, served also to kindle men's passions. Hostility to the Government broke out with renewed force in discourses and libels. Some "horrible" verses, referring to the King, were circulated. They began "Shade of Ravaillac,[1] Awake!" When Louis XV. heard them, he said: "I can see very plainly that I shall die as Henri IV. did." A great many arrests were made. The gates of the Bastille, of the Castle at Vincennes and of For L'Evêque were opened wide for *abbés, savants*, brilliant intellects, professors of the University and doctors of the Sorbonne, all accused of writing or reciting verses against the King, casting reflections on the Government, or publishing books in favour of Deism, and contrary to good morals. Diderot was one of the first arrested, and it was during his detention that he conceived the plan of his *Encyclopædia*.

The Government having supported the Episcopate in its refusal of the Sacraments, confidently anticipated a return of civilities from that body. The difficulty in regard to taxation had led the Ministry to cast their eyes on the enormous riches of the clergy, who possessed about a third of the wealth of the entire kingdom. The subsidies gratuitously tendered by the clergy were thought to be insufficient, and it was proposed to impose upon them the tax of the twentieth. This plan was not at all to clerical taste. In a printed memorial that appeared in 1750, the bishops recalled the Declaration of 1726—by which the Government had admitted that all ecclesiastical property was held by divine authorisation—and respectfully suggested to the King that he was breaking his word. The Ministry had felt confident of the support of the inferior clergy, for upon them the bishops laid the whole burden of the subsidies. But *esprit de corps* and love of

[1] The Jesuit assassin of Henri IV. *(Translator's Note.)*

privilege overcame the enmity which the second order bore
the first, and the two bodies joined forces to resist the Government. The bishops' memorial took effect. In a treatise, published under the form of a series of letters, it was demonstrated
that the Monarch had a right over the "goods" of the clergy, and
that the immunities, of which these boasted, were only usurpa-
tions. This treatise was suppressed by a Decree of Council, the
double object of which was to give satisfaction to the bishops,
and to attract public attention to the letters which had been
published upon the suggestion of the Comptroller-General himself. Two months later the Government decided that the bishops
and all mortmain corporations (*gens de mainmorte*[1]) should
make a full statement of the amount of their possessions. The
bishops addressed a letter to the King, the audacity of which
testified to their sense of their own power. "We will never,"
they said, "permit that which has hitherto been the gift of our
"love, to become the tribute of our obedience." From that
moment the *two Powers* were "at daggers drawn.'"

Strange to say the Government did not, in this matter, receive
the Nation's support. Men saw clearly that its conduct was not
dictated by a desire for reformation, but by the need of money
which, when once obtained, would be absorbed by the Treasury or
the Court expenses, and not spent in alleviation of the condition
of the country. In the few provinces, that had preserved their
right to convoke the "States," the Assembly of the three orders[2]
pronounced against the tax of the twentieth. The Government
then threatened to deprive these provinces of their right. An
eloquent brochure—attributed by some to Montesquieu, and by

---

[1] *Gens de mainmorte*—all corporations and communities (more often
ecclesiastical than lay) which, by the substitution of persons, were always
existent, and consequently the perpetual owners of land, serfs, &c. (*Translator's Note.*)

[2] *Trois ordres* or *états*—the three "states." The first two included
the nobility and clergy ; the third, all free men, small landowners, free
tenants, citizens, and *bourgeoisie*. The lower orders, being serfs or *villains*,
were not recognised at all. (*Translator's Note.*)

others to the Marquis de Mirabeau—on the "Utility of the 'States' of the Provinces" replied to this threat. The Paris Parliament, which had been reproached for agreeing to the tax, raised its voice at last, and seized the occasion of the renewal of certain taxes to remonstrate with the King in terms he was little accustomed to hear, concerning the distress of the people and the prodigality of the Court.

In the meantime, events took place in Paris which might have had most serious consequences. The Government, wishing to increase the population of some of the colonies, had dispatched thither batches of " unfortunate " girls and vagrants. Later on the police—no doubt exceeding their instructions—carried off some of the children of the working-classes. As soon as these raids became known, there occurred a more violent revolt than any that had taken place throughout the reign. Several constables of the police were killed. The crowd swooped down upon the house of the Lieutenant of Police, and, in its fury, would have murdered him, had he not saved his own life by surrendering to the rioters one of his officers. During this period of excitement, the people talked of burning Versailles, which, they said, had been erected at their expense. The Government, not wishing to assume the responsibility of the reprehensible action of the police, refused to believe in the culpability of its agents and hanged three of the rioters. Strenuous precautions were taken to protect the hangman in his work. Just as the execution was about to take place, some voices cried " Mercy ! " and the military immediately charged the crowd with their bayonets. The injustice and cruelty of this *dénouement* sowed fresh seeds of hatred among the lower orders. The upper classes, while they pitied the three victims, were not sorry to see them made an example of. " We must not let the people know their power," they said. For the first time a presentiment of coming disaster was generally felt.

Discontent was rampant ; yet, though all classes complained aloud of the Government, the police could only spy upon the people. If they had begun to make arrests, they would have had to take the whole of Paris into custody. According to d'Argenson, the spirit of revolt was eating "like gangrene" into the national life. People began to hold their own opinions concerning the Government, and to claim that the men who were invested with public authority "ought to repay" the Nation by bestowing upon it "abundance, happiness, and justice." The introduction into the language of new forms of expression was not without its significance. The King received frequent sinister warnings. "Thou "goest to Choisy. Have a care that thou goest not to St. "Denis,"[1] were words printed on some bills posted inside the Palace of Versailles.

In the beginning of the year 1751, another case of a refusal of the Sacrament to a prominent Jansenist, denounced by the Parliament, but supported by the Government, increased the antagonism of the people to the superior clergy. Persons, the least disposed to take part in the discussions, gave it as their opinion that it was "dangerous thus to control all liberty of con-"science, and that persistence in such a system of intolerance might "be the cause, one day, of a *revolution* in favour of Protestantism." At the same time severe measures were prescribed against the Protestants. Special pains were taken to show the clergy that the Government's designs on their property would not diminish its zeal for the faith. But, in the estimation of the bishops, an attack on the temporality of the Church was equivalent to an assault on Religion itself. A Papal brief having implicitly condemned the intentions of the Ministry, the Government feared opposition from Rome and began to parley with the bishops. Instead of the enforcement of the "twentieth," an arrangement was arrived at, whereby the clergy's *gift* was increased to an annual payment of ten millions. In default of the resources anticipated from the clergy, the Government was thrown back upon the Nation. Not daring to create new taxes, it had recourse to the issue of a loan. Three times did the Parliament remonstrate with the King concerning this step, but the Edicts creating the loan were finally registered "at the King's express command." Though this regis-

[1] The burial vaults of the Kings of France are in St. Denis Cathedral. (*Translator's Note.*)

tration was only effected by a majority of ten votes, the public took it in bad part. Everyone commented upon the immoderate expenses of the Court. The incessant journeyings, the *fêtes*, plays, and the constant building and rebuilding of palaces, together with the gifts and pensions accorded by the Crown, absorbed such enormous sums, that, without paying his household expenses, and owing two years' pay to the various Parliaments, Louis XV. spent in one year the revenues of the next. It was no longer mere prodigality, the people said, it was pillage.

A dispute, most imprudently promoted by the Archbishop of Paris, followed hard upon the issue of the loans. This Prelate wished to have the control of the ecclesiastical appointments to the Paris hospitals, which control had previously been in the hands of the administration, and he obtained from the King a Declaration changing the regulations of these establishments. The Parliament registered the Declaration with restrictions that altered its spirit. The King annulled the restrictions by a Decree of Council and informed the magistrates that, though he permitted their remonstrances, he had not given them the right to introduce modifications that completely changed the character of his Edicts. The magistrates dared to reply that, "according to the funda-" mental laws of the State, modifications introduced into Decrees at "their registration remained inseparable to them."

The political questions that these debates gave rise to soon obscured their original cause. As in 1732, the magistrates threatened to send in their resignations, and in the Court circle there was talk of suppressing the Parliament altogether. Called upon, on several different occasions, to register the Declaration in its entirety, the magistrates persisted in their refusal.

The King, in his annoyance, arrogated the cognizance of all matters connected with the hospitals to himself and forbade the magistrates to take any notice of them. More than this, he demanded to see the parliamentary registers, and with his own hand erased all records of the matter. The magistrates ceased their functions. The Ministry, anticipating trouble, hastened to announce a diminution of taxes. This precipitate act betokened fear on the part of the Government; nevertheless, at the King's injunction, the Parliament resumed its duties, but maintained its right of deliberation, prohibited the removal of its registers in the future, and retracted none of its previous protests. Upon this the Government, by letters-patent, transferred the surveillance of the hospitals to the Grand Council. These letters were issued privately for fear of displeasing the public. The whole affair lasted several months and occupied the attention of all Paris, including even the common people. The Parliament itself seemed inspired with the spirit of revolt.

Public sentiment could be fairly gauged by the complete indifference of the populace to the announcement of the birth of a son to the Dauphin. On the occasion of the *fêtes* that celebrated this event, Louis XV. showed himself on the balcony of the Town Hall, but not a cheer was raised. The officers of the guard threw money among the people, telling them to shout, but with no result. Even the strangers in Paris remarked the silence. It was obvious that "the people no longer loved the Kings whom they had loved so long." When the Dauphin and Dauphiness went to *Notre Dame* to thank God for giving them a son, they found themselves surrounded by two thousand women, some of whom cried: "Give us bread, we are dying of hunger!" and others, "Dismiss the harlot who governs the nation. If she remain there "will soon be nothing left of us to preserve as relics."

In the provinces the distress had reached a climax and was occasioning riots in Rennes, Bordeaux, Languedoc, and Touraine. At Arles troops of armed peasants presented themselves at the Town Hall and demanded bread. At the same time, threatening placards multiplied against Louis XV. and the Pompadour.

In the face of this critical situation the necessity for a change in the political regimen of France was widely felt. Among men of reflective minds it was a frequent subject of discussion, and the method of this change was expressed in the one word *Revolution.*

" Nothing is talked of but the necessity for a speedy Revolution," wrote d'Argenson in May, 1751. Many who were averse to all forms of violence judged it impossible for a reform to be carried out by pacific means. But there were others who thought a Revolution could be affected by acclamation; so widespread was the discontent. The country was in such an inflammable state that any riot might have been transformed into a rebellion and that rebellion into a Revolution.

Yet, notwithstanding that Republican ideas were already entertained, it was not proposed to do away with Royalty, but to circumscribe its power. The theory held was that princes reigned over their people by virtue of a contract, real or supposed, which both parties were bound to respect. One of the reforms most wished for was the restriction of the King to a civil list, after the manner practised in England. It was desired above all to separate the Ministry from the pernicious influences of the Court. The alterations proposed for the general political condition consisted in the introduction of Government by Provincial States and States-General. It was the aim of the reformers to re-establish on a wide basis the institutions that Royalty had itself overthrown. These proposals were freely discussed in public places. One day a monk overheard two persons talking in the gardens of the Luxembourg. One said: "It is most opportune that the Govern-"ment oppresses the clergy; these violent measures *hasten the* "*Revolution.*"

At the time these words were uttered, Voltaire was in Prussia at work on his *Century of Louis XIV.;* Diderot had produced only one volume of the *Encyclopedia ;* seven years were to go by before Helvetius published his book on *The Mind;* Rousseau was only known by the discourse which procured him the prize at the Dijon Academy; Raynal was but just emerging from obscurity; Grimm had not begun his *Literary Correspondence ;* d'Holbach had written nothing, and Buffon had published only three or four volumes of his *Natural History.* These facts completely falsify the statements, so often made, that the philosophers were the instigators of the Revolution.

CHAPTER V.

Government of Louis XV.

(1752-1754.)

THE general excitement of the times had transformed France into a theatre, where unexpected scenes continually succeeded each other, and hurried on both actors and spectators, with ever increasing swiftness, to a final *dénouement.*

In January, 1752, the Sorbonne, which still went by the invidious name of the "carcass," condemned a thesis which it had previously applauded, but which, after a more careful examination, it deemed heretical. This thesis was a dissertation by the Abbé de Prades, one of the collaborators of the *Encyclopedia.* In one of his propositions, the author maintained that the miracles of Jesus Christ, apart from the prophecies which announced His mission, no more proved the truth of Religion than the cures of Æsculapius did. The affair was considered serious enough to demand the intervention of the Archbishop of Paris. "People no longer confine themselves," wrote the Prelate in his mandate, "to attacking single dogmas of Christianity, they glory "in opposing all its mysteries. Every year impious brochures, de-"testable libels, and volumes filled with errors and blasphemies "appear. Some audacious writers have concerted together to con-"secrate their talents and their labours to the preparation of poisons, "and they have, perhaps, succeeded beyond their expectations." These last lines were directed against the authors of the *Ency-clopedia.* It could not have been stated in clearer terms that Catholicism, with its dogmas and mysteries, was being menaced by public opinion. All possible publicity was given to this mandate. It was cried in the streets and "sold cheap." Similar mandates by other bishops also appeared. Never had writings of that nature created such a sensation. The Abbé's thesis became the common topic of conversation. Wise men regretted the publicity that spread abroad the knowledge of doctrines hostile to Religion. " The thesis had been condemned by the Sorbonne," they said ; "that should have sufficed. The *Encyclopædia* is a rare " book, expensive, and treating of abstract subjects. It could only "have been read by men of intellect and scientific propensities, the " number of whom is small. What is the good of a mandate that " whets the curiosity of the faithful, and instructs them in methods " of reasoning which may turn them ultimately into philosophers ? " The mandate had been issued at the instigation of the Jesuits, who, in casting reflections upon the Abbé, wished to discountenance the *Encyclopædia.* Nevertheless, the second instalment of that work was published, but there appeared immediately a Decree of Council suppressing both volumes. " His Majesty "notes," so ran the Decree, "that in these two volumes are inserted " various maxims tending to the destruction of the Royal authority, "to the establishment of a spirit of independence and revolt, and, by " use of equivocal terms, to the laying of the foundation stones of " error, corrupt morals, irreligion, and scepticism." The formulation of these sweeping statements was another Jesuit task. The Ministry did more than suppress the *Encyclopædia.* A *lettre de cachet* laid Diderot under the obligation of delivering up all the manuscripts of his great work, but he—having no desire for a second term of imprisonment—left Paris in haste.

In the end the Jesuits triumphed. Their object in raising the storm had been to reduce to silence all the first authors in Paris, and to start a similar inquisition in the realm of thought to that they had already established in the domain of conscience. It was the Jesuits who had overruled the Ministry in the dispute about the " twentieth." It was they also, who, in the recent debates upon the subject of the hospitals, had backed up the Archbishop and humiliated the Parliament. At Court, where they had managed to regain their ascendancy, they had allies in the princes of the blood and the majority of the ministers. They

had also won over to their cause Madame de Pompadour, who
was, at this time, playing the devotee, and who had submitted to
their decision the grave question whether she might continue to
live with the King as his "friend" after having been his mistress.
In March, 1752, the last Sacrament was refused to an aged priest
—Le Mère—because he was unable to produce a "ticket of confession." This refusal led to a train of circumstances similar to
those that had occurred at the demise of the former Rector of the
University. In the end, the poor old priest died without having
received the Viaticum, and the King upheld the Archbishop in
the action he had persisted in taking. This affair produced a
disturbance in Paris greater than any that had occurred since
the times of the civil wars. "There was stirred up," wrote
d'Argenson, "a feeling of hatred for the King and contempt of
"the Government that foreboded nothing but ill." Four thousand
persons had attended Coffin's funeral, ten thousand were present
at that of Le Mère.

The obsequies were barely concluded when other refusals of
Sacraments took place. The magistrates, in remonstrating with
the King, called his attention to the disorders which the *Constitution* had introduced into the Church, and pointed out that
these disorders were the causes of the rapid increase of impiety.
They complained, too, that the bishops, in the name of a Bull,
that openly attacked the liberties of France, were raising "the
"standard of schism." "Nothing," they declared, "was more
"threatening to a State than religious dissensions, and, for their
"part, they were determined to continue to draw attention to the
"perils of the situation." The first President, in a consultation
that he had with Louis XV., said to him, with tears in his eyes:
"Sire, you are being deceived; you should know the truth.
"Schism dethrones Kings more easily than whole armies can uphold
"them." The magistrates did more than remonstrate. Assured of
the support of public opinion, and that of the provincial Parliaments, they resolved to act. On the 18th of April, they issued a
standing order forbidding "all ecclesiastics to commit any act
"tending to promote schism, and especially that of refusing Sacra-

" ments in default of presentation of ' tickets of confession,' or
" submission to the Unigenitus Bull." The penalty for those who
disobeyed this order was prosecution as disturbers of the public
peace, and punishment according to the full rigour of the law.
This Decree was put through the press the same night that it
was drawn up, and, at five o'clock the following morning, it was
posted at all the street corners. The public received it with
transports of delight. Ten thousand copies were sold in Paris
alone. Every purchaser called it his "ticket of confession," and
some had their copies framed. In the face of this demonstration,
the Government did not venture to overrule the magistrates'
Decree, but, in the desire to propitiate both parties, ordered a
general silence in regard to the matter. The magistrates decided to
send a "grand deputation" to inform the Monarch that the Parliament, "animated by that fidelity, which does not hesitate, in
" order to serve its Sovereign, to express at times its indignation at
" the King's conduct, was determined to relinquish its functions
" sooner than let the Archbishop pursue unpunished his schismatic
" manœuvres." The Monarch's response was composed of denunciations and threats. The magistrates registered it, but passed a
Decree maintaining the liberty of their resolutions. All sections
of the public approved the resistance of the magistrates and
violently attacked the conduct of the Archbishop. When the
" grand deputation " returned to Paris, the people gathered in
crowds on the quays and clapped their hands as the magistrates
passed. Whilst this agitation was going on, disturbances of
another kind were occurring throughout the kingdom. Fresh
revolts, occasioned by the scarcity of bread, broke out at
Languedoc, Guyenne, Auvergne, Dauphiné and Normandy, and
the Government had to send troops to Rouen and Mans against
the rioters. Everything conspired to inflame the passions of the
populace.

The clergy became at length so greatly exasperated by the
growing audacity of the Parliament, that they tried by all means
in their power to alienate the public sympathy from it. In the
provinces, many bishops preached publicly against the magistrates.

On the 10th of June, nineteen prelates united in signing a
petition, begging the King to punish the men who had dared to
call the Archbishop of Paris a schismatic. The Parliament replied
to these attacks by issuing Decrees against all " writings " of the
bishops. In the same month, it burned a Latin manifesto, attributed to the Archbishop of Paris, that commenced with the
words, *Ira Dei ascendit super nos.* In this the clergy were
charged to remember that " all the laws of the secular powers
" that were opposed to the precepts and authority of the Church
" were usurpatory and criminal," and that " God was to be obeyed
" before man." Ridicule found a part in these agitations. In a
libel entitled, " Petition of the farmers-general of this realm to
" the King," it was suggested that the " tickets of confession "
should be issued on stamped paper and subjected to the control
of the authorities. The King, so the libel affirmed, would thus
be more thoroughly assured of the piety of his subjects, and an
abundant source of revenue would be obtained for the Treasury.
Besides this, the " tickets of confession " were compared to " per-
mits of transit," and it was added that, if they had existed in
olden times, no doubt Jesus would not have given the communion
to Judas. This squib obtained such a success that copies were
circulated freely in Paris, the provinces, and abroad.

Every day complaints reached the magistrates of fresh refusals
of the Sacraments. In order to give more importance to its
deliberations, the Parliament never sat unless all chambers were
assembled. Thus united, it became a national body, so far ap-
proximating the ideal of the States-General and the English Parliament. On the 19th of August it issued a Decree of banishment
from Paris for three years against a curate of the parish of St. Étienne
du Mont. This daring order was quashed by a Decree of Council
that was cried in the streets on the 22nd. The same day, and at
the same hour, the Parliament had its Decree cried, so that both
Edicts were being published at once, as if they were the productions
of " two equal powers that overlapped in their operations." The
following day the parliamentary Decree was cried again, and a
fresh edition printed—the supply of copies not being equal to

the demand. The likely consequences of all this disorder did not escape the notice of men of reflective minds. " Bit by bit every- "thing is going," wrote d'Argenson. " Public opinion stirs, it "grows, it strengthens, and may bring about a *national revolution.*"

The bishops, having just voted to the Government the "free gift" of eleven millions, took advantage of the Parliament being in vacation to solicit anew the annulling of the Decree of April 18th, which offended equally against their authority, their honour, and their religion. The Government yielded to their wishes and, by a decision of Council, quashed the Decree as encroaching on the legislative power "that belongs to the King alone." But the orders, which had sprung from this Decree, were not cancelled, and the Parliament was allowed to retain the cognizance of all abuses of office, of which the clergy might be found guilty. This decision pleased neither bishops nor magistrates. As soon as the latter had resumed their sessions, they found the *Ira Dei ascendit,* which they had condemned to be burned in the previous July, posted in the sacristies of all the Paris churches. The refusal of Sacraments began again with renewed vigour. A priest, having refused the Viaticum to a Sister Perpétue of the community of St. Agatha, the Parliament ordered his arrest, and requested the Archbishop of Paris to provide without delay for the administra- tion of the Sacrament to the dying woman. This request not being complied with, the Parliament convoked the assemblage of his peers to judge the Archbishop and ordered the seizure of his "goods." The King evoked the matter, granted the prelate the right to replevy his property and forbade the peers to assemble. Shortly afterwards, upon the demand of the Archbishop, he ordered Sister Perpétue to be seized by the police. This time the Episcopate appeared to triumph. Again and again the magi- strates protested against the act of violence of which the Sister had been the object. In regard to the Archbishop, they main- tained that he could be tried only by his peers, and the King, in constituting himself the judge, broke the laws of his country. It was thus that simple questions of catechism degenerated not only into religious quarrels, but into differences of opinion on matters of law. The first President, who, upon these several occasions, was made the spokesman of the Parliament, assumed the attitude of the leader of a revolt, who received his authority from the Nation and not from the King.

The Parliament soon entered into another dispute with the Crown. A refusal of the Sacraments took place at Orléans, and the bishop of the diocese was ordered to pay a fine of six thousand *livres.* The King immediately evoked the affair and quashed the judgment by a Decree of Council. A notice of this ruling was thereupon sent to the magistrates' clerk by an usher of the Council. In this process, the magistrates detected a violation of the forms established by law, and were so bold as to ask the King to destroy both *the original and the copy of the notice.* A fresh scandal having arisen at Orléans, the Parliament summoned the bishop to appear before it. The King, determined to put an end to this sort of action, issued letters-patent, ordering the Parliament to refrain from all action in regard to refusals of Sacraments. The magistrates declined to register these letters until the presentation of their *Grand Remonstrances,* which were then being drawn up, and they continued, as before, to take cognizance of all abuses.

Decree after Decree—condemning both persons and " writings " —emanated from the Parliament. A Sorbonne thesis, containing Ultramontane doctrines, having been pronounced against, two members were sent to inscribe the judgment on the College registers. The King annulled this registration, and the magistrates replied by a Decree enjoining instruction in all the Universities upon the four propositions of the Assembly of the Clergy in 1682. The excitement was so great that, if the Council had revoked this last Decree, sixty voices were ready to accuse the Chancellor of the crime of high treason. As if these troubles were not enough, the Government itself increased the general agitation by its rigorous proceedings against the Protestants. In Paris the people were being more and more ground down by the taxes. From the 20th January to the 20th February, 1753, eight hundred persons died of want in the Faubourg St. Antoine alone. Louis XV., more annoyed than troubled by these events, entered only nominally into the decisions of his ministers, and allowed his "friend," Madame de Pompadour, to reign in his stead, while he found distraction in the disgraceful mysteries of the *Parc aux Cerfs*.

By April 9th, the *Grand Remonstrances* were completed. They formed a complete treatise of twenty-three articles. Even before they were printed, copies were ordered for circulation throughout Europe. The King, on being informed of the Parliament's intention of presenting them, refused to hear them so long as his letters-patent remained unregistered. The magistrates declined to subscribe to this condition. The King took offence, and commanded them anew to register the letters, forbidding them, under pain of rousing his indignation, to take cognizance of matters relating to the Sacraments. The Parliament replied with one voice that they could not *obey* without failing in their duty and breaking their vows. What was there for it but to use force? On the nights of the 8th and 9th of May, musketeers were employed as bearers to the magistrates of *lettres de cachet*, which sent them into exile and gave them only twenty-four hours' notice to quit Paris. The Ministry had flattered itself that the members of the Upper Chamber, by reason of their age and the pensions they received from the Court, would be more docile, but to the great satisfaction of the public, these declared openly that they shared their colleagues' sentiments. Upon this, the Upper Chamber was transferred from Paris to Pontoise.

The disgrace of the Parliament seemed to destroy the last vestige of national liberty. All Paris was in an uproar, and the Government feared a revolt. For eight nights the entire body of police patrolled the city, ready to act if occasion offered. The Palace of the Archbishop was shut up and guarded by soldiers. In divers public places, bills were seized bearing the words : "Long "live the Parliament! Down with the King and Bishops!" D'Argenson, who was a witness of these events, wrote, "One can- "not attribute the decline of religion in France to the influence of "English philosophy . . . . . but to the hatred conceived for the

E

" priests who are at this time running into extremes. The ministers
" of religion can hardly show themselves in the streets, without
" being hooted, and it is the *Unigenitus* and the disgrace of the
" Parliament that have been the causes of this state of affairs."

On May 23rd, the *Remonstrances* which had been so noisily
advertised, were placed in the hands of the public. They fully
justified expectation. In them, the magistrates depicted with
great force the alarming progress of schism, and the necessity of
putting some restraint on the actions of the bishops. They de-
scribed the origin of the Monarchy, retraced the incessant inter-
ferences of the spiritual with the temporal powers, and noted the
persistency of the clergy in claiming exemption from all secular
jurisdiction, as a privilege due to the nature of their order. The
contention of the *Remonstrances* was that the office of the
successors of the Apostles was one of ministry, not of empire.
In recapitulating the history of the Bull Unigenitus, attention was
drawn to the disorders it had introduced into the Church and
State—to the violent measures, the prohibitions, and the debased
condition of the Sorbonne and the University, which had
brought about the all but universal ignorance of the Nation.
Without overstepping the bounds of respect due to the Sovereign,
the authors of the *Grand Remonstrances* reproached the Crown
with having become the ally, or, rather, the tool of the clergy, and
with having abused the system of evocation ; the employment of
which, though it might, in the eyes of the careless, appear to be
a mark of sovereignty, was, in reality, only the subversion of all
political order. " If subjects," they continued, "owe obedience
" to Kings, *Kings, on their side, owe obedience to the laws.*" It was
further represented that deviation from the laws of a State *prepared the way for Revolution.* " So great is the extent of our
" wrongs," said the magistrates, "that we are to-day placed in a
" position, in which sad necessity forces us to reclaim almost all the
" principles of the Constitution and of the Monarchy." Reference
was also made to the 45,000 *lettres de cachet* issued since 1714,
to the refusals of Sacraments, and the troubles of every kind
that were the consequences of the King's action in prohibiting the

Parliament to take procedure on writs of error. "No, Sire," wrote the magistrates in conclusion, "we will not permit the "triumph of a schism that is not only fatal to Religion, but capable "of dealing a violent blow to your sovereignty and to the State. "We will not be persuaded into remaining idle spectators of the "wrongs our country endures, and thus become the accomplices of "those who, in abusing the privileges you accord them, seek to "reduce us to the cruel alternative of incurring your Majesty's dis- "pleasure, or of avoiding the duties which an inviolable zeal for "your service imposes on us. They shall learn that this zeal has "no bounds, and that we are resolved to remain faithful to you, "though we ourselves become the victims of our fidelity."

The prestige of the Parliament had never been so great. The *Châtelet*, the Courts (*des Aides, des Comptes, des Monnaies*),[1] and the University sent deputations to Pontoise to congratulate the Grand Chamber. The provincial Parliaments, stirred by a spirit of emulation, modelled their conduct on that of the Paris Parliament, and carried on the war against the clergy. From their various places of exile, the disgraced magistrates issued memorials which strengthened the resistance of the populace. "Though the "King has 100,000 men," they said, "the Parliament has all the "hearts, all the popular esteem, and the universal goodwill." It was thought that every Parliament in the kingdom would unite to demand the convocation of the States-General. The Government continued its old methods of arresting individuals, quashing parliamentary Decrees, and using measures of extreme violence in regard to the magistrates. The Parliament of Normandy, having ordered the Bishop of Evreux to pay a fine of 10,000 *livres*, a lieutenant of the King's guard went to Rouen and, escorted by several officers, erased the Decree from the registers. A short time after, troops were sent into Brittany, with the object of intimidating the Rennes Parliament. Such proceedings could

---

[1] *The Cour des Aides,* Court of appeal for all civil and criminal actions relating to excise, taxation and duties.

Cour des Monnaies, equivalent to the Court of the Exchequer; and *Cour des Comptes,* the Treasury Court. (*Translator's Note.*)

only foment the opposition.   At Pontoise, the exiled Grand
Chamber had but just begun its vacation when the King,
by letters-patent, nominated a "Chamber of Vacation."   These
letters were forwarded to the *Châtelet* for registration, but the
councillors refused to register them, declaring that they received
their orders from the Parliament alone.   The greater proportion
of the higher local courts imitated this example.   A small country
bailiwick, composed of two officers, had the audacity to protest
against the letters-patent.   The wave of revolt that had engulfed
the towns was spreading to the villages.

The doctrines, that the conditions of the times gave rise to,
were no less audacious than the acts.   With the members of the
Parliament, as with the Jansenists, it was thenceforward an admitted principle that the *Nation was superior to the Kings, as the
Church was to the Popes.*   This idea of the superiority of the Nation
to the Monarch was used by the Ultramontanes as a bogey to
frighten the Government.   Letters were circulated throughout
the kingdom, affirming that the republican principles professed
by the Parliament were more threatening to the Throne than the
maxims of Rome, and that the Parliament, through the influence
that it had acquired, was more likely than was the Pope to depose
the King.   Finally, a bishop published a mandate, in which he
recalled the tragic end of Charles I., and insinuated that the
Parliament of Paris, following the example of that of London, was
capable of bringing its Sovereign up for judgment and conducting
him to the scaffold.

These manœuvres had the desired effect.   The measures of the
Government became more rigorous than ever.   The *Châtelet,*
having committed a libel on the Parliament to the flames, the
councillors who had justified the measure were thrown into the
Bastille.   The Grand Chamber was not permitted to re-assemble
at Pontoise, but was deprived of its functions and exiled to
Soissons.   In place of the Paris Parliament, a "Royal Chamber"
was created.   The *Châtelet,* when commanded to register, "without deliberation," the letters-patent establishing this spurious
Parliament, transcribed them upon its registers " by express com-

"mand of the King," and refused to recognise the "Royal
"Chamber," as it had refused to recognise the "Chamber of Vaca-
"tion." There was then talk of suppressing the *Châtelet.* The
people became more and more incensed against the King, and another uprising was feared. "I know from one of the chief
"magistrates of Paris," wrote d'Argenson at this time, "that the
"Parisians are in a highly inflammable state. Military precautions
"are being taken ; the watch is doubled, and patrols of French and
"Swiss guards are met with in the streets. The same informant
"tells me that, if the *Châtelet* be suppressed, he has no doubt
"that the shops will be shut, that there will be barricades,
"and that, *in that manner, the revolution will begin.*" It was in
December, 1753, that these things were talked of.

It seemed as if the exiled magistrates anticipated some great
change, in which the country would need their counsels, for they
applied themselves to the study of public rights. Many people
said that, "If ever the French Nation should have an opportunity
"of testifying its confidence in them, it would find in the exiled
"magistrates a national senate 'ready-made.'" The provincial
Parliaments communicated with each other by means of emissaries,
and accepted the word of command from the exiled magistrates
of Paris.

In the beginning of the year 1754, the situation became still
more serious. Throughout France refusals of Sacraments multiplied, and in Paris the Archbishop deprived of their powers all
confessors who did not evince sufficient zeal for the *Constitution.*
The Royal Chamber, asphyxiated by public contempt, scarcely
dared to avow its existence by the passing of the most insignificant
Decrees. Revolts were feared in Paris and Rouen. Not content
with stirring up the Government against the magistrates and
Jansenists, the clergy denounced the Protestants as well. In
September, 1753, an army had been sent against the *Cevennes.*
In all parts of France the Protestants were taking up arms, and
in March, 1754, 5,000 of them left the kingdom. "Thus
"are preparations being made for a civil war," wrote d'Argenson
once more, "and yet the King is no longer employing his forces

"against his subjects. It is the priests who are promoting the
"disorders. Discontent is rife, and everything tends to a *great*
"*revolution in religious and in political matters.*"

Military men became at length no more submissive than the
professional classes. Dispatched first against the Protestants and
then given the charge of keeping in check a populace maddened
by want, what wonder that they were disgusted with the part they
were called upon to play ! The *Châtelet* having declared that,
during the absence of the Parliament, it intended to take
cognizance of the refusals of Sacraments and to prosecute their
initiators, four councillors were seized in the night and taken to
the Bastille. As if designed to aggravate the misery of the common people, the *fêtes* at Longchamps had never been more
brilliant. The same week, a Jesuit, preaching before Louis XV.,
declared that blood alone could extinguish heresies, and it would
be well to spill a few drops at once, in order to avoid the flowing
of streams in the future. These words had doubtless but little
effect on the King, who was more than ever occupied with his
evanescent loves. But they were taken up by the public. On all
sides, protests were raised against the tyranny of the Government
"married " to the tyranny of the clergy. War raged no longer
between Jansenists and *Constitutionists*, but between Nationalists
and Sacerdotalists. In the opinion of the country, it was the
union between monarchial and espiscopal despotism that had
been the cause of all the evils, and this fatal alliance alone that
had prepared the Revolution that was then threatening on all
sides.

The Revolution that, in men's thoughts, was already accomplished in 1751, was on the point of becoming a reality in 1754.

A Royal ordinance suppressing the *Châtelet* or the Parliament,
a refusal of Sacraments taking place under special conditions, an
outburst of popular indignation in regard to the taxes, or any
other cause, would have sufficed to bring about an explosion. Since
it was in the destinies of France to sustain the shock of a
Revolution, is it not to be regretted that, instead of taking place
thirty-five years later, it did not occur then ? The Parliament

would, no doubt, have assumed the direction of the movement. It is not likely, as d'Argenson fancied, that a democratic form of government would have been established. The probability is that the King's authority would only have been limited. In the place of a despotism, a constitutional Monarchy would have been established, and the Parliament, enlarged and transformed, would either have assumed an analogous position to that occupied by the English House of Commons, or, preserving only its functions of adjudicating, would have entered into a compact, whereby regular powers would have been granted to the States-General and the provincial States. In regard to the clergy, the abortive work of the Government would have been carried out; and the ecclesiastics, like other citizens, would have been obliged to contribute towards the expense of the State. That which is certain is that the Nation would have broken altogether with Ultramontanism without returning to the ways of pure Gallicanism, for all persecution of the Protestants would undoubtedly have been stopped, and the laws that separated them from society, repealed. D'Argenson was mistaken when he thought that the people would immediately have banished all "priesthood, sacerdotalism, revelation, and mystery," and have been contented to worship God "in spirit and in truth." Inferior in doctrine to that of 1789, this supposititious Revolution of 1754—while falling into excesses, unhappily inevitable—would not have established that "reign of terror," the bitter memory of which still hangs over us, though eighty years have passed. The spirit of Reform would have tempered that of Revolution. Men would not have been in the perilous necessity of having to construct a new system of government, all in a piece, upon the ruins of the old. In one word, France, still feeling attached to her past, would have introduced into Church and State, innovations inspired by respect both for tradition and for progress of ideas, and would have left the door open for still greater changes in the future.

CHAPTER VI.

Government of Louis XV.

(1754-1762.)

IF we are to believe Jean Jacques Rousseau, the sensation, produced in the month of December, 1753, by his *Letters on French Music*, was the means of preventing the outbreak of the Revolution. We are further assured by Grimm that the arrival in Paris of an Italian actor, Manelli, saved France from a civil war. We should be forming an exaggerated estimate of the lightness of the French character if we put faith in these assertions. The true cause which averted an explosion was the sudden tack in the course of the Government—a tack said to have been suggested by Madame de Pompadour.

Towards the middle of the month of July, 1754, letters of recall were forwarded to the magistrates in exile. On the 30th of August, letters-patent suppressed the "Royal Chamber." The councillors of the *Châtelet*, who had been imprisoned, were set at liberty, and on the 4th of September—the day following the birth of the prince, who afterwards became Louis XVI.—the Parliament resumed its deliberations. A Declaration of the King, dated September 2nd, gave to the Parliament the charge of maintaining, in all quarters, an absolute silence in regard to the *Constitution*, and deprived those ecclesiastics, against whom Decrees had previously been issued, of the power of instituting any counter proceedings. By this Edict the complexion of public affairs was completely altered. The clergy were humiliated, and the Parliament triumphed. Of course the bishops protested, and refusals of Sacraments began anew in various dioceses; but the magistrates —having their hands strengthened by the Declaration—did not hesitate to interfere. They demanded an explanation of the Archbishop of Paris, in whose diocese a refusal of the Sacrament had taken place. The Prelate replied that he was accountable for his actions to God alone. Instead of prosecuting him, the magistrates complained of him to the King, who, touched by this mark of consideration, exiled the Archbishop to Conflans. This action, which was considered a "great event," filled the Parisians with delight. Louis XV. banished also the Bishops of Orléans and Troyes and the Archbishop of Aix. He flattered himself that he alone was best able to control the upper clergy, but he left to the Parliament the duty of punishing those of the lower order. Decrees of Council no longer frustrated the designs of the magistrates; the banishment of the Archbishop of Paris had so completely reconciled the Parliament and the Ministry that the magistrates never passed a resolution without first notifying the King of their intention. Never had there been so complete an agreement between the Court and the Parliament. But the clergy still resisted. The Archbishop, from his place of exile, fermented the disturbance, and the King sent him on from Conflans to Lagny. The Jansenists and the public were jubilant, though the firmness of the Government provoked the question : "Why "was not this policy adopted two years ago ? If it had been, the "exile of the Parliament would have been avoided, since nothing "more was then asked than is being given to-day."

The Parliament, more and more emboldened, passed sentences of banishment against several *Constitutionist* priests, and on March 18th issued a Decree denying that the Bull was an Article of Faith, and forbidding all ecclesiastics, of whatsoever rank, to attribute to it that character. In this Decree the clergy—who had fallen into such popular disrepute, that they were afraid to show themselves in the street—saw the *Constitution* set at naught by the Nation. But the King, in view of the approaching General Assembly, at which it was hoped that the customary "free gift" of fifteen or sixteen millions would be voted, quashed the Decree. The Parliament fully understood the meaning of this act, and did not take offence. But the bishops were only half satisfied. What they wanted was the abrogation of the Declaration of September 2nd, and that Declaration formed the chief subject of their deliberations. At their instigation, writings, hostile to the Parliament, were circulated among the public, and sermons denouncing the magistrates were preached in the churches. The excitement of the Ultramontane party was so great that it was feared that some fanatic priest might attempt the King's life.

The Parliament was not in the least disconcerted. It burned the writings and banished or condemned to the galleys all rebellious ecclesiastics. As the Sorbonne persisted in receiving theses calculated to promote the disputes, the Parliament caused the Declaration of September 2nd to be inscribed on its registers. It was in vain that the bishops represented to the Monarch that, if the audacity of the magistrates were not repressed, they would be forced to take extreme measures. The King was firm. He refused to recall the exiled prelates, and, as soon as the "free "gift" was voted, replied "Fiddlesticks!" to all the bishops' demands.

But it was not only in its response to the clergy that the Government manifested its change of feeling. It allowed the *Encyclopedia* to re-appear, and even caused the article on the *Constitution* to be omitted, because in it, it was stated that the Bull was received in France. At this time Boyer, the old Bishop of Mirepoix, who had had charge, since 1743, of the list of livings in the King's gift, died, and was replaced by the Cardinal de Rochefoucauld, who had only a very moderate zeal for the *Constitution*. A spirit of tolerance seemed likewise to inspire the Government in its action in regard to the Protestants. In several localities they were allowed to erect churches, and there was some talk of legitimizing their marriages and re-establishing the Edict of Nantes.

But so sudden a change could not be permanent. A disagreement arose between the Parliament and the Grand Council, and the King issued a Declaration, by which he seemed to attribute to the latter assembly the authority of a sovereign court. The Monarch gave an order that his Declaration should be sent to all the sees, bailiwicks, and seneschals of the kingdom for registration. The Parliament suspended the execution of this order until they should have presented *Remonstrances* to the Sovereign. The dispute very soon assumed quite unexpected proportions. All the provincial Parliaments rallied round that of Paris. The King in his reply to the *Remonstrances* confirmed the Declaration, and the Grand Council forwarded his response to all the bailiwicks. The public, which looked on the Ministry and the Grand Council as "aiders and abettors of the Episcopate and the instru-"ments of tyranny," was inflamed by this action. In the chambers of the *Palais*, numbers of *bourgeois* spoke against the Government, which it accused of joining forces with the Jesuits to degrade the Parliament. Under another form, the struggle between the Nationalists and Sacerdotalists had begun again.

Towards the close of the year 1755, innumerable brochures once more stirred up discord. In one of them it was stated that those culpable persons, who had not succeeded in suppressing the Parliament by violence, were now working for the same end by endeavouring to assimilate the rights of the Grand Council with those of the lower chambers. The Grand Council condemned this brochure to the flames, asserting that it, no less than the Parliament, was the depository of the laws of the Monarchy. This assertion was replied to by the reproduction of the *cahiers*[1] of the States-General of 1560 and 1576, which expressly demanded the abolition of the Grand Council. On the 6th of April the Parliament passed a standing order, which denied the right of the Grand Council to interfere in any affairs of public order and general interest, and limited the jurisdiction of that body to questions of a purely private nature. No one was astounded by a Decree in which the Parliament seemed to perform an act of sovereignty. So great a change had come over men's minds in a few years that the people of Paris and the provinces had come to consider the Parliament to be the "real Monarch of France, in whom "all legitimate power was vested." The war of the "tickets of

[1] Schedules or statements of grievances, needs, and wishes of the three orders, drawn up preparatory to the assembling of the States. (*Translator's Note.*)

"confession" still waged. Not only Extreme Unction, but the Sacrament of Marriage was now being refused by certain priests. Everything conspired to bring discredit on Religion. At the Carnival in 1756, it was noted that the most popular costumes were those of bishops, abbés, monks and nuns. Scepticism proclaimed itself on the pages of many books. One of these was the *Christiade*, in which the history of Jesus Christ was told in the form of a romance; another was Bayle's *Analyse raisonnée*. The Parliament remarked the progress of philosophical ideas with some uneasiness; but, quite absorbed by its struggle with the clergy, it bestowed its chief attention on the Ultramontane writings. Thus it was that the same Decree that struck at the *Christiade* and the *Analyse*, branded more particularly the *History of the people of God* by the Jesuit Berruyer.

As might have been foreseen, the standing orders of April 6th did not terminate the conflict in which the Parisians had been so much interested. A deputation from the Grand Council presented *Remonstrances* to the King. Louis XV. received the deputation with the ceremonial prescribed for the reception of the Parliament, and from that time no one doubted that he would soon substitute the Grand Council for the Assembly of Magistrates, or that the entire Ministry would eventually become Ultramontane. Each provincial Parliament united itself more closely to that of Paris, and sent deputies to consult with the magistrates of the capital as to the best methods of resistance. The provincial assemblies styled themselves in their Decrees, "sections of the Parliament," indicating in this manner that they were all parts of one body. It was said that this association of Parliaments represented something more than a States-General; it was "a fully formed *national government*."

About this time there broke out the fatal Seven Years' War, in which France was allied with Austria against England and Prussia. The King addressed an Edict to the Parliament, ordering the imposition during the hostilities of another "twentieth" tax. The magistrates did not at once endorse this Edict, for they flattered themselves that in the interval the Ministry would

relent in regard to the " Grand Council," but the King forced the
registration in a " Bed of Justice." Thereupon the Parliament
protested against this act of authority and presented *Remonstrances,* in which it formally accused the Ministry of con-
spiring to annihilate the Parliament. This growing resistance of
the Parliaments and these repeated struggles had the immediate
effect of inflaming men's passions. In the ministerial clique
sinister words were pronounced; wrote d'Argenson : " I know
" some members of the Grand Council, who, sharing the views of
" the priests, have said that *blood alone can wipe out all this.*" But
remaining all the time utterly indifferent to the wave of anger
that swept around him, Louis XV. continued to disgrace himself
by his undisguised excesses. Submissive to the ever-changing
will of Madame de Pompadour—who, after abandoning the
bishops for the Parliament, now deserted the Parliament for the
bishops—the King was becoming more *constitutionary* and more
episcopal than even Louis XIV. had been. The clergy were not
slow to take advantage of the Monarch's change of front. In
September, 1754, the Parliament being, according to custom, in
vacation, the Archbishop of Paris promulgated a pastoral instruction, in which he not only prohibited the clergy from administer-
ing Sacraments to those who presented orders issued by secular
tribunals, but also enjoined that such orders should be neither
solicited by the faithful nor distributed by the magistrates. This
stroke of policy was so well prepared that the Prelate announced
as certain the adhesion of over sixty bishops. But, as in 1753,
the *Châtelet* assumed the functions of the Parliament, and, on
the 5th of November, publicly burned the instruction. Upon this
the Prelate issued a mandate that threatened all those who read
the sentence of the *Châtelet,* with excommunication. The
Châtelet, in response, prohibited the printing and circulation of
the mandate under penalty of corporal punishment. As soon as
the Parliament reassembled it prepared in its turn to deal a blow
at the Episcopate, and everyone expected that a writ would be
issued to apprehend the person of the Archbishop.

In the meantime, Louis XV. had written to Benedict XIV. to

ascertain the best means of pacifying the quarrels. The Pontiff, though disposed to be conciliatory, could not entirely divest himself of the sentiments of his predecessors. In the Brief, through which he replied, he recognised the *Constitution* as a law of the Church, which could not be rejected without risk of the loss of eternal salvation, but he decided that, in order to avoid scandal, the priests should administer the Sacrament to the dying, who were merely suspected of Jansenism, and refuse it only to notorious Jansenists. The King sent the Brief to the bishops and ordered them to conform to it. The magistrates courageously suppressed the Brief by a Decree, but this Decree only determined the Monarch to proceed against them. Just at this time many of the provincial Parliaments pronounced against the Edict of the second tax of the twentieth. Indeed, the Pau Assembly refused point blank to enforce it, saying that the distress of the people forbade their registration of such a tax.

The storm which had been gathering, since the commencement of the affair of the Grand Council, at last burst. On December 13th, 1756, the King came to the Parliament and held a "Bed of "Justice," in which he caused three Declarations to be registered. By the *first*, he ordered that the Bull should be respected as a decision of the Church, and ascribed to the ecclesiastical tribunals all cognizance of the refusals of Sacraments, except in cases of appeal by writ of error. By the *second*, he decided that the Grand Chamber alone had cognizance of all matters relating to the religion of the State, that the other Chambers could not assemble without its permission, and that no councillor (or magistrate) could have a deliberative voice in the Assembly of the Chambers until he had served for ten years. By the *third*, he suppressed sixty parliamentary offices and two "chambers of "requests." "You have heard my wishes," said the King. "I "insist on their being carried out, and will support the execution of "them *with all my authority.*" The Parliament was completely crushed. With the exception of those of the Grand Chamber, all the magistrates immediately sent in their resignations. The following day sixteen councillors of the Grand Chamber followed their example. The *Châtelet* ceased its functions, the lawyers shut up their offices, and the course of justice was again interrupted. A magistrate, foreseeing that the disturbance might shatter the Government, said of the "Bed of Justice" of December 13th, that it was "the *last sigh of a dying Monarchy.*" It was at this period that Grimm, who had noted the "imbecile fervour" with which the French had for forty years quarrelled about the Bull, and who now saw the whole of Europe in arms and the world not in the least conformed to the type conceived by Philosophy, wrote : " I "am far from fancying that we have attained to the century of "Reason, and it would take but little to make me believe that "Europe is threatened by some sinister Revolution."

The Revolution which had failed to break out in 1754 was perhaps once more upon the point of bursting forth when, in January, 1757, the attempt made by Damien on the life of the King absorbed public attention and arrested the march of events. The news of the attempt caused a revulsion of feeling among a certain section of the public, similar to that which had taken place in 1744. Everyone was anxious for information, and some persons shed tears. Suspicion fell at once upon the clergy. The Jesuits were first accused of the crime, and then the Jansenists. It was also thought that the assassin might be a parliamentary fanatic. At all events a very general excitement was caused. The evidences of it were most noticeable among the shopkeeping classes; the people were silent. Their one feeling was that of resentment, and it had been stirred up in them by the indignities put upon the magistrates.

In certain parts of the provinces, *fêtes* were held to celebrate the preservation of the King's life, but in Paris no demonstration took place and not a single *Te Deum* was sung.

The Government took fright. Fearing that the attempt might become a signal for uprisings in different parts of the kingdom, it enjoined the commanding-officers in the provinces to stick to their posts and redoubled the military precautions in the capital. Sixteen councillors of the Grand Chamber, who had sent in their resignations, were exiled. Two of the principal ministers—one of whom was Machault, who was in disfavour with the clergy, and the other, the Count d'Argenson, a friend of the Jesuit party—were also sent into exile. Arrests of ecclesiastics and of private individuals, whose only crime was the having in their pockets copies of the *Remonstrances*, were frequent. At last on April 16th, the King issued a Declaration, the first articles of which ran as follows : "All those who shall be convicted of having composed, "or caused to be composed and printed, writings tending to attack "religion, to assail our authority, or to disturb the order and tran-"quillity of our realm, shall be *punished with death*. All those who "shall print the aforesaid works, all booksellers, colporteurs and "other persons who shall circulate them among the public shall "likewise be *punished with death*." This Declaration was only a threat. The Government sent the booksellers and printers into banishment, and condemned all obscure writers, convicted of contempt of court, to the galleys. But it dared go no further. The promulgation of a law, the barbarity of which rendered its execution impossible, only disgraced its initiators. After some months the excitement seemed to subside. The Government deemed it possible to relax some of its severities. Though the Declarations registered in the "Bed of Justice" were not revoked, they were not acted upon ; the magistrates had their resignations returned to them, the sixteen councillors of the Grand Chamber were recalled, and the Parliament was re-established under the same conditions as had existed before the "Bed of Justice." At the same time, the Archbishop of Paris was recalled from his place of exile, and all the priests banished by the Parliament were authorised to return to their parishes. The Government hoped that these gentle measures would conciliate the public mind, but they only aggravated it by their inconsequence. Yet the Ministry showed itself consistent in one thing. It continued to disallow the renewal of religious disputes. In November, the Sorbonne was commanded by the Ministry, in the King's name, to cease thenceforward to refer in any way to the *Constitution*. These orders being directly contrary to those previously received, the Sorbonne took offence and decided that, in view of the oath taken by its members, "to defend the Catholic, Apostolic, and Roman "religion *usque ad effusionem sanguinis*," it could not conform to the prescribed silence. The Dean of the faculty was immediately sent into exile, and the Archbishop of Paris, who had secretly encouraged the rebellion of the Sorbonne, was once more banished; on this occasion to Périgord. At the same time the Parliament condemned some Jesuitical writings to be burned. This was the first blow struck at the Jesuits, and a precursor of the thunderbolts that were soon to fall upon them. These severities produced their effect, and all parties were silenced. The election of Clement XIII., who had been supported by the Ministry and opposed by the Jesuits, so greatly disconcerted the partisans of the *Constitution*, that it seemed as if the Bull were, at last, forgotten. But, in default of religious quarrels, public opinion was kept alive by other grievances.

The defeat of Rosbach in November, 1757, was the source of much annoyance, sorrow, and shame. These feelings were deepened in June, 1758, when news came of the loss of the battle of Crevelt. The expressions of dissatisfaction were all directed against the Court, and what the populace gave tongue to, the ministers secretly thought. "The worst of it is," wrote the Abbé de Bernis on the day following the defeat of Rosbach, "that "private individuals direct our affairs. We have neither generals "nor ministers. What we want is a Government." The Abbé was only repeating words written by d'Argenson in 1743. But in 1758 the disorganisation was still more serious, the evil deeper, and France possessed no longer a General Saxe. Louis XV., more disgusted than ever with public affairs since the attempt made on his life, only sank into deeper debaucheries. Madame de Pompadour was the real King. She nominated generals and ministers, received the ambassadors, regulated political moves, and decided upon alliances. The expenses of the humiliating defeats had, of course, to be met. As in the time of Louis XIV., a "free gift" was exacted of all towns and boroughs of the kingdom. Thereupon the discontent burst forth with renewed force. The people were loud in their condemnation of the Government. Whilst the

F

anger of the lower classes was expressed in the first "call to
"arms" yet placarded in Paris, the members of the upper ranks of
society did not restrict themselves to decrying the Government;
they disparaged France, and praised to the skies free England,
victorious Prussia, and even China, which country nobody knew
anything about, but which was believed by all to be the home of
wisdom. The "upper ten" spoke freely of the general "break
"up" of their country and the decadence of their nation. The
attempt made upon the life of the King of Portugal, in which the
Jesuits of Lisbon were concerned, had not only thrown the Society
of Jesus into discredit in France, but had cast a slur upon Religion. *Convulsionnaires* were once more to the fore with their
transports and miracles, and in the midst of all this disorder in
the Church, the Philosophers propounded their doctrines as sub-
stitutes for the religious traditions which were being shattered.
Aware of the process of disintegration that society was under-
going, and being no longer able to blame the clergy, whom it had
effectually silenced, the Parliament began to accuse the Philosophers and to treat them with the same severity that they had
been employing against the *Constitutionists*. The Advocate-
General, Omer Joly de Fleury, in condemning Helvetius's book,
De L'Esprit, together with the *Encyclopedia*, Voltaire's poem,
Natural Religion, and many other works, brought a very
wholesale charge against the Philosophers. He said: "It
"cannot be denied that a project has been conceived and a
"society formed to support materialism and destroy religion, to
"inspire independence and promote the corruption of morals.
"The book, *De L'Esprit*, is, as it were, an abridgment of
"that too famous work, which, according to its true object, ought
"to be the book of all knowledge, but which has become that of all
"errors." He accused the Encyclopedists of pretending "that the
"method of adoring the true God ought never to be in opposition
'to reason, because He is, Himself, the Author of Reason;" of
claiming liberty of conscience, and, "by a necessary consequence,
"universal tolerance;" of insisting that the authority of Kings has
its origin either in violence or in a contract, real or supposed,

between the people and their masters, instead of recognising, with the Apostle, that all power comes from God, and that He has established all those who are in authority upon the earth.

All the works denounced in this harangue were condemned to be burned by the common hangman. The *Encyclopedia* alone was exempted, a body of lawyers and theologians being commissioned to examine it. This action was approved by devotees, by Jansenists, and by those men of the world who distrusted ideas that seemed too bold, but it lowered the Parliament in the eyes of the numerous partisans of free thought. "What a fuss "about Monsieur Helvetius's book!" wrote Voltaire; and, referring to a work by the Abbé Caveirac called *Apology for the Massacre of Saint Bartholomew*—the publication of which the Parliament had permitted—he added: "Monsieur Helvetius is "persecuted, and monsters are tolerated." Grimm, who disapproved of *De L'Esprit*, was filled with indignation by a Decree that joined to it in a common censure Voltaire's poem *Natural Religion*. Some months later a Brief from Rome condemned the *Encyclopedia*. At the same time the Parliament committed to the flames Voltaire's *Précis of Ecclesiastes and the Song of Songs*. In spite of these surprisingly rigorous measures, the Philosophers did not relinquish their work. Attacked, as they had been, in the name of Religion, they became thenceforward the most persistent assailants of the Church. By a contrast worthy of notice, the Parliament which, in religious questions, did not go beyond the doctrines of the Gallican Church, continued in politics to act up to principles which the Philosophers themselves could find no fault with. The resistance of the Parliament of Besançon in reference to the levying of fresh taxes, drew from the Sovereign several *lettres de cachet*. The Parliament of Paris protested against the employment of these letters as contrary to the laws, to the dignity of the magistrates, and the *rights of the Nation*. It was the first time that the Parliament had upheld before Royalty the "rights of the "Nation." Not long after this, disasters to the French arms at Minden and in Canada and the loss sustained by the navy at

Belle Isle called for more funds from the Treasury. The Government suspended payments of its bills, and Louis XV. sent his plate to the mint and called upon his subjects to follow his example. When in February, 1760, fresh imposts were created, the Parliament constituted itself the organ of public opinion, and announced its intention of requesting the ministers to submit to it their accounts. The magistrates maintained that, until they had assured themselves that the sums of money that had for years past been poured into the Treasury had been really spent in the service of the State, they could not register edicts imposing fresh taxes upon the people. The King refused to listen to any remonstrances, but relaxed some of the orders contained in his edicts.

Whilst public opinion was being stirred up against Royalty in regard to the tax question, the Archbishop of Paris returned to the capital after twenty-one months' absence. Thereupon brochures appeared complaining of the silence enjoined by the King in regard to the *Constitution*. At the same time fresh attacks were made on the Philosophers. A play by Palissot was brought out at the *Comédie Française*, in which the men who, in the eyes of Europe, were the chief glory of France, were represented as blackguards. The closing lines of the comedy characterised the whole. "At last all Philosophy is banished from "the house, and we have among us only honest men." "Things "have come to such a pass," wrote Grimm, "that there is not a "single man in office to-day who does not consider the spread of "Philosophy to be the source of all our woes. One would have "thought that the causes of our losses of the battles of Rosbach "and Minden, and of the destruction of our fleet were sufficiently "immediate and apparent; but, if you take the opinion of the "Court, you will be told that all these misfortunes must be attri- "buted to the new Philosophy ; that it is Philosophy that has ex- "tinguished our military ardour, our blind submission, and all that "has hitherto produced the great men and glorious actions of "France." Thus an opinion was formed that established itself by degrees and has been perpetuated until the present day.

The conduct of the Government was, at this time, exciting the most violent denunciations. The scarceness of money, the multiplicity of taxes and consequent general distress exasperated the people. Everywhere there was an outcry in respect to the depredations of the finances, and a desire to be avenged of them. The *Remonstrances* of the Parliament of Rouen were printed. In them " the unity of the Parliaments of the kingdom, the constitution "of the French Government, and the fundamental laws of the " Monarchy," were subjects of discussion that tended openly to place the authority of the Parliament of France above that of the Sovereign. The Government did not dare to take action in the matter. It knew well that the entire province of Normandy was for the Parliament, and, at a time when the English were only awaiting an opportunity to invade the coasts of France, it feared to excite a revolt in a seaboard province. The King contented himself with commanding the attendance at Versailles of several of the Rouen magistrates, and with addressing them in the following manner : " I am your master and I ought to punish you for " the audacity of your principles. I am more occupied than you " imagine in caring for my people, and in devising means to ac- " complish my task. Return to Rouen. Register my Edicts with- " out delay. I will be obeyed ! "

All this time, the Parliaments of France had never ceased to remonstrate with the King in respect to the *lettres de cachet* that had exiled the Besançon magistrates. The Parliament of Toulouse maintained that their exile infringed the right of all citizens to be punished only in conformity with the laws, after a judicial examination held by their legal judges, and protested that, in reversing the forms observed by all civilised peoples, the *way was prepared for anarchy and independence.* Never had any section of the Parliament made use of such plain language. The Parliament of Rouen also remonstrated. To it, the Chancellor replied : " His " Majesty orders me to remind you that his authority being sover- "eign, no one in the kingdom can share it with him. Though the " King be willing to receive the remonstrances of the Parliaments, "he does not permit them, upon that pretext, to suspend, still less

" to forbid, the execution of his orders.   They should wait till they
" receive from his justice the reformation of the pretended abuses
" which they denounce.   These are the true principles of Monarchy
" —unalterable principles that you are endeavouring to destroy."
This conflict proved to be a more serious one than any that had
previously arisen between the Parliaments and the Crown.   The
question of principle outweighed the question of fact.   Royalty
was openly attacked in the heart of the magistracy, and the *revolutionary spirit* entered even into those who most protested
their fidelity to existing institutions.   Yielding to repeated ap-
plications, the Government at last recalled the exiled magistrates.

The Nation had begun to long for peace at any price—anxious
only for the termination of a war, by which France had gained
nothing save humiliation and ruin.   In the month of April, 1761,
it was announced that a Congress was to be held to conclude the
peace.   As the anxiety on that head subsided, all attention was
turned to a trial proceeding in the Upper Chamber, in which the
Jesuits were implicated.   Father La Valette, Superior of the
Missions of Martinique, who carried on considerable trade with
the merchants of the south of France, had just gone into bankruptcy for nearly 3,000,000 *livres*.   The creditors first addressed
their claims to the chief of the Jesuit Society at Rome, and subsequently made an application to the Parliament.   In May, the
Grand Chamber unanimously condemned the Society to pay the
3,000,000.   The Jesuits were also ordered to submit their
statutes to the Advocate-General for examination.   On the 6th of
August, 1761, the Parliament issued two startling Decrees.   The
first condemned twenty-four Jesuit books to be burned as " sediti-
"ous, destructive of Christian morals, and teaching a murderous
"and abominable doctrine, not only in respect to the lives of
"citizens, but also in regard to the sacred persons of Sovereigns."
The second forbade the Jesuits to continue to teach, and
prohibited all subjects of the King from frequenting their schools,
until judgment had been passed in respect to the status of their
Society.   These two Decrees created an immense sensation in Paris.
The King, without disapproving of the second one, commanded

that its execution should be deferred for one year. The magistrates, fearing that so long a delay might put off the whole question, altered their original date from October to April, and allowed six months' grace. The Jesuits made every endeavour to profit by the respite. The Superiors of their three houses in Paris witnessed before notaries deeds in which they protested their fidelity to the person of the King and repudiated the imputations cast upon them by the magistrates. The superior clergy declared loudly that a society " that had in all times promoted the welfare " of Religion, and the maintenance of the Royal authority," ought not to be subjected to the animosity of the Parliaments. Following the example of the Paris magistrates, those of Rennes, Rouen, Aix, Bordeaux, Besançon and Grenoble demanded the submission to them of the Society's statutes. The Parliament of Paris threw out an Edict, forwarded to it by the King, that aimed at reforming the Society and, by that means, at preserving it. In justification of its conduct, it presented the Monarch with an *Extract* of dangerous doctrines taught by the Society, and contained in its books. On April 1st, 1762, the term fixed by the Parliament, the Jesuits found themselves constrained to give up teaching, and a seal was put on all their papers. On August 6th, exactly a year after the promulgation of the first Decree against them, the Parliament condemned to be burned 163 more books of their's, and announced the dissolution of the Society. Up till the last moment, the Jesuits did not abandon hope, and when the announcement was made, they appeared to be completely non-plussed. The King did not interfere with the action of the Parliament. The Lisbon plot, in throwing a light upon the attempt made upon his own life, had quite changed his disposition towards the Jesuits.

Voltaire correctly estimated the real cause of the abolition of the Jesuit bodies. " It was," said he, " neither Sanchez, Lessius, "nor Escobar, nor the absurdities of casuists who destroyed "the Jesuits; it was Le Tellier, it was the Bull, that exterminated "them." This extermination provoked among the people an excessive and almost indecent outburst of joy.

In the dissolution of the hated Society, the Parliaments recognised the results of their combined efforts. The Jansenists exulted as if the victory had been of their achieving, and the Philosophers also took to themselves the credit of it. " I seem," said Diderot, "to see Voltaire raising his hands and eyes to " Heaven, as he repeats the *Nunc dimittis*."

In reality the abolition of the Jesuits was an achievement belonging neither to the Parliaments, the Jansenists, nor the Philosophers. It was the triumph of Public Opinion.

CHAPTER VII.

Government of Louis XV.

(1762-1770.)

The abolition of the Society of the Jesuits was the first conquest of the Revolutionary Spirit.

But the parliamentary opposition to the old order of things, which had for its object the diminishing of the Royal authority and the maintenance of Gallicanism, did not go far enough for the more intelligent members of the community. Without any clear plan or purpose, these followed the guidance of the Philosophers, who, themselves, but vaguely aimed at the establishment of a new *régime*. As a thoughtful writer has said: "At this "crisis the real events were not acts, but books." On November 3rd, 1762, the preliminaries of the peace between France and England were signed, and to the war of force without succeeded a war of thought within the kingdom. Two celebrated books, *Émile* and *The Social Contract*, inaugurated this period. *Émile* was burned by the Parliament and censured by the Archbishop of Paris. The terms of both condemnations were, however, more moderate than had been those which greeted the appearance of *De L'Esprit*. It was said that the Archbishop published his mandate against *Émile* as a mere matter of form, and the magistrates denounced it because, having just taken proceedings against the Jesuits, they were afraid of being accused of indifference to the Faith. *The Social Contract*, which upheld the principle of appeal to the people and of the sovereignty of the Nation, and which transformed the Government into a sort of revocable commission, was incomparably more daring politically than *Émile* was in religious matters. Even among certain supporters of Philosophy, it was deemed dangerous. "It is most "important," remarked Bachaumont, "that a book of this kind "should not be allowed to ferment in minds that are easily excited." But, in spite of its temerity, *The Social Contract* was not burned by the Parliament. Printed in Holland, it was known in Paris by only a very small number of copies, whilst *Émile*, on account of its denunciation by the Parliament, was read by everyone. A writ was issued against Rousseau for the seizure of his person, but the Ministry made its evasion easy. At the same time, the *Encyclopedia* was most inconsequently allowed to re-appear, and *De L'Esprit* was sold openly. Six months later, *Émile* and *The Social Contract* were also obtainable at all booksellers.

Ever since 1759, when Omer de Fleury pronounced his famous speech against them, the writers of the *Encyclopedia* had, in self-defence, joined forces, with the object of establishing upon the ruin of all dogmas, an empire of reason. From Ferney, whither he had retired from the range of persecution, Voltaire stimulated their zeal and directed their actions. From Ferney he sent forth his *Sermon of the Fifty*, and the *Testament of the Priest Meslier*— first fruits of the innumerable brochures that were about to proceed from his indefatigable pen. But, unlike Rousseau, who laid himself open to persecution by signing his works, Voltaire disavowed his. "Try," he said to Helvetius, "to serve the human "race without harming yourself in the least." Faithful to this maxim, he attacked his enemies without exposing himself to their counter-thrusts. Yet his ulterior aim was noble. The ardent friend of humanity, he declared war against all fanaticism; and it must not be forgotten, that at the moment that he gave to Helvetius this piece of ignoble advice, he was preparing his *Treatise of Tolerance* and winning the sympathies of the whole of Europe for the innocent Calas.[1]

Notwithstanding that the Jesuits had been crushed, they still attempted to stir up public opinion. They accused the

[1] *Calas*—a Protestant merchant of Toulouse, accused of strangling his son for becoming a Catholic, condemned to the punishment of death by breaking on the wheel, and his family to imprisonment and banishment. The latter, through the exertions of Voltaire, were subsequently pardoned. Louis XV. gave them as compensation, 3,000 *livres*. (*Translator's Note.*)

Parliament with having violated all principles of right, and insisted that the pretended *Extracts* from the doctrine of the Jesuits were nothing but a tissue of misrepresentations. They circulated the most outrageous libels on the Parliaments, and these bodies replied by committing the libels to the flames. One of the writings that made a great stir was the *Three Necessities.* These *Necessities* were to hound down the Jesuits, destroy Christianity, and assassinate the Dauphin. This pamphlet, which was much talked of, but which no one seems ever to have seen, and which was very likely never written, was attributed by the public to dissimulating Jesuits, who desired to prove that their enemies were also those of Religion and of the Throne. But in February, 1763, the King confirmed the dissolution of the Society by an Edict, and the Jesuits were soon forgotten.

The close of the hostilities did not immediately bring about an abatement of the taxes. But, in the month of May, the King held a "Bed of Justice," in which he forced the registration of certain Edicts which suppressed some taxes and created others. Thereupon the Parliament issued a Decree, declaring that these enforced registrations "tended to the subversion of the fundamental laws of the kingdom." The King, in despite of the Parliament, persisted in upholding his Edicts, and the magistrates prepared fresh remonstrances, threatening, as in 1760, to insist upon the Ministers surrendering to them their accounts. A conflict between the rights of the Throne and those of the Magistracy was hourly expected.

"If the Government succeeds in diminishing the authority and "asserted rights of the Parliaments," wrote Barbier, "there will "no longer be any obstacle in the way of assured despotism. If, "on the contrary, the Parliaments unite to oppose this move with "strong measures, nothing can *follow but a general Revolution.*" This Revolution, which Barbier then foresaw, and which, in *Émile,* Rousseau averred was menacing the whole of Europe, was also announced from the pulpit. "In a realm, where the sceptre and "censer continually clash," said a priest, "sooner or later a Revolu-

"tion must break out.   The crisis is a supreme one, and the
" *Revolution cannot be far off.*"

The excitement caused by the promulgation of the Money Edicts
spread from Paris to the provinces.   Most of the Parliaments
refused to register them, and asked the Monarch to submit to them
statements of the revenues and debts of the kingdom.   *A propos*
of these Edicts, mention was made in the Assembly at Bordeaux of
the "end of monarchies, and the downfall of empires."   The " sec-
"tion of the Parliament in session at Rouen " declared that it was
time to put an end to a disorganised administration, " under pres-
"sure of which the Nation groaned."   It refused also to contribute to
the ruin of the country and the triumph of the oppressors of the
public.   For its part, the Parliament of Paris maintained that an
Edict was not executory unless freely registered by all the Parliaments of the kingdom.   By these incessant, and ever bolder
claims, the magistrates, while believing themselves to be keeping
to the political traditions of the past, were preparing the way
more and more for the Revolution.   Louis XV. resolved not to
yield.   He quashed the Decrees of the Parliaments, and enjoined
the commanding officers in the provinces to enforce the registration of his Edicts, *manu militari.*

This order was rigorously carried out, and the magistrates
replied by issuing writs for the apprehension of the officers.   At
last the Paris Parliament represented to the Monarch that measures
of violence could only shatter the stability of the Throne, and that,
" to sustain a Government by force, was to teach the people that
"force could overturn it."   The Ministry, intimidated by this bold
language, relaxed its strenuous measures.   The difficulty in regard
to taxation gave birth to a number of brochures.   Grimm affirmed
that the greater part of them were of so futile and puerile a
character as to excite pity.   But the Government regarded them
from another point of view.   It considered them likely to produce
in men's minds the germs of sedition, and, by a Declaration of
March 28th, 1764, forbade the publication, for the future, of any
writings relating to the State or the national finances.

This Declaration was no better observed than had been those

issued concerning the *Constitution.* People were beginning to laugh at these orders of silence which the Ministry so greatly abused. It was at this time that Voltaire wrote the passage which has since become so celebrated : " All I now see *sows the "seeds of a Revolution which will infallibly spring up,* but I shall " not be a witness of it. The French are slow in accomplishing " anything, but they achieve it in the end."

In the midst of the tumult the Money Edicts gave rise to, the Archbishop of Paris tried to revive the quarrels concerning the Jesuits. He published a pastoral instruction in which he strove to demonstrate that the accusations made against the Society concerning its doctrine had no legitimate basis, and that the magistrates in their action in the matter, had audaciously encroached upon the jurisdiction of the Church. The Parliament committed this instruction to the flames, and requested the King to chastise the incorrigible Prelate. The King, fearing that the Parliament might itself take the initiative, commanded the Archbishop to retire from Paris for a short time. This pastoral instruction was succeeded by other mandates, and by brochures conceived in the same spirit, which were all condemned to be burned. The Pope joined his authority to that of the bishops and published two Briefs, in which he associated the cause of Jesuitism with that of Religion itself. The Parliament ordered the suppression of these Briefs and renewed the prohibitions against the introduction without authority into the kingdom of any Act of the Court of Rome. The recriminations of the clergy resulted only in the hastening of the total ruin of the Jesuits. In the month of November, 1764, Louis XV. at last declared the Society to be totally suppressed throughout the realm. The Parliament, supported by the authority of the King, pronounced against another of the Pope's Briefs, and boldly insinuated that if the Court of Rome continued to sow discord, it must beware of the enmity of France. The Parliament of Aix was also guilty of an unparalleled audacity in publicly committing to the flames an Act of the Holy See.

All this time the Encyclopedists were publishing their propaganda. From Ferney, there emanated successively the *Catechism of an Honest Man*, *The Examination of Religion*, and the *Philosophical Dictionary*. In the fight in which he was engaged, Voltaire looked upon large works as arms too heavy to be employed. He preferred little booklets which were easily circulated, as they were not sold, but given to trustworthy persons, who distributed them to young people and to women. It was, in reality, less a party than a Church which the poet sought to build up, and in which he wished to unite in a new apostleship all enemies of fanaticism and superstition. When he saw his *Treatise on Tolerance* circulated throughout the kingdom, and read even at Court by Madame de Pompadour and some of the ministers, when, above all, he saw the Council of State quash the Decree pronounced by the Parliament of Toulouse against the unfortunate Calas family, he experienced the holy joy of a man who propounds on earth a new creed. " God " bless our budding Church," he cried. " Scales are falling from " men's eyes, and the reign of Truth is near."

The bishops, in their turn, seemed to be taking alarm at the ardent propagandism of the Philosophers. In August, 1765, the General Assembly of the clergy published an extract of its deliberations, in which it gave expression to its anxieties. This was the first time that the superior clergy had joined in protesting against the new Philosophy. "A multitude of fearless writers," they said, " have trodden under foot all laws, both human and " divine . . . . Nothing has been respected either in the civil or " spiritual order. The majesty of the Supreme Being and that of " Kings is outraged . . . In the realm of faith, in that of morals, " and even in the State itself, *the spirit of the century seems to* " *threaten a Revolution that presages on all sides total ruin and de-* " *struction.*" This exordium—which may be considered the first announcement of the Revolution set forth in a document of a public character—was followed by the condemnation *in globo* of all the books that had recently appeared against Religion ; notably, the works of Helvetius, Diderot, Voltaire, and Rousseau. By a stroke of the pen the whole of literary France was placed under a ban. The Parliament did not entirely approve this censure, and reproached the bishops with having said nothing of the scandals of which the Jesuits and their partisans had been the authors; thus inferring that, if Religion was then being combatted by the Philosophers, it was because the men who should have taught and defended it had, by their own conduct, caused it to be dishonoured. But the denunciation of the Philosophers was not the most important part of the manifesto; it did but precede a long *exposition of the rights of the spiritual powers*, in which the prelates maintained that the ecclesiastical ministry was completely independent in all the "things of God," and, particularly, in the administration of the Sacraments. Following on to this came a declaration upon the *Unigenitus Bull*. This was exhuming all the old quarrels with Jansenism. In his capacity as President, the Archbishop of Rheims addressed a circular letter to all the prelates of the kingdom, in which he invited them to give their adherence to the *Acts of the Assembly of the Clergy*. At the very time that these *Acts* were being published, the Archbishop of Paris refused the Communion to a nun at St. Cloud, who had solicited before dying the consolation of the Church. She managed to evade the surveillance under which she was placed, and to forward her plea to the Parliament. Upon the order of the magistrates, a priest of the chapel of St. Cloud presented himself to administer the Sacrament to the dying woman. But the Mother Superior, acting upon the injunctions of the Archbishop, refused to open the doors to him. Force was obliged to be used, and the priest carried the *viatica* into the convent, escorted by a lieutenant of police and two officers of the Parliament, whilst outside, mounted troops, surrounded by an excited multitude, filled the avenues. No one doubted that these fresh intrigues were the work of the Jesuits. The Parliament, declaring that the bishops had exceeded their powers, suppressed the *Acts of the Assembly of the Clergy*. The bishops complained to the King, who, as he was just then desirous of obtaining subsidies from the clergy, quashed the Decree. Emboldened by this mark of favour, the bishops circulated the suppressed *Acts* throughout their dioceses. Libels were spread abroad asserting that the

magistrates were designedly aiming at the subversal of the Throne
and the Altar.   Other writings demanded the re-establishment of
the order of the Jesuits.   But the Parliament feared a renewal of
those disorders which had so profoundly troubled the kingdom
and prohibited all adherence to the *Acts*.   The Government also
took alarm, and published a Decree of Council, in which it com-
mended the observance of the Gallican maxims of 1682, fixed the
bounds of the *two powers*, and recalled the Declaration of 1731,
which had prescribed an absolute silence upon these questions.

At the same time, some difficulties arose in another quarter,
the consequences of which the Government had equal reasons
for apprehending.   At the close of the conflict which the
Money Edicts had brought about between the Government and
the Parliament of Brittany, all the members of that body had
sent in their resignations.   Upon the order of the King, six of
the magistrates, including the Proctor-General, La Chalotais, were
arrested, and three Councillors of State, and twelve " Masters of
Requests," were sent to Rennes to institute proceedings against
them.   The Parliament of Paris protested, in a Decree, against
the establishment of a tribunal, resembling " those which so
"many historical events had consigned to public contempt."   On
March 3rd, 1760, Louis XV. appeared in the midst of the Parliament and had this Decree erased from the registers before his
eyes.   "In *my person alone*," he said, " resides the sovereign
"power.   It is *to me alone* that the Courts owe their existence and
"their authority.   *To me alone* belongs the legislative power in-
"dependently and indivisibly.   All public order *emanates from me*."
He concluded by declaring that if the Parliament continued to
present " the scandalous spectacle of a rival contradiction of his
"sovereign will," he would be "reduced to the sad necessity of
"employing the power he had received from God to preserve his
"people from the baleful consequences of such proceedings."   Never
had Royalty asserted its rights with so much vigour, for never
before had it been so sensible of its weakness.   The Parliament
would not allow itself to be intimidated.   It renewed its remonstrances and threatened to resign.   The Ministry feared to try it

too far and once more made a compromise. The commissioners were recalled from Brittany, and La Chalotais and his colleagues, who had been imprisoned in different fortresses, were transferred to the Bastille.

In spite of the prohibition of the Parliament and the Decree of Council, adherents to the *Acts* continued to multiply. The Paris Parliament issued writs for the apprehension of the various priests who had disobeyed its injunction, and the Assemblies of Bordeaux, Aix, and Toulouse followed suit. War raged once more between the bishops and the magistrates. Louis XV., with the object of conciliating both parties, evoked to his Council the cognizance of all disputes relative to the *Acts*, and quashed the parliamentary Decrees. This conduct of course displeased the magistrates. Some fresh refusals of Sacraments having taken place, the Parliament, in a Decree dated January 1767, ordered the seizure and the banishment of those ecclesiastics, who were responsible for the refusals. Whereupon the bishops rushed in a body to Paris and held conventicles to decide upon a new course of action. The Parliament informed the prelates that they must return to their dioceses, under penalty of the seizure of their personal property, and forbade their holding any assembly without permission of the King. The bishops prayed the Monarch to annul this Decree and to preclude the Parliament from interfering in the affairs of the Church. The King felt that they were asking permission to stir up the kingdom according to their will, and, in quashing the Decree, he followed the example of the Parliament and ordered them to return to their dioceses. It was thus that the designs of the clergy miscarried. The bishops, by their mistaken zeal, only succeeded in furnishing their adversaries with fresh arms. It was upon this occasion that Voltaire, referring to the *Unigenitus*, wrote : "One must be either a priest or an ignor-"amus to make of this Jesuitical and Romish harlequinade a law of "the Church and State."

But the bishops did more than brand the productions of the Philosophers in their *Acts*. At their instigation, the last volumes of the *Encyclopedia* were seized and some of its authors sent to

G

the Bastille. The Encyclopedists retaliated with fresh writings. The death of the Chevalier de la Barre—the victim of religious intolerance—who was beheaded at Abbeville in accordance with a sentence confirmed by the Parliament, served to increase the ardour of the Philosophers. They had not forgotten the cruel end of Calas, and did not hesitate to accuse the Parliaments with making themselves the instruments of fanaticism and superstition. From that time forward the Philosophic school held clergy and magistracy in equal enmity.

The news of the tragic event at Abbeville quite overwhelmed Voltaire. "The inquisition is mild in comparison to your "Jansenists of the Grand Chamber and of *la Tournelle*," he said. "We are rescued from foxes to be delivered up to wolves." When the storm was passed, he set to work again. As, after the punishment of Calas, he preached tolerance, so, after the death of La Barre, he taught respect of human life, and, inspired by the recent work of Beccaria, he wrote his *Commentary on the Book of Misdemeanours and Penalties*. The police seized this brochure, but Voltaire's voice found an echo. In November, 1766, a magistrate developed the same ideas in a *Discourse upon the Administration of Criminal Justice*. In February, Marmontel produced his *Belisarius*—a warm plea for tolerance. This book was condemned by the Faculty of Theology and by the Archbishop of Paris, both of whom declared that religious intolerance was one of the essential principles of Catholicism. They added that, by virtue of the bond which united the *two Powers*, Sovereigns ought to place the sword at the service of the Faith. Such declarations did not arrest the stream of publications directed against the Church. In vain was a stricter watch put upon the book-trade. In vain did the colporteurs encumber the prisons. Whilst in certain writings, the legitimacy of the wealth of the clergy was called into question, and in others the King was advised to abolish convents, there appeared one after another—*Priests Unmasked, The Spirit of the Clergy, Sacerdotal Imposture, Doubts on Religion, Portable Theology, Catechumen,* and *The Soldier Philosopher.*

Whilst strictly proscribing the philosophical books, the Government was, nevertheless, partly inspired by the ideas of their writers. It openly blamed the Sorbonne for its censure of *Belisarius*, and could not be got to endorse the principles that transformed the weapon of the law into an arm in the service of the Church. Towards the close of 1767, the ministers presented to Louis XV. an Edict which restored to the Protestants their civil status. Three times the King rejected this Edict, but, at the same time, the governors of the provinces and the proctors-general were commanded not to molest the "religionists." A commission was also established to reform the convents, and several abuses were done away with. A more significant event bore witness to the new disposition of the Government. The Duc de Parma—Ferdinand de Bourbon—had expelled the Jesuits from his dominions, and promulgated a regulation which limited the action of the Papacy in religious matters. Clement XIII. quashed the regulation, excommunicated the author, and declared himself the sole sovereign of the States of Parma and Plaisance. The Parliament suppressed the Brief and forbade its publication as an act of high treason. Louis XV. confirmed this sentence, addressed the Decree to all the bishops of the kingdom, and seized upon Avignon[1] and the Comtat Venaissin.[1] This move, which was loudly applauded by the populace, testified to the progress that the Revolution had already made in men's minds in religious matters. The Pope was, in a manner, hunted out of France by the King.

Yet if in regard to Church questions, the Government partly followed the direction of public opinion, it did not do so at all in politics. An Edict of January, 1768, announced the re-establishment of the Grand Council upon the basis which had been organised thirty years before under Cardinal Fleury, when that minister, to please the Jesuits, had been on the point of sub-

---

[1] *Avignon*—In 1309, the Pope's Court was removed for a period from Rome to Avignon; subsequently Avignon became the residence of the anti-Popes, who were driven out in 1408. The Pontiff, however, still retained his sovereignty over the town. *Comtat Venaissin*—a district ceded to the Popes in 1229. (*Translator's Note.*)

stituting it for the Parliament. Public disapproval, as much, and
perhaps more, than the combined resistance of magistrates, princes,
and peers, caused the breakdown of the King's attempt, and less
than six months after promulgating his Edict, Louis XV. revoked
it implicitly by a Declaration.

At this time there began those artificial famines created by the
monstrous association called the *pacte de famine,* which counted
Louis XV. among its members. In the first half of the year
1768, revolts, occasioned by the dearness of bread, took place in
parts of Brittany and in Normandy. The Parliament of the
province wrote to Louis XV., describing " entire villages " as
being devoured by maladies caused by the bad quality of the
grain, and calling his attention to the hunger that decimated the
workmen in the towns. The dearth was also felt in the capital.
Towards the close of the preceding year, the Parliament had sent
a deputation to the King, beseeching him to look with compassion
on his people. "I love my people tenderly," replied the Monarch,
"and your ill advised action will serve only to encourage their
"complaints." In the months of October and November, 1768,
placards, posted in the most frequented streets of Paris, threatened
to set the city on fire, if the price of bread were not lowered. In
one of these placards the King was accused of constituting himself a "merchant of wheat," and it was more than hinted that
Damiens might find his imitators.

Still the bombs continued to fall into the "house of the Lord."
The cannonade was composed of *Sacred Contagion, The Examination of the Prophecies, The Life of David—the Man after God's
own Heart,* etc., etc. In their war against Catholicism, it must
be owned that the Philosophers attacked, without caution or reserve, all the traditions and ideas which formed obstacles in their
path. They imposed their doctrines, too, in the same dogmatic
manner that they so much condemned in their adversaries. The
publishers, following the example set by the writers, made themselves anonymous and inaccessible, and severities were, therefore,
redoubled against colporteurs. In default of colporteurs, the
prohibited works were passed from hand to hand. Certain mem-

bers of the Parliament, irritated by the licence permitted to authors, wished to have Voltaire arrested. The Patriarch, who flattered himself that he was more adroit than Socrates, and who had not the slightest ambition to pose as a hemlock-drinker, publicly received the Communion in the church at Ferney. This action stirred up a " devil of a row " in Paris. Twice in 1768 and 1769 he took part in this spiritual farce. If he had lived at Abbeville, where De la Barre was executed, he would, so he said, have communicated once a fortnight. The philosophical propagandism continued so fast and strong that the Lieutenant of Police himself avowed that he could not control the shower of pamphlets. Encyclopedist ideas filled the minds of the nobility, the *bourgeois*, and the magistrates. Even the clergy began to take the infection. In 1769 two monks declared to Diderot that atheism was the current doctrine in their cloisters. At the same time, many people were demanding other rules of family life than those prescribed by Catholicism. Some revolted against the institution of marriage, and wrote in favour of divorce.

Whilst the Encyclopedists stirred men's minds by their writings, the discontent provoked among the lower classes by the dearness of bread was far from being appeased. The Parliament began to consider means of remedying the evil, and demanded information concerning the monopolists. On their side, the *Economists*—a newly-formed sect of "political Philosophers," who aimed at upsetting all received principles of Government and establishing a new order of things—set forth their views upon the subject. The creation of fresh taxes, declared necessary in order "to close the wounds which long and ruinous wars had made in the State," augmented the popular indignation and increased the misery. But the Government, pressed by a debt of nearly 3,000,000,000 *livres*, sought only to create fresh resources. The Abbé Terray, lately nominated Comptroller-General, undertook the task of bleeding the Nation. In January, 1770, Edicts were issued by the Council which so heavily taxed pensions and incomes, that Voltaire had to hand out from his own pocket 100,000 *livres*.

This measure brought many families to ruin and excited universal animosity. The Parliament, constituting itself the mouthpiece of public opinion, presented *Remonstrances*, to which the King replied that he was certainly touched by the situation of his subjects, but that his paternal sentiments must yield in this case to the necessities of the State. At this crisis, the King was advised in a pamphlet to extinguish the debt by immediately appropriating the wealth of the clergy, which, valued at a third of that of the kingdom, represented, so it was affirmed, a revenue of 3,000,000,000 *livres*. This suggestion made all the more impression because it was not put forward in a party spirit, but with every mark of respect for Religion, in the name of which, the author exhorted the bishops to observe the rules of poverty prescribed in the Gospels. But the Government repudiated the doctrines that it had previously encouraged and took proceedings against the publishers of the work. It could, however, see for itself the universal distress. During the year 1770, the dwellers in the country districts lived on beans, bran, oats, and herbs. Seditious placards multiplied in Paris. One of these contained the words : "If the price of bread is not diminished and order "introduced into the affairs of the State, we shall know how to "perform our part ; we are twenty against each bayonet ! "

The clergy were, at this time, holding their General Assembly at Paris. Neither the critical state of the country, nor the distress of the population was the subject of their deliberations. Apart from questions of ecclesiastical administration, the bishops were solely occupied in devising means to dam the torrent of writings directed against the Church. At the commencement of their session, they laid before the King a *Memoir of the Baleful Consequences of the Liberty of Thought and Publication.* They complained particularly that a new edition of the *Encyclopedia* was being at that moment published. Yielding once more to their plaints, the Government caused all the volumes of the new edition, that had already appeared, to be taken to the Bastille. No one, however, doubted for a moment that these volumes would be returned some months later to the publishers. Besides this, the bishops voted an annual pension of 2,000 *livres* to an erudite ecclesiastic—the Abbé Bergier—who undertook, for that price, the charge of refuting all the important works of the Encyclopedists. Before separating, the bishops published a Manifesto, entitled *Warning to the Clergy of France and to the Faithful of the Kingdom against the Dangers of Incredulity.* In this Manifesto, the prelates strove to interest the Monarch in the cause of the Church by pointing out that Religion taught the people to bear the yoke with meekness, and wear unresistingly the chains of despotism. The Government was no doubt touched by this declaration, no less than by the " free gift " of 16,000,000 *livres* accorded to it, and, in acknowledgment of this gift, the Parliament was requested to seize all impious works. The magistrates responded to this request by committing to the flames *Sacred Contagion, Christianity Unveiled, The System of Nature,* and other books. But in spite of all these severities, it was apparent that Philosophy, thenceforward victorious, had exhausted its adversaries. The *Warning* of 1770 had none of the vigour that was still remarked in the *Acts* of 1765, and the magistrates, contrary to custom, would not allow the speech of the Advocate-General, on the occasion of the condemning of the philosophical works, to be printed. In order to publish it, the latter had to obtain the King's permission.

In this speech, the power of the Philosophers, whom it was proposed to annihilate, was unskilfully thrown into strong relief. " The Philosophers," said the Advocate-General, " have consti-" tuted themselves the preceptors of the human race. ' Liberty of " Thought' is their cry, and this cry has made itself heard from one " extremity of the earth to the other . . . . Their object has been " to direct the minds of men into another channel in regard to all " civil and religious institutions, and thus *the Revolution, so to speak, " has been accomplished.* Kingdoms have felt their ancient founda-" tions totter, and nations, astonished to find their principles anni-" hilated, have asked themselves by what fatality they have become " so different from their former selves. It is against Religion above " all that these innovators have aimed their deadliest blows. In writ-

" ings without number, they have poured forth the poison of unbelief.
" Eloquence, poetry, histories, romances, and even dictionaries have
" been infected. And these writings are scarcely made public in
" the capital before they spread like a torrent to the country.
" The contagion has penetrated even to the workshops and
" cottages."

It would have been impossible to attest, in clearer terms, the
triumph of Philosophy, and, in particular, of the doctrines that
attacked Catholicism. This public avowal, emanating from a
magistrate, confirmed the declarations made by the Philosophers
themselves. According to Voltaire, to whom a statue was about
this time erected by his admirers, the Revolution, in its victorious
course, had already overstepped its mark. The Patriarch had
aimed at cleansing the Temple of Divinity of its stains, but had
not thought of overthrowing it. Yet the Temple was fast falling
to pieces. Of the edifice of the *ancien régime* there remained only
the tottering walls, beneath which Royalty took shelter. The
moment was drawing near when those walls would in their turn
crumble into dust, and not a vestige of them remain.

CHAPTER VIII.

End of the Government of Louis XV.

(1770-1774.)

AFTER more than a year of captivity, La Chalotais and the five other magistrates of the Parliament of Rennes had been sent into exile. But, though banished, they had not ceased to protest against the harsh treatment to which they had been subjected. La Chalotais, who, in spite of his advanced years, had been the most severely dealt with, deemed himself the prey of the "Society of Jesus," against which body he had formerly pronounced a celebrated *réquisitoire.* This idea was readily embraced by a prejudiced public. At Paris, as at Rennes, it was believed that there existed a vast Jesuitical plot directed against La Chalotais and the Parliament of Brittany, in which the Duc d'Aiguillon, Governor of the province, was himself concerned. Only a small number of the magistrates who had resigned had subsequently resumed their seats, and the vacancies had been filled by magistrates chosen by d'Aiguillon. The Parliament had protested against these arbitrary nominations, and had requested to be re-established in its entirety. In July, 1769, its desire was granted, and, as soon as the magistrates were installed, they instituted inquiries into the "facts of bribery, false witness, and other crimes imputed to the Duc d'Aiguillon." D'Aiguillon, wishing to refute these allegations, solicited the jurisdiction of the court of Peers, and, by order of the King, the Paris Parliament was convoked.

The proceedings opened at Versailles with great solemnity. Louis XV. presided at the debate in person, and the magistrates congratulated themselves upon their liberty of deliberation in so grave a matter. The debate lasted for two months, and was then summarily interrupted by letters-patent that annulled the proceedings, and gave the Duc d'Aiguillon a complete discharge. This act was both a serious miscarriage of justice, and an affront to the dignity of the Parliament. On their return to Paris, the magistrates issued a Decree, declaring the *Duc* "deprived of the " rights and privileges of the peerage until he had cleared himself " of the suspicions which tarnished his honour." The King quashed this Decree, and, repairing to the Parliament, caused all the records of the case to be expunged from the registers. Great was the indignation of the provincial Parliaments, and had not the Government hastened to prevent any united action, of which it foresaw the danger, the King's conduct would, no doubt, have again given rise to wholesale resignations, and a " confederation "of resistance " in the name of the unity and indivisibility of the Parliament. At the instigation of Chancellor Maupeou, the King issued an Edict, by which he forbade all the Parliaments, thenceforward, to make use of the terms " unity," " indivisibility," and " sections," to correspond with each other except in certain cases specified in the Statutes, or to resist his will, whether by cessation of service, or collective resignations, under penalty of having their members deprived of their offices and punished as rebels. The Parliament refused to register an Edict, the adoption of which would have covered it with ignominy in the eyes of the public. The following day, a " Bed of Justice " was held at Versailles, at which the Chancellor stated, in the King's name, that if no barrier were opposed to the actions of the Parliaments, authority would no longer emanate from the Throne, but from the magistracy. After some useless representations from the first President, the Edict was registered. At this memorable session Royalty, by "divine right," uttered its last protest against the doctrines which were assailing it on all hands.

The people, who were suffering so severely from scarcity of bread, warmly took the part of the magistrates, and the princes of the blood-royal testified their disapproval. The magistrates besought Louis XV. either to withdraw an Edict that so disgraced them or to receive their resignations ; and they further resolved to suspend their functions until he acceded to their request, saying that "they had no longer sufficient mental freedom to enable "them to regulate the 'goods,' safety, and honour of the King's "subjects." The Monarch's only response was an order to them to resume their duties. Four times he reiterated this order in "letters of command ; " four times the magistrates refused to obey. At last, on the night of January 20th, 1771, musketeers served them with papers upon which they were forced to write " yes," or " no," to signify if they consented or not to resume their functions. The greater number wrote "no." Forty, who signed "yes," re-tracted the following day. The night after, one hundred and thirty magistrates received letters of exile, and were notified, by Decree of Council, that their seats were confiscated and they and their children declared incapable of holding any judicial offices in the future. On January 21st, thirty-eight members of the Parliament, on whom no writs had been served, came to the *Palais de Justice,* followed by an enormous crowd, and solemnly pronounced themselves to be at one with their colleagues. They were immediately sent into exile. From that moment, no Parliament existed. The Chancellor requested the Grand Council to replace it ; the Council hesitated. He then made overtures to the *Cour des Aides,* but met with a rebuff. Eventually the Grand Council complied with the Chancellor's request, and on January 24th, was installed in the place of the old Parliament, assuming both its title and attributes. This *coup d'état* excited a storm of indignation against Chancellor Maupeou. Insulting and threatening placards were posted at Paris and Versailles, and on the day that the new magistrates took their seats, it was necessary to employ the military to protect them from the anger of the mob. During the first days of their sitting, the *Palais de Justice* was transformed into a veritable camp. Soldiers filled it within, and on the outer walls people wrote inscriptions, referring in insulting terms to the new magistrates. The princes of the blood, all of whom, except the Comte de la Marche, had blamed the action of the Ministry, received anonymous letters, imploring them to "come to the help of the Nation," for fear of a catastrophe.   "I affirm," wrote a man, who was in a position to judge of events, "that if, at this critical moment, a chief could have been found, "a most terrible Revolution would have broken out."

Whilst Paris trembled, the provincial Parliaments protested by Decrees, by letters and by remonstrances.   At Paris, the *Cour des Monnaies* and the *Châtelet* also uttered protests.   The *Cour des Aides*, over which Malesherbes—the future defender of Louis XVI.—presided, asked the King to convoke the States-General. "The incorruptible testimony of the representatives of the Nation," so ran the *Remonstrances* of the latter body, "will tell you if the "cause we support is that of the people, by whom, and for whom you "reign."   In a few days, copies of these *Remonstrances* had multiplied to such an extent that they were to be found in every house, and Malesherbes was sent into exile.

Since the accession of Louis XV., there had never been such a stirring up of public opinion against the Government.   At private gatherings and supper-parties, nothing was spoken of but the impudent violation of the "fundamental constitutions" of the kingdom.   Even women took part in discussions about "public "right," and transformed their *salons* into miniature States-General, from which they rigorously excluded "the traitors or the cowards" who from weakness or interested motives abandoned their country's cause.

Maupeou fancied he could calm things down by introducing into the judiciary system some of those reforms for which the public had long clamoured.   Under the title of "Superior Councils," he created six new courts of justice within the jurisdiction of the Paris Parliament, the extended scope of which had long been a source of ruin to all suitors.   He abolished all venal posts and announced that, thenceforward, justice should be administered gratuitously[1] to all the King's subjects.   The Parliaments of the

---

[1] This gratuity of justice was more apparent than real.   The payments for fines, stamps, etc., were all left as before, and, at the request of a hundred advocates—newly created and devoted to the interests of the Chancellor— the lawyers' costs were augmented.

provinces objected to the establishment of "Superior Councils," and the Rouen magistracy demanded the convocation of the States-General. The Duc d'Orléans presented to the King a memoir, signed by sixty peers and five princes, which protested against all the action taken by the Government since December 7th, 1770.

But instead of relaxing, Maupeou increased his severities. The *Cour des Aides* having refused to recognise the new Parliament, he suppressed it, and he also ordered the princes of the blood to withdraw from the Court. As the initial step in these proceedings Maupeou had exiled those among the ministers who would have been likely to withstand his designs. He now nominated in their places men of whom he felt sure, and, in defiance of public opinion, he recalled the Duc d'Aiguillon to the Ministry. In the end, Louis XV., in a "Bed of Justice," sanctioned the action of his Chancellor by word of mouth, and asserted that *he would never change.* These words called forth the angry demurs of his people. Many declaimed against injustice and tyranny in the streets, and women, more passionate than men, announced the downfall of the Monarchy. Some verses were published, in which it was set down that France was thirsting for the Chancellor's blood. Numerous notices, placarded throughout Paris, bore the words: *"Bread for two sous and the Chancellor hanged, or revolt in Paris."* The political emotion was greatly deepened by the agitation caused by the dearth and distress.

Again there poured forth a deluge of libels, amongst which the *Correspondence between M. de Maupeou and M. de Sorhouet* dealt the hardest blows at the Ministry. This *Correspondence* was composed of spurious letters, addressed by the Chancellor to his friend Sorhouet, developing his plans, ideas, and morals—"which were not always "those of honest men"—and holding up their supposed writer to ridicule and contempt. Maupeou defended himself in brochures, written by authors whom he employed for the purpose, of which more than one hundred were given to the world before the close of the year 1771. It was unfortunate that some of these writings betrayed a zeal so indiscreet that the Chancellor had to request his Parliament to denounce them !   This Parliament pursued with severity the numerous writings that attacked the Minister, and the police, for their part, were not inactive.   Every day persons were arrested for distributing libels or speaking idle words of gossip. Raids were made on the booksellers, and, as another means of putting an end to the publications, a tax was put on paper.

In the absence of a Paris Parliament, the provincial Assemblies, united by a common feeling of resentment, threatened to become centres of resistance.   However, in the last month of 1771, they were all suppressed ; some to be re-established, others to be modified, diminished, or replaced by Superior Councils.   This measure was everywhere carried out by the same means.   The commanding-officer of the province assembled the magistrates, proclaimed the Edict of suppression, and employed military force to compel the evacuation of the chamber of deliberation.   In Normandy, where the Parliament had been dismembered and two Superior Councils substituted, many of the new magistrates, nominated by the Chancellor, were in danger of their lives.   Some of them were hung in effigy, and troops had to be sent to keep the populace in check.   A *Manifesto to the Normans* appeared, in which it was asserted that the King, having broken the contract made with the province when it was joined to the rest of the kingdom, the Normans had the right to detach themselves from France and choose another Sovereign.   To keep Louis XV. in a severe frame of mind, which, it is only just to say, was not his natural mood, the Dubarry—who had succeeded the Pompadour, and whom the Chancellor had won over by humouring her whims and by flattery—was entrusted with the task of inducing in the King a dread of the possible proceedings of the Parliaments.   She placed in her rooms a portrait of Charles I. by Vandyck, which she had bought for 20,000 *livres*, and whenever the King showed signs of relenting, she recalled to his mind the tragic end of the English Monarch.

At the same time that the Ministry made its attacks upon the Parliament, it suppressed the *Châtelet* and reconstructed it on a new basis.   The *Cour des Comptes* was threatened with abolition, and a number of inferior courts were done away with. The Nation began to be seriously concerned. All around them, the people saw their laws and institutions crumbling to pieces and a despotic empire arising from their ruins ; they were further incensed by the clerical reaction which followed immediately upon the restoration of absolute government.

The clergy did not hide their joy at the turn events had taken. They thundered from the pulpit against the ancient Parliament, and the Jesuits returned to the capital in crowds. A Royal Declaration, issued at the entreaty of the Archbishop of Paris, recalled all the priests banished or arrested for refusals of Sacraments since the "Bed of Justice" of December, 1756. This Declaration was clearly intended to pave the way for the re-establishment of the Jesuits. The Cardinal de la Roche-Aymoun, who was devoted to their interests, having been charged with the list of benefices, promoted several Jesuits to livings. The according of these favours to the clergy created the belief that the *coup d'état* had been the work of the Jesuits, who hoped, by the overthrowal of the magistracy, to regain their old ascendancy. In truth they had helped it forward by all the means in their power, but the initiative had been taken by the Government alone. Neither was the *coup d'état* forced upon the Chancellor by the disagreeable position in which the d'Aiguillon case had placed the Ministry. According to several contemporaries, that violent measure was taken by Maupeou in order to extricate himself from the all but insurmountable difficulties of the financial situation. Louis XV. had refused to declare himself bankrupt, and, as he would not reduce his expenses, it had become necessary to create fresh duties, to which the Parliament would assuredly have offered a most determined resistance. On that account alone, it was said, the destruction of the magistracy was resolved upon, and the King allowed himself to be led into a measure, for which the d'Aiguillon case afforded an easy pretext. From the moment that the Parliament of Paris was suppressed, the financial operations commenced. Money Edicts multiplied to such an extent that, in the year 1771 alone, the Monarch's revenue amounted to 100,000,000 *livres* more than

his customary income.   But, in spite of this fact, not a single
State debt was discharged.   Yet, though it was so firmly believed
that the confused state of the finances alone accounted for the
great political changes, there were, in truth, other causes.   It
had for a long time been evident that the King, irritated by the
incessant attacks made upon him by the magistracy, would some
day attempt to crush this resistant force.   The situation was so
strained that it could only be relieved by a *coup d'état*, and Louis
XV. had recourse to one, as soon as a minister presented himself
who was bold enough to execute it.   No one believed that the
Chancellor had been led into it, as he pretended, by ideas of reform.   Indeed, the only immediate result of the innovations was
the destruction of the magistracy.   The Parliaments had not been
merely judicial bodies, led, by force of circumstances, to deal with
political subjects; they had come to be the sole barrier between
the Nation and absolute Government.   In the authoritative Act
that destroyed them, France recognised the overthrow of her sole
defence against despotism.

One of the most characteristic results of the *coup d'état* was the
concentrating of thought and doctrine upon a single object.   To the
religious war, which the Encyclopedists considered finished, there
succeeded a political conflict, but it was not the Encyclopedists,
properly speaking, who conducted it.   Voltaire, who never forgave
the Parliaments for their persecution of men of letters, and who
did not cease to reproach them for having tortured Calas and the
Chevalier de la Barre, actually applauded the action of the
Chancellor.   He had, it is true, no enthusiasm for political liberty,
liking better, as he said, "to obey a fine lion, much stronger than
"himself, than two hundred rats of his own species."   It was the
Patriots—theorists more nearly resembling the Economists than
the Encyclopedists—who placed themselves, at this juncture, at
the head of the movement.   The Jansenists themselves turned
against monarchial despotism all the forces that they had hitherto directed against papal despotism, and allied themselves to the
Patriot party.   Thenceforward, side by side with the libels, which
were showered upon the Ministry, there appeared pamphlets, in

which the authors endeavoured to unite and develop theories, propounded before their time, concerning "the natural liberty of "man, the imprescriptibility of his rights, and the origin of Kings "and the social contract."

These new theorists hurled forth brochure after brochure, thinking, by repeated efforts, to attain their end more easily, and to baffle the severe measures of the Government. It was in the second half of 1771 that these writings began to be circulated. They attacked first some of the principles so often put forward by the King. "Does the sovereignty reside in one "individual or in the whole body of the nation?" was one of the questions they propounded, and they denied that Royalty *held its authority from God*, and that the legislative power was rested solely and indivisibly in the Monarch. Further they declared all acts of the Sovereign, that infringed the fundamental laws of the State, to be *ipse facto* null, and they insinuated that, in regard to such acts, the people had the right of resistance.

Thus passed the year 1771, undoubtedly the most troubled period of the reign of Louis XV. In 1772 the agitation, though less tumultuous, still continued. The libels on the Chancellor became more and more aggressive, and the author of the *Secret Correspondence* published a new series of letters, in which irony was supplanted by insult. All this time the *Gazette de France* never ceased to affirm that the changes decreed by the Ministry worked smoothly in all quarters and had gained the approbation of the public. There were brought out some "Supplements" to the *Gazette de France* which, under pretext of correcting the frequent untruths retailed by this journal, occupied, from a political point of view, the same position that the *Ecclesiastical News* had held in religious matters. By a Decree of March, 1772, the Parliament condemned to be burned the *Secret Correspondence* and one of the supplements, declaring the authors to be guilty of the crime of "divine and human petty treason." This sentence was parodied by a "Decree of Parliament," supposed to be pronounced at the request of the Advocate-General against "a furtive pamphlet, the "production of an obscure cabal of 18,000,000 persons."

Far from intimidating the libellists, the last Decree of the Parliament seemed only to stimulate their audacity. Whilst bitter epigrams and insolent prints multiplied against the Chancellor, there appeared, one after the other, pamphlets so violent that they stimulated Maupeou's anger to the highest pitch. Together with the libels, political brochures also appeared. In one, *The Maxims of Public Right*, it was declared that Kings were made for the people and not people for Kings. In another, in which enquiry was made into the origin of Monarchy, it was established that "the King and the Law received their authority "from the same source . . . . the unanimity of the wishes of the " Nation," and that the latter "had the right to assemble of its "own accord" to deliberate upon the affairs of the State. In face of these persistent attacks, Maupeou, who felt the need of creating allies, did not neglect the means of inducing the friendship of the clergy. At the request of the Archbishop of Paris, letters-patent suspended the execution of the Decree of the old Parliament, which forbade the introduction into France, without authorisation, of any Act of the Court of Rome. This concession was apparently made to prepare the way for the re-establishment of the Jesuits, and their return was feared more than ever. Associating himself with the Episcopate in its enmity against the Philosophers, the Chancellor ordered that part of the Bastille, in which the copies of the last edition of the *Encyclopedia* had been deposited, to be walled up. Two partisans of the Encyclopedists, Suard and the poet Delile, who had just been nominated by the Academy, had their election cancelled by the King.

Maupeou still continued to issue brochures in reply to the writings directed against him, and his Parliament, by measures so exceptionally severe, as to be almost inquisitorial, attempted to avert the deluge of pamphlets. It took proceedings not only against the authors, publishers, and distributors of these writings, but also against "their adherents and accomplices," among whom were included those who only read them. Thenceforward the public found itself exposed to the most tyrannical proceedings. Houses were searched, and if a man was found with one of the libels about his person, he was liable to immediate arrest. Paris swarmed with spies. Yet, in spite of these rigorous measures, the publication of pamphlets went on. As in the times of Jansenism, the entire Nation was an accomplice in this plot to deceive the Government.

Nevertheless, the Comptroller-General still continued to bleed the people. "Unlike a leech, which at least drops off when "full," he persisted in imposing fresh taxes. All the new Parliaments had been forbidden to present further *Remonstrances*, and no more were issued until after the death of Louis XV. Delivered up like spoil to ministers, who had no longer any check put upon them, and each of whom was an absolute master in his own department, France presented the appearance of a conquered country, upon which a foreign power had imposed new laws. In less than a year 100,000 persons, despoiled of their fortunes, or threatened with the deprivation of their liberty, quitted the capital, bound either for the provinces or for foreign lands. The venal posts, so noisily abolished by Maupeou, reflourished under another form. The Abbé Terray and another minister, the Duc de la Vrillière, allowed shameless women to traffic openly with the appointments that were at their disposal.

Louis XV., "shut up in his seraglio, and plunged in de-"bauchery," bestowed the revenues of his kingdom upon the Dubarry. Provided that he had enough money for his pleasures, he was but little concerned by the disordered state of his finances.

At this time the Abbé Raynal published his *Philosophical and Political History of the Establishments and Commerce of the Europeans in the two Indies*, in which he attacked all persons in authority—Ministers, Priests, and Kings—with equal violence. The sensation created by this book determined the Government to condemn it. But, as the Ministry paid more attention to phillipics than to doctrinal works, it was only suppressed by Decree of Council. The Government likewise contented itself with merely suppressing the *Philosophical Reflections upon the*

System of Nature, a book, no less audacious than the other, in which it was maintained that it was not the people's *right* alone, but their *duty*, to rise up against despotism. The Chancellor seemed to be very uneasy in regard to the rapid introduction of free thought into politics. His prudence led him to go so far as to forbid the printing of the *Capitulaires* of Baluze, for fear lest that collection of old French laws should become a weapon in the hands of Patriot authors. His Parliament, for its part, was pursuing inquiries in regard to anti-Chancellor books. In reference to these, fifty-two persons found themselves drawn into a case which lasted for nearly the whole of the year 1773.

While these events were taking place in Paris, revolts, provoked by the scarcity of wheat, broke out in various parts of the provinces. The peasants came in thousands to the towns to demand bread, and it was feared that the continuous dearth might bring about a general rebellion.

In the midst of all these legitimate causes of discontent, the public had one satisfaction. A Brief from Clement XIV., dated July, 1773, definitely suppressed the Society of the Jesuits, and this body was obliged to consider itself annihilated, since its Ultramontane maxims forbade it to rebel against Rome. In this matter the Government had been unable to separate itself from other Catholic Courts, all of which had solicited the Pope to grant this fiat of abolition. Besides, Maupeou was no devotee, and, following on the storm of opposition which he had just been contending against, he had no desire to stir up public antagonism a second time by the re-establishment of a detested institution. And he perhaps thought, by favouring its complete suppression, to win the sympathies of the Nation. In truth, the Brief had to be paid for by the restitution of Avignon and the Comtat Venaissin, and the Chancellor felt himself called upon to show that the disbandment of the Jesuits would not have the effect of making the Government more indulgent to the enemies of Religion. In January, 1774, the Parliament which had, up to that time, burned none but libels directed against the Chancellor, committed to the flames two books which it stigmatised as impious; one of them being a

posthumous work of Helvetius, called *Concerning Man : His In-
tellectual Faculties and Education.*

At the close of the year 1772, the princes of the blood, though still
adhering in a certain degree to their original protests, were recalled
to the Court. Most of the members of the suppressed provincial
Parliaments, after having refused for a long time to accept compensation for the loss of their offices, yielded, and the public opposition began to subside. Pamphlets, too, became less numerous
and pointed. For two years the country had looked forward to a
new order of things. Every month the news had spread abroad
that the Parliaments were going to be re-established and the
Chancellor disgraced, but the constant renewal and disappoint-
ment of their hopes had at last worn out the people's enthusiasm.

Thus it happens too often that a Nation, that has been oppressed
by the heavy hand of despotism, is seized in the end by a "species
"of torpor and lethargy." To this lethargy soon succeeded the
fever of pleasure and dissipation. "Never have there been so
"many pastimes and spectacles," remarked a contemporary. At
Court, and in the capital, pleasure reigned in a manner all the
more indecorous because it seemed designed as an insult to a people
succumbing on all sides to poverty, and dwelling in the midst of
overturned fortunes and widespread bankruptcy. When, in 1774,
there appeared *The Almanack Royal*, in which a certain Mr. Mir-
lavand was characterised as " treasurer of the grain on account of
"the King"—which was an open declaration of the traffic in which
the King was engaged—the protest of the Parisians took the feeble
form of a comic song.

This state of dejection accounted for the absence of any objections to the restitution of Avignon and the Comtat Venaissin.
With equal indifference, the public received the news of the dis-
memberment of Poland. If a few people were concerned by the
latter event, it was because they foresaw the war which might
break out in consequence—some fearing it as the climax of the
evils that had come upon the country, others, on the contrary,
desiring it as a "salutary shock."

Yet, though the opposition of the people appeared to be exhausted, their hatred was still unappeased. The proof of this was found in the case of one, Beaumarchais, against whom a councillor of the Maupeou Parliament had brought an action for the recovery of fifteen *louis*, which the former affirmed he had already repaid. The whole of France was stirred by the debate, which put to shame the detested Maupeou Parliament. Beaumarchais was looked upon as the organ of national vengeance. When he was censured in a Decree that deprived him of all civil rights, he was the recipient of an ovation. "All Paris" hastened to call upon him, and the Duc de Chartres and the Prince de Conti gave a *fête* in his honour. The effect of these proceedings was such a disgrace to the councillors that it was popularly said, with that touch of raillery so peculiar to Parisians: "If Louis XV. destroyed the old Parliament, fifteen *louis* will destroy the new one." But a much more important event was about to change the political situation.

In April, 1774, Louis XV. was struck with a malady that threatened to put an end to his existence. The news of his illness soon became the sole topic of conversation. The public rejoiced at the prospect of a new reign. The lower orders, especially, did not hide their satisfaction at the idea of changing masters. One fact alone shows how much, in the space of thirty years, the disposition of the Parisians towards their Monarch had changed. On the word of a canon of *Notre Dame*, six thousand masses had, in 1744, been requested at that church for the restoration to health of the King, then ill at Metz. In 1757, when Damiens made his attempt, the number of masses demanded was only six hundred. In 1774 there were but three. Louis XV. expired at last after a reign that had lasted too long for France.

That principle of "Divine right," which, four years before, he had made such a desperate attempt to enunciate, he proclaimed once more upon his dying bed. On receiving the Communion, he said that he repented having scandalised his subjects, though he *owed an account of his conduct to God alone.*

He died in the midst of public apathy, and had for his funeral oration the obloquy of his people. During the month that followed, he was spared neither placards, satires, nor detractory epitaphs. No one remembered him, except to insult his memory.

With Louis XV. the prestige of Royalty faded away, never to reappear. Monarchy by Divine right was thenceforward condemned. Those four years, in which a Dubarry reigned by the side of a Monarch sunk in debauchery—that short and shameful period when principle, morality, and duty were all alike forgotten— were the result to which the entire reign of Louis XV. contributed. The scandals with which those years were filled prepared all minds for the reception of the political maxims of Philosophy. They did for Monarchy what the agitated period of the refusals of Sacraments did for the Church. In them the Revolution was accomplished in idea, from the political standpoint, as it had already been from that of Religion, and the old system of Royalty was buried by the side of the Church that had succumbed before it. The time had come for Revolutionary ideas to be transformed into Revolutionary facts.

CHAPTER IX.

Reign of Louis XVI.   The Turgot Ministry.

(1774-1776.)

On the 10th of May, 1774, Louis XVI. ascended the throne, the
cynosure of the high hopes of the Nation. Following on to an
oppressive reign which had terminated in shame and disorder, the
advent of a Prince—who, in spite of his youth, had already won
the esteem of the public by his virtues—was welcomed as a
pledge of the many reforms for which the Nation sighed. Not
that the country had formulated any special wishes, the immediate realisation of which it imposed upon the successor of
Louis XV. For that matter, the minds of men had been so
greatly agitated during a long period of years, and public opinion
so much misled by conflicting theories, that there had come to be
more diversity than unanimity of thought in regard to the changes
necessary to be introduced into the political system. But the
general public, at least, had in mind some definite ideas of reform.
The dismissal of ministers whom they detested, the recall of the
ancient Parliament, prompt reconstruction of the finances, and a
speedy termination of the famine, were the first satisfactions that
they demanded of the young King. Louis XVI. was, at heart,
fully disposed to walk in the way of reform. But, though he was
a good and honest man, he possessed a limited intelligence and an
undecided will. The first Edict of his reign revealed his true
sentiments. It remitted all "accession dues," which amounted
to 24,000,000 *livres*, and cost the tax-payers some 40,000,000 *livres*.
In it, he invoked the support of the "Most High" to sustain him in his youth and inexperience, announced that his reign
would be founded on principles of justice, promised to maintain

order and economy in the finances, and spoke of his desire to
make his people happy in terms that, according to Grimm, moved
the whole of Paris to tears. The young Queen, wishing to
associate herself with the sentiments of her husband, renounced,
in her turn, a right called the "dues of the Queen's girdle." In
these initial acts of the reign, men saw the promise of other
benefits, and across the pedestal of the statue of Henri IV. some
one wrote "Resurrexit."

Nevertheless there were murmurs mingled with the expressions of delight. Some astonishment was felt that, in spite of
the assurances of reform, contained in the Royal Edict, the
Maupeou Parliament was allowed to remain in office and to congratulate the King upon his accession. This fact was considered
a bad omen. The people were no less dissatisfied with the
changes that were made in the Ministry. Louis XVI. sent away
some of the ministers, whose dismissal was desired—notably the
Duc d'Aiguillon—but he allowed Maupeou and the Abbé Terray
to remain in power. The Nation was impatient to be avenged of
the men who so ground it down, and mistrusted promises, which
were not endorsed by the discharge of these two ministers and
the recall of the old Parliament.

The Archbishop of Paris, and other prelates, represented to
the King that, if he recalled the former Parliament, Religion
in France would be completely done for. Mistrusting the
influence of Marie Antoinette, to whom it attributed the dismissal of the Duc d'Aiguillon, the clerical party tried to alienate
from her the King's affections. At table, Louis XVI. found, on
his plate, notes containing the words: "Sire, put no trust in the
Queen," and attempts were made to persuade him that she was
unfaithful. Thus, from the very steps of the Throne, emanated
the first attacks on Marie Antoinette—attacks which were but
the precursors of more terrible assaults. At the same time, the
clergy strove—by posting threatening placards and circulating
lying scandals against the King—to set Louis XVI. against the
people and the people against him. Between the representations
of this cabal, which hemmed him in with its intrigues, and

the desires of his people. the Monarch hesitated.   That hesitation greatly impaired his popularity.   .

The public was already oscillating between the conditions of indecision and defiance, when, on the *Fête*-day of St. Louis, August 25th, it was informed of the banishment of Maupeou and the disgrace of Terray.   In a single moment, the King regained his popularity, and there was an outburst of universal joy. Paris was illuminated, and transparencies with the words : " Long live the King ! Long live the Queen ! Long live the ancient Parliament ! " were lighted up.   To these testimonies of delight were joined other demonstrations.   On the *Place Dauphine*, the mob burned Chancellor Maupeou in effigy, and on the hill of St. Geneviève a figure, representing the Abbé Terray in full ecclesiastical costume, was affixed to a gallows.   The Government took alarm at these manifestations.   Hearing that the people intended to burn in front of the statue of Henri IV. the figure of the Chancellor, clothed in all the insignia of his dignity, the horse-patrol was sent to disperse the crowd.   Some difficulty was experienced in carrying out this design.   With cries of " Long live the King ! Long live the ancient Parliament ! " packets of inflammable fusees were thrown at the horses' heads, and the multitudes had to be charged with drawn swords, whilst a detachment of French and Swiss guards made a pretence of loading their guns.   As for the members of the Maupeou Parliament, they could only reach the *Palais* in disguise, and had to be protected, during their sittings, by soldiers.   Similar demonstrations took place in the provinces.   It was thus, in the first months of the reign of Louis XVI., that the people of France anticipated the tragic scenes of the Revolution.

The recall of the old Parliament followed hard upon the dismissal of the ministers.   The *anti-parlimentaires* moved Heaven and earth to prevent this recall, and the clergy, especially, " gnashed their teeth " in their rage.   Voltaire and the greater number of the Philosophers were astounded that the King " wished to sacrifice the new Parliament, which had always known " how to obey, to the old one, which had done nothing but defy."

Conforming to the wishes of the Nation, however, Louis XVI. wrote to the exiled magistrates to return to Paris and to repair to the *Palais* on the 12th of November in their robes of ceremony. There the King met them, and, in a " Bed of Justice," registered Edicts by which he suppressed the Supreme Councils and re-established the former Parliament.

On coming away from this assemblage, both King and magistrates were saluted by the acclamations of the crowd, and that evening the whole of Paris was illuminated. In a few months, all the provincial Parliaments were reinstated, and the *Châtelet* and the *Cour des Aides* re-established.

The King endeavoured also to conciliate the interests with which his Edicts clashed. The Grand Council, which had been suppressed since 1771, was revived in order to receive the members of the Maupeou Parliament, but notwithstanding this measure, Louis XVI. found himself exposed to the resentment of the party, whose defeat he had accomplished. Placards, that threatened the King's life, were posted at the Luxembourg and in other parts of the capital. The very men who had so often declared that the recall of the old Parliament would imperil the Crown were the first to stir up the people against the person of the Sovereign. The Archbishop of Paris had thought that the Parliament would, at least, have been deprived of the cognizance of ecclesiastical affairs, and, when he found his hopes deceived, he made no attempt to conceal his displeasure. There was reason to fear that he might have recourse to the means he had employed in the previous reign and endeavour to stir up the public mind by refusals of Sacraments. Louis XVI. sent for him, and made him understand that, if he attempted to renew the troubles he had formerly excited, he would not only be banished but subjected to the full severities of the law. This action showed clearly that, in accordance with national desires, the Government had resolved to keep a firm hand on the clergy. At the same time, Louis XVI. opened wide the door for reforms.

On the evening of the day on which he had dismissed the two hated ministers, he nominated Turgot—one of the most prominent chiefs of the Economist party—Comptroller-General. His choice was much applauded, for Turgot was well known to be a man of great honesty, if somewhat of an innovator. In Limousin, where he had held the post of Intendant, he was adored by the inhabitants. Upon his acceptance of the office of Minister of Finance, he resolved to have recourse neither to increased taxation nor to loans, but to approximate the State expenditure to the receipts by the practice of the strictest economies. Belonging to a school, which, since 1767, had announced its intention of changing the conditions of society, he attached himself, in that respect, to Revolutionary ideas. The innovations, which he meditated, did not, properly speaking, have any political character, but appertained more particularly to social and administrative institutions. He was not in the least in favour of an Assembly that should share the legislative power with the King, and he had opposed the restoration of the former Parliament. He was also hostile to the States-General. From this point of view, he entirely ignored the aspirations of the country; and it cannot be denied that, in spite of praiseworthy intentions, he became an ardent supporter of absolute Monarchy. As an Economist, he was the partisan of indefinite liberty in industrial and commercial matters, but he committed a grave error in the planning of his reforms by not sufficiently taking into account either traditions or customs. Having failed to find in the Nation evidences of that public spiritedness that makes good citizens, he conceived a plan of education, by which, he flattered himself, he could, *in ten years*, transform France.

The first act of Turgot was to proclaim freedom of trade in grain, and, in order to cut short the *pacte de famine*, to suppress all purchasing and warehousing of wheat, on behalf of the State. This measure, which was, at once, an attack on the monopolists and a pledge of the cessation of the dearth which their manœuvres had caused, was received with acclamation. The Decree of Council which notified the reform was, in itself, a novelty; for in it the minister propounded the principles of his economic measures, and endeavoured to demonstrate the salutary effects of commercial liberty. This was the first time that the Government had thus submitted its decisions to the judgment of public opinion. The Edict was barely registered when Turgot began to prepare another that was destined to create no less a sensation : this was the Edict of the suppression of *corvées.*[1] He projected at the same time a reform of all taxes ; and the first ameliorations he effected in this connection greatly softened the condition of the people in the country districts.

The men, with whose interests or prejudices these changes clashed, soon roused themselves. The financiers, the hangers-on of the Court, all those whose existences depended upon the old abuses, arrayed themselves against Turgot ; and the clergy, on their side, neglected their former foes to attack the minister. The Parliament, itself, took part against him. The long exile that the magistrates had endured had damped their patriotism and enfeebled their views. Re-established under conditions that deprived them of their old ascendancy, they had experienced a profound feeling of bitterness, and seemed to have but one care, that of preserving their own privileges. They were, besides, aware of the fact, that the minister was their enemy, and that he wished to restrict them to purely judicial functions.

In the spring of 1775, some unexpected disturbances created fresh difficulties for the Government and suspended Turgot's beneficent activity. The price of bread went up and the people began to murmur. In various parts of the kingdom, and in the environs of the capital, seditious movements took place. At Pontoise, thousands of individuals assembled on the banks of the river, and stopped and plundered the boats laden with grain. At Saint-Germain bags of wheat were emptied and their contents strewn about the streets. Even at Versailles, under the eyes of the King, similar disorders took place. The movement spread, at last, to Paris. On May 3rd, the people rioted in the market-places, and, all in a moment, a general uprising took place. Every house of business was promptly closed, but the crowd forced its

[1] All feudal dues including gratuitous labour or service due to the *Seigneur* by peasant or tenant. (*Translator's Note.*)

way into the bakers' shops and pillaged them.   An entrance was
also effected into many private residences, the people stealing all
the bread they could find.   The Government was obliged to resort to military measures.   Troops were drawn up in the markets
and on the *places*, and soldiers posted at all the bakers' shops.
But the employment of force did not terrify the mutineers. They
spat in the faces of the sentinels and threatened the troops with
paving-stones.   The Government was obliged to prohibit the
assembling of crowds in the streets and to authorise the soldiers
to fire when necessary.   In the midst of this tumult, a "horrible"
placard was posted, bearing the words : "Louis XVI. will be
crowned on June 11th and assassinated June 12th."   Another at
Versailles had the inscription : "If the price of bread is not
"diminished and the Ministry not changed, we will set fire to the
"Palace."

The scarcity of wheat seemed to be less the cause than the
pretext for these disturbances.   Both the public and the Government suspected a plot in which were concerned Maupeou, Abbé
Terray, the Jesuits, the superior clergy, the financiers, the grain
monopolists, and all other enemies of the Ministry and of reform.
Numerous indications testified to the existence of a concerted
movement, got up with the object of exciting the people against
the King.   Superior-looking men, clergymen, and even ladies of
position had been seen encouraging the mutineers.   False Decrees
of Council had been circulated in Paris and the provinces.   Only
a year had passed since Louis XVI. had become King, and already threats of death were being launched against the Bourbon
dynasty.   "Unless I am much deceived," said de Mirabeau—the
uncle of the future Tribune—"revolts of this kind have always
"preceded Revolutions."

Towards the end of May the "flour war" came to an end and
order reigned once more in the streets.   The restoration of tranquillity enabled the coronation ceremony, which had hitherto been
deferred, to take place.   On this occasion, another glimpse was
afforded of the passions which surged around the Throne.   Upon
the pretext of sparing the King the fatigue of too many formalities,

the clergy suppressed that part of the ceremonial, at which, according to tradition, the priest seemed to ask the people's consent to the election of the King, but retained the old oath, by which the Monarch pledged himself to exterminate heretics. This double fact did not pass without exciting a protest. On the return from the coronation, Turgot handed to the King a memorial, in which he represented to him that he had no right over the consciences of his subjects, and besought him, therefore, to leave to everyone full liberty to follow and profess their individual beliefs. The Patriots, too, published brochures, in which they reminded the Monarch that he held his crown not from God, but from the Nation; and not content with declaring that the King's authority had limits that must not be overstepped, they represented revolt against despotism as an effort of the sublimest virtue. Yet, bold as these writings were, they did not put forward any views that had not been advanced before. *The Citizen's Catechism*, in particular, reduced to the comprehension of the simplest and dullest minds the doctrine that *The Spirit of the Laws* and the *Social Contract* had "enveloped in metaphysics difficult to understand." This fact was characteristic of the age. At this epoch, the revolutionary education of the people was being undertaken politically, as it had previously been undertaken in religious matters. This tendency, more, perhaps, than the principles propounded in the brochures, made the Parliament uneasy.

The President of the *Cour des Aides*—Malesherbes—addressed some *Remonstrances* to the King, in which he drew up a complete table of the system of taxation under which France groaned, and of the numerous abuses that accrued in consequence. He showed how the people were ground down by, and completely at the mercy of, the fiscal agents, and how all the guarantees which citizens had formerly enjoyed, had been, one after another, destroyed. He complained too that, in regard to these matters, everything was secret, and to a certain extent mysterious, and that this concealment extended to tariffs and regulations as well as to the personality of the agents, who were entrusted with the onerous task of determining the fortunes, the liberty, and sometimes the lives of the taxpayers. Malesherbes demanded, therefore, that these clandestine methods should be put an end to, and proposed the regular recourse to the States-General, or, at least, to the provincial States. It was Turgot's wish that these *Remonstrances* should be published, in order to influence public opinion in favour of the projected changes. But, upon the representations of Maurepas, who always jealously opposed Turgot's ideas, the Monarch decided against publicity. He assured the *Cour des Aides* that it should be the work of his reign to put an end to the abuses to which his attention had been drawn, but he maintained that it would be imprudent to make the abuses public until the Government was prepared to announce the remedy. Thus, by the pernicious influence of Maurepas, the voice, that first demanded of Louis XVI. the convocation of the States-General, was stifled. That the King, in spite of all, was not averse to hearing the truth, was proved a short time after, when he summoned to his Council the author of the *Remonstrances*, the publication of which he had interdicted.

The addition of Malesherbes to the Ministry strengthened the authority of Turgot, which his enemies had deemed completely undermined by the "flour war." These men esteemed and loved each other. If there were a few political points on which they differed, they were of one mind concerning the necessity for reform. Honourable and pure as was the reputation of Malesherbes, the bishops were displeased at his nomination, and at the placing in his hands of the administration of the affairs of the clergy and of the "reformed religion." Indeed, the alliance between two ministers, both of whom had been won over by the doctrines of Philosophy, rather alarmed the superior clergy. They were especially fearful that the ministers might be leagued together to constrain the clergy to furnish a statement of their wealth and possessions. The public, on the contrary, received the news of the elevation of Malesherbes with unbounded joy. The union of these two men of worth seemed to them the happiest of omens.

Malesherbes fully justified the confidence which his character had inspired. Upon his entrance into the Ministry, he requested the King to abolish *lettres de cachet.* He even considered it a point of honour to repair the injustices committed by their means. Accompanied by a lieutenant of police, he went to the Castle of Vincennes, and to the Bastille, and set at liberty a number of prisoners. Turgot, for his part, was again occupied with the measures of reform, which had been interrupted by the "flour war." He lightened the burden of taxes by more equal distribution, suppressed dues, revoked privileges that oppressed trade, introduced some important ameliorations into the administration of the finances, and restored the national credit, which had fallen during the foregoing reign. A law to validate the marriages of Protestants was announced, and many people persuaded themselves that the Government would shortly accord to all "religionists" full freedom to exercise their cult.

The attributing of these designs to the Government alarmed the clergy, who were then holding their General Assembly. Instead of fostering a reform, in favour of which public opinion was becoming more and more pronounced, the bishops opposed it in a memorial which was presented to the King by a grand deputation. The question of the Protestants was not the only one touched upon in this memorial. The bishops complained of the system of education that had been introduced into the colleges since the suppression of the Jesuits, and begged the King to make his reign illustrious by restoring these seminaries of learning to the control of the clergy, who, by their enlightenment and the disinterested nature of their ministry, seemed to have a special call for the education of youth. The main object of the memorial was to express, in a roundabout way, a desire for the recall of the Jesuits, and to combat, in advance, the plan conceived by Turgot for the establishment of a national system of instruction. It included also a protest against the liberty accorded to literary men, and denounced the number of books that attacked Religion, begging the Monarch to interdict their sale and punish their authors. The influence of the clergy had so much decreased that this memorial

I

was scarcely noticed by the public. The King did not appear to
take it into serious consideration, and returned only evasive re-
plies to their demands. In a special audience, accorded to them
by the Monarch, the clergy laid before him a copy of the work entitled *Portable Theology*, for which they solicited his censure.
This was the one point on which the Monarch yielded.   He
ordered the book to be burned by the common hangman.

But if in the King the clergy lost an auxiliary that had hitherto constantly supported them, they found an ally where they
least expected one.   A request, on the part of the bishops,
had resulted in the suppression by Decree of Council of Voltaire's
Diatribe against the Author of Ephemerides, which contained
an eulogy on Turgot and some "unseemly" allusions to the
part which the clergy had taken in the late disturbances.
The Parliament, in turn, dealt with the condemned work,
and committed it to the flames.   The Advocate-General—
Ségnier—in his *réquisitoire*, declared that the moment had arrived in which "the clergy and the magistracy ought to join
"forces and to repulse the attempts of impious hands to overturn
"the throne and the altar."   It was clear to the public that, by
this declaration, the Advocate-General made avowal of the existence of an alliance between the Episcopate and the magistracy.
Nominally contracted to safeguard the throne and the altar, this
alliance was, in reality, directed against the innovating spirit of
the Ministry, which threatened to deprive both clergy and Parliament of their influence and privileges.   The *Châtelet* followed the
example set by the Parliament and condemned a work of Delisle
de Sale, entitled : *Concerning the Philosophy of Nature*.   Thus
did the Government encounter opposition in the quarters from
which ideas of innovation and reform had formerly proceeded.

All this time clouds were gathering against Turgot at Court.
The Queen, whose conduct already exhibited marks of that
frivolity, of which she subsequently gave such lamentable proofs,
was most impatient with the Comptroller-General's plans of
economy.   Seconded by Maurepas, she had obtained for one of
her favourites, the Princess de Lamballe, the post of mistress

of her household with the stipend of 150,000 *livres*. Turgot had most reluctantly consented to this appointment, and by his reluctance had incurred the royal displeasure. He managed too to give offence in another quarter. Upon his advice, Louis XVI. had nominated an officer of approved merit—the Comte de St. Germain—Minister of War, and the great nobles had angrily protested against the elevation of a simple *gentilhomme* to so high a post.

In the midst of all these difficulties, Turgot pursued his reparative work. At the close of the year 1775, the Edict to abolish *corvées* was ready for registration. A second Decree, on which he had worked for some time, and that had been inspired by his principles of economy, was also completed. This was the Edict for the suppression of *jurandes*.[1] Others were promised, which were to establish a single and proportionate method of taxation and to reconstruct the judiciary system. There was talk of a "Bed of Justice," in which the King, in spite of the opposition of the clergy, would solemnly abrogate the laws promulgated against the Protestants by Louis XIV.

The inevitable consequence of these widespread reforms was the overthrow of the fortunes of a large number of individuals. Cabals, more determined than ever, were formed at Court against Turgot; and the Parliament, siding with the adversaries of the Comptroller-General, prepared to declare openly against him. Louis XVI. having forwarded the Edicts suppressing *corvées* and *jurandes* to the Parliament for registration, a deputation of forty-two magistrates waited upon him, to beg him to withdraw them. In regard to the duty-service, they made the following remarkable declaration: "The duty of the nobility is to defend "the country against its enemies, that of the clergy to edify and "instruct the people, and the lower classes, not being able to render "such distinguished service, ought to acquit their obligations to the "State by payments in industry and personal labour." Well did Louis XVI. say: "I see very well that only Turgot and

---

[1] *Jurandes*—wardenships. The *jurandes* were the sworn heads of the trade guilds which possessed some mischievous privileges. (*Translator's Note.*)

" I love the people." The merchant class, for its part, displayed a lively opposition to the Edict abolishing *jurandes*. They published brochures, pleading for the maintenance of their privileges, but a Decree of Council suppressed their plaints. This action gave rise to the remark that *Messieurs les Économistes*, who preached liberty for themselves, would not give it to their enemies.

The entire Parliament was stirred up against Turgot; his person, ideas, and administration, were all turned into ridicule. At Court, his enemies characterised the prefaces of his Edicts as "undignified." They said that the giving of reasons for the promulgation of orders was a degradation of the authority of the Crown. Walpole, who was a witness of these events, wrote:—"The resistance of the Parliament to the admirable reform pro-"jected by *Messieurs* Turgot and Malesherbes, is a greater scandal "than the most ferocious caprices of despotism. The action of "these magistrates, in opposing the welfare of several millions of "men, partly justifies Chancellor Maupeou for having suppressed "them." Louis XVI. held firm, and, in order to put an end to all resistance, he had the Edicts registered in a "Bed of Justice," held on March 12th, 1776. Praiseworthy as were the intentions of Turgot, the step which, on this occasion, he suggested to the King was an authoritative one, for which he was greatly blamed by those who were certainly not in the position to reproach him for such conduct. The Advocate-General Ségnier, in drawing a picture of the disorder which would follow the carrying out of these Edicts, commenced his discourse with the words: "*The "Royal Authority knows no bounds save those which it is pleased to "create for itself.*" No magistrate under Louis XV.—not even Maupeou—had dared to make use of such language.

On the evening of the "Bed of Justice," there were illuminations in various quarters of Paris. "Long live the King and Liberty" was written across a good number of transparencies. But, unfortunately, the enemies of the reforms were made to appear in the right, by the immediate outbreak of a considerable amount of disturbance. On the very day of the "Bed of Justice," and during those which followed it, violent altercations took place between journeymen, "maddened by their liberty," and their masters, and troops had to be sent to repress the revolts. In the country districts, similar disturbances took place. Excited by the idea that all feudal dues were to be abolished, the peasants, in different localities, rebelled against their lords. In view of these troubles the Parliament issued a Decree, by which it enjoined "all "subjects of the King, copyholders and vassals of lords to continue, "as in the past, to pay—whether to the King or to the said lords "—all dues and obligations according to the statutes of the kingdom." Besides this, the Decree expressly forbade anyone "to promote, "whether by unguarded remarks or by indiscreet writings, any "alteration of the said dues and usages, under penalty of the "offenders being proceeded against as rebels to the laws, and dis- "turbers of the public peace, and punished with an exemplary "punishment." This Decree, posted throughout Paris, was looked upon as a sort of embargo put upon the projects of the Ministry. As a matter of fact, only the lower classes and the Philosophers applauded the recent measures of Turgot.

As for Louis XVI., he early began to evince concern in regard to the opposition of the Parliament. He feared that he had made a mistake. With great reluctance he had imposed the registra- tion of the Edicts by an act of authority. At the "Bed of "Justice," even his brothers declared against him. Throughout the whole of the proceedings he had been unable to overcome a sense of sadness. Shortly afterwards, he said to his minister : "Monsieur Turgot, you speak to me of nothing but the happiness "of my people and the general welfare of my subjects, how is it, "then, that arrangements so useful and advantageous, as you tell "me they are, call forth so many objections ? "

The number of the minister's enemies had visibly increased. To the court, the clergy, the magistracy, the financiers, and de- votees, were joined the *anti-économistes*—who counted amongst them some determined spirits—and the entire body of the in- dustrial and commercial *bourgeoisie*.

On May 3rd, the Parliament dealt a last blow at the Ministry by committing to the flames a work entitled, *The Accomplished*

Monarch, which contained an eulogy of the Emperor, Joseph II. In this eulogy, the author gave utterance to some impassioned reflections upon the state of society. He drew a lugubrious picture of the distress of the people, and called upon them to revolt and *slaughter the monsters that devoured their substance.* He further averred that the affairs of the French Nation had reached a crisis, incident to certain forms of Government—"a "terrible, bloody crisis," which was yet the signal of liberty. "This crisis of which I speak," he added, "is civil war." The Advocate-General, in denouncing "this murderous doctrine," said : "We cannot disguise the fact that the country owes the "shocks that agitate it to those enterprising geniuses who work "only in the light of their own knowledge, to those dangerous "innovators who, without studying the progress of the human "mind, think that they are fitted to lead it, and to those insane "and furious demagogues, who dare to destroy Governments under "the pretext of reforming them." Nobody doubted that in these words the Advocate-General referred to Turgot. Some Court intrigues, in which both Maurepas and Marie-Antoinette had a hand, consummated the effect produced by these attacks.

On May 12th, 1776, Louis XVI. ordered Turgot to retire from the Court. Malesherbes, disgusted with the many cabals he saw formed around him, had already sent in his resignation.

For some time, all persons of reflective minds had expected that these two wise men would quit their offices. Their downfall was inevitable. Apart from the measures inspired by Turgot's schemes of economy, their innovations ran counter to so many usages, interests, and prejudices, that they could not carry them out. The "amputations" they proposed ought to have been begun under Louis XV. Under Louis XVI., it was too late. Yet society, in consequence of its unwillingness to submit to the manipulations of the two surgeons, who then presided over France's destiny, was given over on a future day to more relentless operators.

CHAPTER X.

Reign of Louis XVI.—The Necker Ministry.

(1776-1781.)

AT Versailles the news of the disgrace of Turgot gave rise to an outburst of joy. But the people at large, though they disapproved of Turgot's systematic ideas, regretted him on account of his honesty. Only a few of the more enlightened citizens showed signs of real dismay. This disgrace, which affected the minister more than the man, was followed, as might have been expected, by the sweeping away of the reforms he had instituted. The Edict that had abolished *jurandes* was revoked and *corvées* were re-established. Other measures were also abandoned. Nothing remained—or at least scarcely anything —of all that Turgot, had done for the relief of the Nation and the re-organisation of the finances. The Economist party fell into disfavour. Louis XVI. destroyed the work of Turgot, just as he had destroyed that of Louis XV., without stopping to consider that such sudden variations brought discredit upon the Royal Authority. The Decree that re-established the *jurandes* was accompanied by conditions that gave it the character of a money-edict, and called forth such violent antagonism, that the Court was made quite uneasy by the agitation, and became more so when the renewal of the *corvées* all but excited a revolt.

The changes in the Ministry increased the expressions of discontent. In the place of Turgot, Clugny, a man of no moral character, had been appointed to the Comptroller-Generalship by the King's mentor, the old Comte Maurepas. When yet barely installed, the new minister took advantage of his situation to live freely and establish sinecures for the benefit of his mistresses and other parasites. In order to do away at once with the State debt, Clugny proposed to go into bankruptcy. This proposition, to which the ministers seemed inclined to assent, might perhaps have been carried out, if Louis XVI. had not forcibly repulsed it. Just when the loss of Turgot was being more keenly felt, people began also to find fault with the creature—a mere tool of the clergy—who had replaced Malesherbes. Only four months after the dismissal of Turgot, the discontent became so widespread that it was said that if Louis XVI. did not discharge some more of his ministers, a general uprising was inevitable.

The death of Clugny put an end to a situation that was becoming perilous. Maurepas himself saw the necessity of changing his tactics, and suggested as Clugny's successor, a man who was antagonistic to the Economist school, but much in favour with the commercial classes. This was "Genevan Necker," who had acquired a great reputation for ability as a banker. There was all the more need for an experienced administrator to direct the finances, since the events then occurring in America seemed likely to lead to a war with England. By this nomination, Louis XVI. made another concession to the new school of thought, for Philosophers congregated in Madame Necker's *salon*, and certainly under Louis XV., a Protestant would not have received an official appointment. The Archbishop of Paris and other prelates were not slow to remind the King that, by virtue of the revocation of the Edict of Nantes, a Protestant could not fill any important governmental post, and Louis XVI. yielded to their representations to the extent of nominating Necker "Director of the Treasury," and later "Director-General of Finances," without raising him to the rank of Minister. But, in spite of this distinction, the cabinet at Versailles was known to France and Europe as the "Necker Ministry."

A considerable rise in stocks attested the confidence which the choice of Necker inspired in the public. Of a more limited genius and less elevated mind than Turgot, and withal a little presumptuous, Necker was honest, economical, and exact. Imbued with the philanthropic ideas that did honour to the Philosophy of the day, and sensible of the glory of being useful, he came to power with the sincere desire of doing good. An enemy of Parliaments, as his illustrious predecessor had been, he gave, like him, fresh force to that form of government which had come to be called "ministerial "despotism." Though he had in view divers beneficent measures, inspired by his philanthropic sentiments, it was his intention to concentrate his best efforts on financial reform, thinking er- roneously, that the greatest, and perhaps the only evils from which France suffered were connected with her finances. Though given the name of statesman, Necker was in reality only a financier.

As had already been remarked, during the Ministry of Turgot, the works published at this period were but repetitions of former ones. All political ground had been so thoroughly broken up, that, as Mairobert noted, there remained nothing new to be said. Nevertheless, essays, made up of plagiarisms and repetitions, abounded, and, by sheer force of numbers, carried the bold doctrines of Philosophy into all corners of France. Newspapers also multiplied. Voltaire, receiving a gazette at Ferney, com- plained that its space was almost exclusively given up to politics. By sowing in detail the theories developed in books, the journals rapidly became powerful vehicles of Revolutionary ideas.

At the same time that the newspapers, by the nature of their tenets, were rapidly unsettling the Nation's respect for Royalty, a quantity of pamphlets were published that cast discredit on the reigning house. The members of the Royal Family, the Queen, and Louis XVI. himself were attacked in libels, the circulation of which it had become quite impossible to restrain. The Queen es- pecially was defamed in writings a hundred times more scurrilous than any that had branded the mistresses of Louis XV. Of such pamphlets as *The Amours of our Queen, Life and Loves of the Empress, her August Mother,* etc., the titles alone were an outrage. In vain were colporteurs prosecuted and libraries searched. These attacks, born of fierce party spirit, or of the corrupt fruits of Court intrigues, and personal spite, only increased in number and effectually helped forward the downfall of the Monarchy.

If the new minister deserved reproach for not having a better understanding of the evils of the political situation and the re- medies it demanded, how much more did the clergy, magistracy, nobility, and Royalty itself merit censure! All of these divisions of the class in power seemed stricken with that blindness which ordinarily precedes catastrophe. Ever since the disgrace of Turgot, the Jesuits had been making the greatest possible efforts to re-organise themselves, under the name of "The Brothers of the Cross." The statements in a brochure, circulated among the public, and styled *The Plan of the Apocalypse*, left no doubt of their designs. Both in Paris and Lyons they were very numerous. Occupying pulpits and disbursing large revenues, they used all their influence to secure the exclusive control of a seminary that there was then talk of creating, the purpose of which was to train chaplains for the Army. By this means, they trusted eventually to gain the support of the military. The Parliament committed *The Plan of the Apocalypse* to the flames, and begged the Government to proceed with severity against the detested body. Without going as far as the magistrates wished him to, the King, in May, 1777, published an Edict which, while conciliating the Jesuits, declared that their *society would never be re-established*. Just at this time, the *Châtelet* brought to a close the proceedings that had been commenced under the Turgot Ministry against the author of the *Philosophy of Nature*. The heads of the accusation brought against Delisle de Sale, were that he had a tendency towards "Spinosaism;" had designated the cult of a certain party the "prevailing cult of citizens;" had said that, in the life of a State, there were moments of ferment, when each citizen held an office, and Kings were of no more account than ordinary men; and finally, that he had dared to maintain that the four cardinal virtues might be reduced to one. These points being established, a discussion had followed in the *Châtelet* as to the mode of punishment to be dealt out. Every severity and indignity, short of death, were first suggested, but eventually perpetual banishment was decided upon by 14 votes to 7. Delisle de Sale appealed against this sentence to the Parliament. Public indignation offered a further protest, and the *Châtelet* prison became, for the moment, an arena of triumph. The most noted Philosophers and the distinguished women of their party went thither to congratulate De

Sale, and his book acquired a popularity that it would never have obtained upon its own merits. The Parliament perceived the ridiculous severity of the *Châtelet* sentence, and reduced it to a mere admonition.

But, in spite of this act of common-sense, the Parliament's usual proceedings were not remarkable for wisdom. Though it forbade the celebration of the *fête* of the *Sacred Heart*, burned some writings in which the Jansenists were attacked, and set a watch upon the movements of the Jesuits, it paid no attention to the real wants or wishes of the country. Its chief task was the demolition of the Grand Council; while the members of that body, for their part, complaining of being treated as a commission and not as a sovereign court, joined forces with the inferior courts in accusing the Parliament of having acquired too formidable an authority. Such were the miserable quarrels that occupied the attention of the magistracy in this crisis of France's destiny, and the Court presented a no less piteous spectacle. The nobles, in their cupidity and paltry ambition, sought only to seize upon lucrative posts; and no exterior dignity veiled their mean plots. Under the influence of the ideas propagated by the Philosophers, the Court etiquette that Louis XV. had, at least, known how to maintain, lost all its rigour. The Queen was the first to throw off the restraints of ceremonial, and to tolerate a familiarity that militated against her own dignity and the prestige of the Crown. She outstepped the bounds of prudence and chose her favourites according to her own whims and fancies without reference to their worth. Added to this, she threw herself with feverish delight into an uninterrupted round of *fêtes* and dissipations. Although all games of chance were forbidden by law, lansquenet and faro were played at Versailles, Fontainebleau, and Marly until four or five in the morning. Divested of all decorum and reserve, the Court of Louis XVI., though of purer morals than that of the previous reign, greatly resembled a "free and easy" club, or a gambling "hell."

But Necker stuck to his work. Like Turgot, he had resolved not to create fresh taxes, but determined to have recourse to the loans which his forerunner had proscribed. In January, 1777, he opened one of 24,000,000 *livres*, which was succeeded in the course of the same year by many others. The Parliament, in registering the loan Edicts, raised some objections, and even people least antagonistic to all forms of change passed criticisms, saying that what France wanted was not fresh expedients, however well chosen, but a total change in financial usage and an entirely new system of taxation. Yet if, on the one hand, Necker burdened the Treasury with loans, he sought, on the other, to relieve it by economics. He simplified all services under his direction, suppressed some offices, and announced his intention of reducing the number of Receivers-General of Finances and of Farmers-General. But these wise exploits only drew down upon him fresh criticisms. The financiers made such an uproar that, from July onward, the downfall of the Genevan appeared inevitable. Necker, fancying that he could silence his enemies and popularise his administration by some beneficent measures, appointed a commission to reform the hospitals. The lamentable condition of these institutions was at that time exciting just complaints. A little later on pawn-shops were started, but usurers and money-lenders being numerous among men in office, these useful establishments were not opened without some opposition.

Yet Necker had more partisans than adversaries. He was not "a man of schemes" like Turgot, and the common people, who saw at once the bearing of his acts, effusively applauded them. But it was evident that the clergy feared a seizure of their property and were very uneasy; they did not, however, enter into an organised form of resistance. The Parliament also held itself in reserve—a reserve instinct with malevolence, for in Necker, as in Turgot, the magistrates discerned an enemy. Upon the surface, the opposition to Necker appeared to be unimportant enough, nevertheless there was opposition.

The inconsequent treatment of Voltaire, who returned to Paris about this time, gave rise to some comment. The King refused to receive the poet at Versailles, but permitted the people to make much of him. On his death, which occurred soon after, the Monarch, at the request of the clergy, ordered a complete silence in regard to him, but six months later he allowed the *Apotheosis of Voltaire* to be celebrated at the *Comédie Française*. Another of the inconsistencies, with which Louis XVI. may be taxed, was his support of the American colonies in their war against England. In the preamble of the celebrated Declaration of Independence signed at Philadelphia on July 4th, 1776, occurred the following words: " All men are created equal and endowed by their Creator "with certain unalienable rights. To secure these rights, Govern-"ments are instituted among men, deriving their just powers from "the consent of the governed; and whenever any form of Government "becomes destructive of these ends, it is the right of the people to "alter or to abolish it."

Taking only the text of this Declaration into consideration, it may well be said that, in allying himself with men who gave utterance to these principles, Louis XVI. furnished his subjects with arms against himself. The American doctrines found an echo in France and forwarded the progress of revolutionary ideas there. Yet this revolt of colonies against their parent country seemed to resemble more nearly a war between two peoples than the insurrection of subjects against their Sovereign. The feeling of the French in regard to this war was characterised less by sympathy with the insurgents than by a national hatred of England. The revolt of the American colonies was welcomed as a promise of the humiliation of the British and the destruction of their pride and power.

Nevertheless there were in France a great many partisans of peace. Louis XVI., who was, by nature, indisposed to make war, had been slow to declare it; and Necker, in view of the state of the finances, desired a truce. The King had hitherto only secretly assisted the Americans, but when he saw fortune favour their arms, he decided to receive Franklin as an Ambassador, and thus formally recognise the American Republic.

Some months later he openly broke with England. The length of the war, which could not be foreseen, rendered Necker's work more difficult. He was forced to have recourse to fresh loans, but, at the same time, he resolutely hunted down all abuses and useless expenses, carrying economy not only into big matters, but into the smallest details. One of his most useful works was the suppression of the Royal pay-offices—the dispersion of which was a fruitful source of disorder—and the gathering in of all funds to the Treasury. This reform was a severe blow not only to the Treasurers-General, but to all the ministers of departments, with separate treasuries. The reform of the Royal household followed. This was, in truth, the quarter in which the most crying abuses were to be met with; it was also that in which the most obstacles were thrown in Necker's way.

. The nobles, who did not wish to be checked in their depredations, joined with the financiers in opposing him. The Financier-General had, indeed, only the King on his side, for the Parliament continued to find fault with his financial arrangements and to sanction, most reluctantly, all his other reforms. At Court, Necker had not only to combat opposition, but to witness abuses that partly destroyed the result of his economies. The Queen, always infatuated by play, lost 14,000 *louis* in the year 1778 alone, and she continued to recompense by costly presents, extravagant pensions, and appointments, representing sometimes salaries of 80,000 *livres*, persons, whose only title to consideration was that they ministered to her taste for dissipation. In February, 1779, she came with the King to Paris, to be present at the singing of a *Te Deum* to celebrate the birth of the Princess, who afterwards became Duchesse d'Angoulème. Nearly everywhere, the Royal pair was received by a silence, which was attributed solely to the bad effect produced upon the public mind by the expenses and dissipations of the Queen. Having dedicated the whole of her resources to pleasure, she had no money left for good works, and it was Madame Necker who assumed her duties as patroness of the charitable institutions of the kingdom. It was quite in vain that the Director-General represented to her the enormity of the charges she made upon the Treasury. But if Louis XVI., in his indulgence of his consort, allowed the continuance of abuses that he ought to have reprimanded, he, at least, seconded all the wise and beneficent schemes that were submitted to him by Necker. In

August, 1779, he promulgated the celebrated Decree, that abolished all rights of servitude and mortmain [1] within his domains. " We "should have desired," he said, in the preamble to the Royal Edict, "to abolish, without distinction, all vestiges of a rigorous, feudal "system, but our finances do not permit of our purchasing this "right from the *seigneurs*." He expressed, however, the hope of seeing his example copied by the rest of the kingdom. Some of the nobles were honourable enough to follow the King's lead, but a large number of men remained for some time attached to the glebes and deprived of the liberty of their persons and the prerogatives of proprietorship. [2]

Feeling sure of the confidence and support of the Monarch, Necker continued to carry on the work he had begun. He introduced more and more stringent rules into the administration of the finances, and started a new system of book-keeping, which showed, at a glance, the balance of receipts and expenses. He diminished the number of Farmers-General, and reduced from sixty to twelve, that of Receivers. He also continued the difficult work of reforming the King's household. The various purses for the table, for minor pleasures, for the hunt, the stables, etc., were united in a single fund. But in proportion as his reforms were effected, so did hostility to them become more and more threatening. Some of the ministers, whose independence was affected by Necker's measures, began to complain, and whilst they secretly plotted to impede the execution of his reforms, libellous pamphlets appeared, accusing him of all kinds of public and private vices.

The bishops had good reason to fancy themselves threatened by Necker's reforming spirit, since the idea of assessing the property of the clergy had come to be an universally admitted principle. In face of the financial embarrassments of the Government, it was a matter of surprise that the Episcopate still refused to contribute to the expenses of the State.

[1] *Mainmorte*, in this instance, refers to the right of *seigneurs* to the real estate and personal property of their serfs, which property escheated on their deaths to their lords. (*Translator's Note.*)

[2] In 1789 there were still 1,500,000 left in France.

When the General Assembly of the Clergy opened in June, 1780, the King's commissioner, in consideration of the war with England, made an application for a "free gift" of 30,000,000 *livres*. But the President of the Assembly expressed his surprise that "so excessive a demand" should have been made, and it was agreed in the end that, in return for the sum asked, the King must pay back annually, for fourteen years, the sum of 1,000,000 *livres*, and further, that he must promise not to claim another subsidy until 1785.   According to custom, the bishops presented the King, in the course of their deliberations, with memorials containing their wishes in regard to the Religion of the country.   In one of these they expressed regret that, in spite of the laws against them, Protestants had been admitted to public posts ; this was, of course, an attack on Necker.   In another, they complained of "Anti-Christian productions" circulated everywhere with impunity, and instanced especially a famous writer, "less known "for the beauty of his genius than for the implacable warfare he "has waged for sixteen years against *the Lord and His Christ*." After having thus designated Voltaire, they referred to the Abbé Raynal as "a former priest, still wearing the sacred livery of the "Church," who has just published a new edition of a work "teem- "ing with revolting blasphemies."   "Sire," they added, "the time "is come for your Majesty to safeguard Religion, Morality, and "Authority," by making a law to confine "that most noble of all "arts—writing—to the bounds of a generous but discreet liberty." As in 1775, the King's reply was couched in evasive terms, and from the public the bishops' desires did not obtain even that feeble attention which had been accorded them five years before.

Whilst the superior clergy were giving the world these fresh proofs of their intolerance, the young Monarch, following his own totally different disposition, was instituting some long-needed ameliorations in the prison system, and abolishing the "preparatory question."[1]

In January, 1781, Necker published, with the King's permission,

[1] Examination by torture.   Questions put to the accused while on the rack previous to condemnation.   (*Translator's Note.*)

his famous "Accounts" of the finances. In this publication he did not confine himself to drawing up a table of the receipts and expenses, but also explained his previous measures, announced his projects, and exposed the disorders and abuses that he had made it his mission to repress. Until then, as he said, a great mystery had always been made of the state of the finances, and now, for the first time, the veil was lifted. An immense effect was produced by this statement of the accounts. On the day it appeared 6,000 copies were printed, and it was soon reproduced in every European language. Prints and sets of verses were published in honour of Necker. But together with the praises, criticisms were also to be heard. It was pretended that, in delivering up to the knowledge and, in a certain degree, to the control of the public, all the actions of the Sovereign, the honour of the Crown was detracted from, and its authority lessened. The enemies of Necker, rendered desperate by the announcement of his projected reforms, united all their efforts to overthrow him. They overruled the King's timidity, stirred up the entire Court, issued innumerable pamphlets, and, in the end, availed themselves of means still more efficacious and decisive.

Necker, borrowing the idea from Turgot, had established in Berry, Haute Guyenne, and Dauphiné, and wished to establish, by degrees, throughout France—under the name of "Provincial Administrations"—elective commissions composed of deputies from the three estates. These, according to his design, were to assemble at certain periods, and to be entrusted in each province with the assessment of taxes and the oversight of the interests of the population. But, before putting his plan into execution, he presented a sketch of it to the King, and his enemies made use of this sketch to bring about his ruin. In it, very diverse matters were touched upon, and, it must be owned, that, side by side with many useful ideas, some principles were advanced that directly favoured absolute Monarchy.

In order to diminish the *gabelle*—tax on salt—throughout the country, Necker proposed to deprive all the members of the sovereign courts of their immunity from this tax. He wished also to abolish tithes, to raise the stipends of country clergymen to the fitting sum of 12,000 *livres*, and to provide the means for the increase of these salaries out of the incomes of the "big wigs" of the Church and the rich endowments. His plan also abolished all Intendancies, as offices "onerous to the State and tyrannous to the "people," and deprived the Parliaments of the right of registration, thus reducing them to purely judicial functions. The publication of these propositions did not fail to stir up against Necker the anger of the officials, the aristocracy, and the clergy. The sketch of his reforms was secretly printed and communicated to all the Parliaments of the kingdom. This was the signal for an outburst of clamour. A league was formed in opposition to the Director-General that was made up of all those whose interests were menaced by his plan. Louis XVI. was quite overwhelmed with complaints of Parliaments, Intendants,[1] clergy, and court officials.

Necker soon came to the conclusion that it would be impossible for him to keep the direction of the Finances, unless he received some distinguished mark of his Sovereign's confidence with which to overawe his enemies. He, therefore, requested the King either to admit him to his Council, under the title of Minister, or to accept his resignation. Louis XVI. might have held his ground. He had no longer—as at the time of his dismissal of Turgot—the excuse of his extreme youth, and it could not have escaped his notice, that the opposition directed against Necker was neither so serious, nor so considerable, as that which had been formed against Turgot. Yet in his extreme weakness he failed to fulfil his duty and accepted Necker's resignation.

When the news of this resignation broke upon Paris on the morning of May 20th, it caused general consternation. A panic was created on the Bourse, and the price of the Royal Bonds fell considerably. The public deplored the event as a national calamity, and that evening at the *Comédie Française*, a reference to Necker excited a veritable tumult. The King himself evinced

---

[1] *Intendant*—A Treasury-commissioner or provincial Treasurer-general. (*Translator's Note.*)

signs of regret at the departure of a man, whose stubborn character must oftentimes have aggravated him, but who had, nevertheless, won his esteem. For several days, the public cherished the hope of his recall, and some efforts were made to induce the King to retain him. But the fear of his return only revived the cabals against him. On the 4th of June, Joly de Fleury, the man whom the enemies of Necker had designated as his successor, joined the Council as Minister of Finance, and all hope that the Monarch would retract his decision was thenceforth abandoned.

CHAPTER XI.

Reign of Louis XVI.—The Joly de Fleury, d'Ormesson, and Calonne Ministries.

(1781-1786.)

ON the day following the retirement of Necker, Louis XVI. declared that "though he had changed his ministers he had not "changed his principles." But the appointment of Joly de Fleury showed how much this Declaration was to be believed

In August, 1781, an Edict was promulgated, which raised the taxes on all articles of consumption two *sous* in the *livre*. This was a return to the fiscal system in vogue in the time of Louis XV., which Necker and Turgot had both repudiated. The measure excited universal murmurs. Among the lower classes, who were most affected by it, the discontent more particularly showed itself. The Parliament, in gratitude for the sacrifice made to it of the "dangerous Genevan," registered the two *sous* in the *livre* without uttering a single remonstrance on behalf of the people. Other money-edicts followed. Returning, without scruple, to the old abuses, the minister caused a loan to be raised by the city of Paris to supply the personal needs of the Comte de Provence and the Comte d'Artois. He re-established the forty-eight offices of Receivers-General, the posts of Treasurers and Farmers-General, and all the suppressed appointments in the Royal household. The King was, in fact, made to undo all Necker's work, as he had previously undone Turgot's, and thus, by his weakness and incessant self-contradictions, to lower himself more and more in public opinion.

Almost at the same time that the Government was annoying the public with its financial measures, it published a regulation,

by which all commoners were interdicted from serving as lieuten-
ants in the army, and no one, whose nobility did not date from
four generations, could be raised to the rank of captain. Just
when the War of American Independence was fostering the ideas
of equality propounded by Philosophy, and when the reforms of
Turgot and Necker had opened all eyes to the injustice and abuse
of privilege, it would have been difficult to commit a more impoli-
tic act. The impression produced by it was so great, that many
contemporaries have counted it among the secondary causes of the
Revolution.

Yet, to judge by appearances, it might have been thought that
many hearts were still attached to the Monarchy. In October,
1781, Marie-Antoinette gave birth to a Dauphin, and, at the news
of this event, the Parisians seemed to forget all their grievances.
Louis XVI., on his way to *Notre Dame*, was received with loud
acclamations. At the opera, where a gratuitous performance was
given to the crowd, the auditorium resounded with cries of " Long
"live the King ! long live the Queen ! Long live *Monseigneur* the
" Dauphin !" The address of the market-women who, according to
custom, went to congratulate Louis XVI., finished with the words:
" We charge ourselves with the task of teaching our children to
"love and respect their King." But, besides these attestations of
rejoicing, other and very different sentiments were also expressed.
A certain number of people were put into the Bastille for having,
upon this occasion, written or spoken scandalous words against
the Queen. Many people, too, highly disapproved of the *fêtes,*
which the Mayor of Paris had arranged in celebration of the birth
of the Dauphin.

Some bishops who looked upon the disgrace of Necker only as
an event favourable to their own interests, attempted to raise
the alarm against Philosophy. Their mandates, however, found
no echo. The Ministry, to whom the Faculty of Theology
had complained of the publication of Voltaire's works, declared
that such affairs should be referred to the police. Not only were
Voltaire's works printed, but a new edition of the *Encyclopedia*
was authorised by the Government. A little later, Palissot's piece

was brought out again at the *Comédie-Française*. It was a complete failure, and when Crispin entered on all fours to represent Jean Jacques, there was a general expression of indignation from the floor of the house. In the place of the old Archbishop of Paris, who died in 1781, Louis XVI. had nominated an ardent Jesuit partisan, who tried his best to exact the complete submission of the various ecclesiastics of his diocese to the *Unigenitus*. But his superannuated zeal only disturbed a few old Jansenists. All events tended to show that the doctrinal *rôle* of the Church was played out. Bishops themselves had been won over to philosophical unbelief, and a certain party of them—having ceased to invoke "religious phantoms"—abandoned doctrinal matters for questions of administration. These went by the name of " Prelate-" Administrators " or " Bishops of the new school."

In spite of the hopes of peace, to which Washington's victories and the French maritime successes had given rise, the war with England was still prolonged. The Ministry, running short of resources, employed the method, for which Necker had been so severely reproached, and opened a loan at a higher rate of interest than any issued by the former Director of Finance. The King renewed his generous promises, and announced that—the peace once concluded—he would be in a position to accord his people "the measures of relief which he was impatient to procure them." These promises, however, did not re-assure the public. They began to murmur at the duration of a war, of which they could not clearly see the utility, and which had already cost over 700,000,000 *livres*. At the news that a considerable portion of the navy had been destroyed at an engagement near Guadeloupe, their murmurs changed to consternation. But hatred for England triumphed over alarm, and subscriptions were opened on all sides to aid the Government and furnish it with vessels. The King, in a public letter, declared himself disposed to accept the offers of provinces, towns, and the different corporations of the kingdom, but refused those of private persons as " the financial situation did not make this " resource a necessity." But immediately afterwards there appeared an Edict, which established, for the duration of the war and three years after, a tax of a third twentieth on all "goods."

The Parliament registered this tax with the same submission that it had displayed in registering the two *sous* in the *livre*. But the provincial Assemblies—more jealous of the interests of the people—began to make a stir. The Besançon Parliament registered the two *sous* in the *livre* with restrictions, repulsed the tax of the third twentieth, and drew up some *Remonstrances*. But before these *Remonstrances* were presented to the King, the commanding-officer of the town, by order of the Ministry, enforced the registration of both acts in their integrity. The magistrates protested and declared that it was a mere farce to submit Edicts to the Parliament and then to deprive it of the power of verifying them. They contended also that the King commanded by virtue of the law, and that the men, to whom he delegated his power, were bound, like other citizens, to respect it. Thereupon a deputation of the rebellious Parliament was commanded to appear at Versailles. The members of the deputation, in addition to the registers, brought with them a fragment of oat bread as an evidence of the extremities to which the rural populations were reduced. The King, however, did not allow the magistrates to state their grievances, but reproved them for their insubordination, informing them that they had exceeded their powers, and that "all that "was done in his name, was done by his order." He further enjoined them to erase from their registers all their recent Decrees. But the time had gone by when Royalty could always have the last word. Upon the return of the deputies, the Parliament of Besançon passed a resolution declaring that the magistracy was reduced to impotence and the people deprived of their interpreters by ministers who despised the law, and claiming for the Franche-Comté the assemblage of the Provincial States, and for the kingdom the convocation of the States-General. Thus, upon the first occasion that Louis XVI. revived the despotic measures of his forerunners, claims were formulated that directly tended to Revolution. The accusation brought by the Parliament of Besançon against the ministers was well founded, for since the accession of Louis XVI., the rights of the magistracy had been less considered than ever.   A confederation of the various Parliaments of the Kingdom was now initiated by the magistrates of the Besançon.   More disinterested than the coalitions that had been formed in the previous reign, this one aimed at greater things than the restoring to the magistracy its former influence.   Acknowledging—perhaps not without remorse—" that they could not, of " themselves, regain their lost ascendancy," the Parliaments decided to return to the underlying principles of Government, and to demand unanimously the convocation of the States-General.

But in September, 1783, an apparent change of the conduct of the Government, and the general satisfaction caused by the conclusion of the peace with England, somewhat calmed the general agitation.   Immediately after the signing of the preliminaries of peace in the beginning of the year, the Government had printed and " profusely distributed " a regulation concerning the administration of the finances, in which the suppression of some of the taxes was promised.   The dismissal of Joly de Fleury seemed to confirm this assurance.   In his place, the King appointed a young Councillor of State, d'Ormesson, who, without great financial aptitude, had, at least, the reputation of being an honest, hardworking man.   Since the beginning of the reign, this was the seventh administrator who had been placed at the head of financial affairs, and the public began to be alarmed at the continual change of ministers which so palpably demonstrated the indecisive views of the Government.   In April, 1783, d'Ormesson was nominated to his post; in November he quitted it.   Assailed by expenses he was powerless to control, and forced to satisfy the whims of the King himself, who, oblivious of his economical designs, had—among other extravagances—just bought Rambouillet at the price of 14,000,000 *livres*, d'Ormesson had secretly borrowed money from the *Caisse d'Escomptes*—*i.e.*, Discount Office.   This fact transpiring, the owners of bills crowded to the office, which soon found itself unable to disburse.   D'Ormesson authorised the suspension of payment, but this measure only increased the general uneasiness. It was this maladroit action of the young Comptroller-General that appeared to be the cause of his disgrace. In reality, he was forced to retire because, in default of capacity, he evinced some patriotism, and had endeavoured to deter the King and his courtiers from their reckless expenditure.

Those "perverse" spirits, who had overturned d'Ormesson, persuaded the weak-minded Louis to appoint a minister after their own hearts—one who had long coveted the post of Comptroller-General. This was Calonne: a man of no morals and bad reputation; but clever, amiable, and seductive; one who played with difficulties, but who displayed such dexterity in business affairs, that—according to his flatterers—he had in him "sparks of true "genius." In his first interview with the King, he confessed to having unpaid debts to the amount of 220,000 *livres.* "A "Comptroller-General," he added, "can easily find means of dis-"charging obligations, but I prefer to leave all to your Majesty's "kindness." Louis XVI. took from a desk 230,000 *livres* in shares of the Paris Water Company and gave them to Calonne, who kept the shares and found other means of getting rid of his debts.

The appointment of this man annoyed the public, but Calonne was too careful of his popularity to have recourse to measures that might bring him into disrepute. He began by dismissing from office several clerks, who had been guilty of notorious misappropriations, and when he went to take his oath at the *Cour des Comptes* he pronounced a discourse, full of sentiments of the purest patriotism, in which he promised to shield the Parliaments from authoritative measures. As a substitute for fresh taxes, that would, undoubtedly, have stirred up objections, he issued, under the form of a lottery, a loan of 100,000,000 *livres,* and he further established a Sinking Fund, by means of which, he said, the National Debt would be cancelled in twenty-five years. It is unnecessary to say that this Fund was never really started. Calonne spoke of his methods of amelioration in a tone of such complete conviction, and prophesied such happy results from them, that it was impossible not to believe that a new era was beginning for finance. No one, outside of the court circle, knew the amount of Calonne's expenditure. Still less did anyone guess

that the means he employed to sustain it were calculated to ruin
France in about three years' time.   Only later were discovered
the thousand secret expedients, amounting to fraud, and the
disastrous methods of anticipation, to which he had recourse.
For the moment, money poured forth from the Treasury as from
an inexhaustible source.   Credit was re-established, and wealth
seemed to abound.   The populace were dazzled, and the Parliaments astounded   At Court, whence the words "economy" and
"reform" seemed at last to be banished, everybody was en-
chanted.   This sudden appearance of prosperity was not wholly
fictitious.   Peace once concluded, trade by a natural consequence
revived   The Independence of America created fresh outlets for
commerce and industry, and Calonne knew how to take advantage of the circumstances that combined to favour him.

No wonder that in the years 1784 and 1785 the people of
France made to themselves an illusory future !   Deceived in
regard to the real state of the finances, gladdened by the proclamation of peace, and filled with pride at the thought of
England's humiliation, France—under a *débonnaire* prince, and
restored to her former rank among the nations, from which
the Seven Years' War had ousted her—appeared, for the first
time, to give herself up to the charms of a civilisation, which
the progress of ideas only served to polish.   The privileged
classes still existed, but the various divisions of society seemed
all but effaced.   If Faith were extinguished, Tolerance reigned in
its stead.   People wrote and spoke freely on all sorts of subjects.
In response to Mirabeau's book on *lettres de cachet*, which a few
years before would, without doubt, have been committed to the
flames, the Government ordered the emptying of the donjon at
Vincennes, and all Paris assembled to see the odious traces of an
antique barbarism.   Everywhere, at the suggestion of the Ministry, useful establishments were founded.   Men seemed seized
with a veritable fever of philanthropy.   In the rigorous winter
of 1784, the tokens of benevolence exceeded all previous manifestations of that virtue.   The Abbé de L'Épée obtained the
support of the Government for his work of instructing deaf mutes,

and Valentin Haüy, his emulator, founded the "Institute for the "Blind." Never had the poor people been the objects of such solicitude. Bishops established lying-in hospitals in their dioceses, and in different provinces, intendants presided at open air *fêtes*, where prizes for agriculture were distributed amid cries of "Long "live the King!" However much men's dispositions may have been influenced by fashion, these charitable enterprises indicated, none the less, that more humane ideas were permeating society. No one could have imagined that a period of violence and class hatred was at hand. Rather did the people of France seem to hail the dawn of those millennial days predicted by Philosophy.

Unexpected discoveries and marvellous novelties seized upon men's imaginations and helped to blind all eyes to the imminent catastrophe. In 1784 the invention of balloons startled the world. Princes, nobles, priests, and magistrates were enraptured by this novelty. At once they fancied themselves masters of the empire of the air. It was a century of wonders. The word "impossible" seemed no longer to be in the vocabulary of the French. "Talk-"ing heads" and "birds that flew" were manufactured. Mesmerism became the rage: the same excitement prevailed, the same miracles took place, that had once been induced at the tomb of "Monsieur "Pâris." The serious accomplishments of men of science were no less remarkable. Lavoisier discovered the composition of water, and La Pérouse made his preparations to explore the undiscovered regions of the globe. Intoxicated by these marvels, and carried away by chimerical ideas of philanthropy, the imagination of the people of France was exalted at the expense of reason. Dreams were substituted for realities. The hour was approaching when those ideas which, though so grandiose, were humane, generous, and intrinsically true, were to be transported to the sphere of politics and induce there the same illusions, the same flightiness, and the same beliefs that the conditions of society might be changed as instantaneously as the conditions of life already seemed to have been. An innovation, dating from this period, had much to do with the training of those orators, who were destined so soon to speak not only to France but to the whole of Europe. In '83 and '84 clubs were founded. Men joined them at first for beneficent purposes, or simply to dine, play cards, or read the gazettes. These clubs, to which, as a rule, only men belonged, rapidly became the fashion and were substituted for the *salons* over which women had presided. Whilst some of them degenerated into gambling Hells, others became miniature Academies, where conferences were held, speeches delivered, and, in the end, politics were freely discussed.

In the minds of those who felt that they were being borne towards a future full of promise, ancient institutions and the principles of the past appeared to be nothing more than ridiculous errors, while the Church which had for so long dominated men's deepest passions seemed only a ludicrous phantom. Yet, in the midst of this mirth and these illusions, the *dénoûement* rapidly drew near.

In January, 1785, Calonne started a fresh loan of 125,000,000 *livres*, the conditions of which were made out to be so advantageous to the lenders that they were promised a doubling of their capital at the end of twenty-five years. The *Chambre des Comptes* remonstrated, and the Parliament felt bound to protest, representing to the King that a loan had never yet been contracted at so high a rate of interest, and that, in spite of the promises inscribed on the previous Edicts, the National Debt was perceptibly increasing. Then, for the first time, Calonne was attacked in pamphlets; but a more serious onslaught was that contained in Necker's book on *The Administration of Finance.*

In this work Necker gave figures to show how considerable had been the increase of the National Debt since his retirement, and called attention to the renewal of the disorders that he had succeeded in arresting. He concluded by insisting upon the necessity for reform. Calonne tried to turn the blow aimed at him. But his brochures and threats only served to increase the popularity of Necker's work. By the end of January 12,000 copies had been printed. So great was the sensation produced that the author was requested not to show himself in Paris, as his presence would have undoubtedly excited a tumult. This book put the finishing touches to the picture of the finances that had been painted for the public four years before in the "Account."

Calonne's credit, but not his audacity, was now almost shattered. He asked the clergy for a "free gift" of 20,000,000 *livres*, but obtained only 18,000,000, and that, on condition that he suppressed the new edition of Voltaire's works. Calonne accepted the conditions, and a Decree was published and posted. But there is no doubt that the Government secretly facilitated its evasion. The loan of 125,000,000 was not easily raised. The financial companies that Calonne had greatly favoured, in order to produce a fictitious circulation to mask his own movements, attracted all available money to themselves. The jobbing which he had promoted recoiled on him. He attempted to decry the companies in brochures, and Mirabeau, more eloquent than honest, consented to put his talents at the minister's service. Calonne soon bethought himself of a method, inspired by the worst of monarchial stratagems, and undertook the recoinage of gold specie. By this operation he hoped to bring in about 50,000,000 *louis*, but, by a series of frauds, he managed to lay hands on much more. The Parisians, deceived by a promise of twenty *sous* for the old *livre*, crowded to the mint. Many received only fifteen, thirteen, or twelve *sous*, and some had to furnish silver over and above their gold. The Ministry, instead of giving new *louis* in the place of old ones, returned bills on the *Taisse d'Escomptes*, and later on, gave only acknowledgments. The public took alarm. The *Cour des Monnaies* protested, but was reprimanded by the King, who ordered its Decree to be erased from the registers. After this another Edict appeared, starting a fresh loan of 80,000,000. The Parliament entreated the King to withdraw it, but Louis XVI. imperatively commanded its registration. The magistrates obeyed, subjoining clauses calculated to discredit the loan. The entire Parliament was thereupon ordered to appear with its registers at Versailles, and the King with his own hand struck out the added clauses. "Under-"stand," he said to the magistrates, "that I am satisfied with my "Comptroller-General, and that I will not permit my plans for the "good of my State and the welfare of my people to be interrupted "by unfounded alarms." From that moment there was an open schism between Calonne and the Parliament.

The Parliament of Besançon was just then disputing the possession of twenty-two leagues of alluvial soil which the State, in spite of the rights of proprietorship and the unanimous protest of the inhabitants of the Province, wished to seize upon. The Rennes magistrates having had a registration illegally forced upon them, were also offering protests. Their representations were met with an assertion worthy of Louis XV. himself. "In me alone," said the King, "resides, undivided, all legislative power." It was, thus, clearly shown that the arbitrary methods of Louis XV. were again to be put into force. At the same time there were unmistakable signs that men's sympathies were becoming more and more alienated from the Royal Family. The cruel attacks made on Marie-Antoinette, in regard to the affair of the necklace, proved this fact beyond a doubt. The whole of France became interested in the trial of the Cardinal de Rohan, the scandalous details of which compromised Marie-Antoinette as woman and as Queen. No one believed in the morality of the proud prelate, who was known to be both a spendthrift and a libertine, but so great was the hostility of the people towards the Queen that he was universally commiserated, and his acquittal excited general expressions of joy. Not the Queen alone, however, but the entire Royal Family, the Court, and the Episcopate, were disgraced by this affair. In July, 1786—a month after the acquittal of the Cardinal—the clergy, by the King's order, held a General Assembly. On this occasion the Ministry made a fresh attempt to bring up the subject of the assessment of the "goods" of the clergy. But the bishops—who could not have been ignorant of the alarming state of the finances —proved, by unanswerable arguments, that neither they nor their possessions were subject to any taxation or feudal dues.

The breach between the Court and the magistracy continued to widen. The affair of the alluvial soil, in regard to which the Bordeaux Parliament still combatted the unjust pretensions of the Ministry, had assumed the proportions of a national conflict. On May 30th a "military session" imposed upon the Assembly at Bordeaux the registration of letters-patent, that gave the ground in litigation to the State. The magistrates protested, and declared that usurpation, sanctioned by letters-patent, was the fruit of a system of depredation maintained " by men whom uni- " versal indignation would have denounced, had they not known " how to shelter themselves behind the sacred name of the Monarch." The Parliament of Toulouse issued a Decree, in which it solemnly adhered to that of the Parliament of Bordeaux, and all other Parliaments prepared to follow this example.

The magistrates of Bordeaux were commanded to appear in a body at Versailles. Ninety-six of them obeyed the summons. Only those who were infirm or ill remained behind. The Ministry wisely took the precaution to prohibit their passing through Paris. Arrived at Versailles, the King held "a species of 'Bed of Justice,'" and ordered them to expunge from their registers the Decrees that attested their resistance. But, in reality, he yielded. Under pretence of making his intentions more thoroughly understood, he caused explanatory letters to be registered, in which he cancelled the first ones, and recognised the owners whose claims the Bordeaux Parliament had so valiantly maintained. The ovation with which the magistrates were received on their return to Bordeaux was a fresh humiliation for the Power that had planned to rebuke them. Other Parliaments began to send deputations to Versailles. On the roads to the capital, magistrates were constantly to be met with, going either to complain to the King or to receive reproofs from the Royal mouth. In the midst of these grave events, Calonne's financial embarrassments steadily increased, and the illusions of the public were at last dispelled. The shares in the last issued loan had not been taken up, and, upon the other hand, the third twentieth was just about to expire. Under pretext of embellishing the capital, Calonne attempted to open, through the city of Paris, a loan of 30,000,000, which he intended, in reality, to pour into the Treasury. He had recourse at last to smaller measures. He put a stamp on music-paper, and thought of taxing lacqueys, carriages, and other articles of luxury For 15,000 *livres* he sold to every under-sheriff the title of King's

Councillor, and talked of supplementary taxes, to be exacted from notaries, attorneys, and process-servers. It was even asserted that the Government was going to accord civil liberty to the Protestants, who offered to pay a large sum for the concession. A thousand rumours circulated, testifying to the distress of the Treasury and the embarrassments of the Government. Calonne himself did not hide his desire to be relieved of the burden of the finances by being called to another office. In December, 1786, a quantity of Edicts and Declarations establishing fresh taxes were laid before the Parliament, but the magistrates refused, in the name of the people, to register any "New Year's gifts." Thereupon, everyone expected the announcement of a "Bed of Justice." Instead, the startling and wholly unanticipated news was spread abroad that Calonne had asked from the King, and the latter had accorded him, permission to convoke an *Assembly* of *Notables*.

The Prologue of the Revolutionary Drama had begun.

CHAPTER XII.

The Assembly of Notables and the Convocation of the States-General.

(1787-1789.)

The idea of convoking the Notables had been suggested to Calonne by the desperate state of the Finances. The dishonest minister was at his wit's end. He had exhausted all resources and made use of every imaginable expedient. The same temerity that had prompted him to conduct France to her ruin now led him to fancy he could extricate her from it. After having promoted every kind of disorder and protected all sorts of abuses, he was obliged, in the end, to revert to the project of reform conceived by Necker and Turgot.

He proposed to institute throughout the entire kingdom Provincial Assemblies, which should not only make a more equal assessment of the taxes, but should prevent the numerous illegalities practised in collecting them. Among other methods of effecting the first of these reforms, he created a land-tax, to which the clergy were to be subjected in common with other landlords, and made some alterations, notably in introducing a stamp-tax, in the duties imposed on commerce. He proposed also to alienate some of the Crown domains and to reduce by 20,000,000 *livres* the annual expenses of the King's household. Louis XVI., according to his custom, adhered to the propositions of his minister. The plan adopted, means for carrying it out had to be devised. It was at this point that Calonne borrowed from the past the undreamt-of expedient of assembling the Notables. He thought, not without reason, that if he obtained the approbation of this body, he could overrule the objections of the clergy, Court, and Parliament. The Assembly, which was to be composed of 140 persons, and included

L

the most important members of the Church, the nobility, and magistracy, and the mayors of the principal towns, was to meet on the 29th of January. Calonne, who feared that his plan might arouse opposition, had kept his intentions so secret that the announcement of them surprised some of the ministers themselves and caused a sensation in Paris and throughout the country.

Whilst the ministerial journals applauded the generous initiative of a Sovereign, who "deigned to make advances to the Nation," the public could not throw off a feeling of uneasiness. The question was asked : "Does the Ministry really intend to do good, or "are these proceedings only a pretence ?" Many persons looked upon the event in the darkest light, and on 'Change there was a great fall in Royal Bonds. There were those who said that it was one of Calonne's projects to repeal the law of registration in order to prevent the Parliament's resistance to fresh imposts. And these clear-sighted ones entreated the public not to be deceived, for the Government was convoking this Assembly for the sole purpose of obtaining its adherence to fresh taxes "which it did "not dare to impose upon the Nation single-handed." It was further urged that nothing could be expected of men appointed by the ministers and influenced by them through the granting of pensions and favours.

In the midst of these uncertainties, one distinct thought was borne in upon the minds of reflective men. It was foreseen that this Assembly would bring about, by an inevitable consequence, important changes in the condition of the country and "even in "the form of the Government." Mirabeau, who was then in Berlin, wrote that the Convocation of Notables would, no doubt, soon be followed by a National Assembly. This was also the idea in the mind of Bailly, the future Mayor of Paris. Though no one could forecast the violent shocks that would be the outcome of these events, it was, at least, believed that the country was on the eve of a Revolution. Calonne sought to destroy these annoying suppositions and to dissipate all anxiety. He said publicly at Versailles that the King was too much attached to the fundamental laws of the Monarchy to dream of diminishing the authority of the Parliaments. And, by his order, there were distributed in the *cafés* and all public *rendezvous*, manuscript bulletins, in which it was stated that the King was not convoking the Notables with the view of obtaining help, either in money or taxes; his object being to submit to them a plan destined to make his people happy. This plan, so it was declared in the bulletins, was worthy of so beneficent a Monarch, and *would acquaint the country with the wisdom and superiority of the Minister of Finance.* But in spite of all contrary assurances, the Nation was persuaded that the Ministry's sole reason for having recourse to this Assembly was want of money.

On February 22nd, the Notables assembled at Versailles. After a short harangue from Louis XVI., who spoke of his love for his people, and recalled the example of Henri IV., whom he was "pleased to imitate," Calonne addressed the Assembly. He stated that the imperative circumstances augmenting the expenses had produced a deficit of 80,000,000 *livres*, and intimated that, in order to reconstitute the finances, loans must no longer be resorted to, since they aggravated the evil instead of repairing it. He declared, therefore, that the increase of taxes upon the established system was thenceforward impossible, and that, economy itself being an insufficient resource, the remedy lay in the reformation of abuses. After this he gave a sketch of his proposals, using all the artifices of rhetoric, which he so well knew how to employ, to persuade the Assembly to his way of thinking. With that audacity, which the preambles of his addresses had so often exemplified, he stated that a new era had begun for France, and the ancient formula, "*What the King wills, the law wills,*" would from that day forward be replaced by the motto, "*What the happiness of the "people demands, the King wills.*"

But, in spite of these claptrap assurances, it was evident from the first that the Government desired less to consult the Notables, than to avail itself of their consent to force upon the country some measures already determined upon. Calonne had said in his discourse that his plans, which were known to and approved by the Monarch, "had become a personal matter with his Majesty."

These words, in which he insinuated that it was the duty of the Assembly to subscribe to his projects, induced a lively altercation between himself and some of the Notables. The Assembly had been divided into seven committees, each one presided over by a prince of the blood. The minister professed to have taken this measure with the view of cutting short all questions of precedence. In reality, he thought that the princes, by their ascendancy, would be enabled to extort suffrages. The Government had counted so surely upon a favourable vote that the Edicts were all printed beforehand. It was then that the wags started the joke, thereafter reproduced under various forms, in which a farmer was reputed to ask the animals he was about to slaughter, "what "sauce they would prefer to be eaten with." A similar pleasantry was attributed to the Archbishop of Narbonne. "Monsieur de "Calonne," he said, "proposes to bleed France—already bled "several times before—and he asks the Notables for their advice "as to whether it is best to bleed her in the foot, arm, or jugular "vein." Calonne, however, did not find in the Notables that entire docility which he had flattered himself he should meet with. They consented, without resistance, to the institution of Provincial Assemblies and the suppression of feudal service. But the proposed territorial subsidies did not meet with the same favour. Though one section of the Notables highly approved of this attack on the privileged classes, others, though they dared not own it, did not. But all were, at least, agreed upon the necessity of knowing the exact amount of the deficit before voting fresh taxes, and demanded, therefore, information regarding the state of the finances. Calonne refused this information, saying that the Assembly ought to vote upon the form and not the grounds of taxation. The Notables persisted in their demands. Their contention was that the King had desired to consult free men, and some of them declared that, sooner than subscribe blindly to what was being exacted from them, they would demand the convocation of the States-General. At Court, this unexpected resistance took everybody by surprise. The public, for its part, after having made great sport of the Notables, applauded their energy, which appeared to be dictated to them by patriotism. The King, who had fully made up his mind that everything would work smoothly, did not disguise his displeasure. The princes were no less annoyed, and some of them forsook their committees for the hunting field. Calonne too had to suffer for his audacity. Already he had been forced to avow that the deficit was not 80,000,000 *livres* but 112,000,000. Shortly after this he had the effrontery to maintain that the Assembly agreed with him in regard to the principle of his project, and only differed respecting some unimportant details. This lying assertion so irritated the Notables that they accused Calonne to the King of prevaricating. The minister began, at last, to distrust the Assembly on whose support he had too readily counted, and he attempted to turn public opinion against it by distributing throughout Paris a printed leaflet, on which it was asserted that the Notables were animated by views contrary to the generous designs of the King and subversive of the people's happiness. A storm of indignant protests broke from the Notables, when they found their sentiments so cruelly misrepresented to the country. In a memorial addressed to the Monarch, they accused Calonne of appropriating considerable sums, and of making the King pay 15,000,000 *livres* for the estate of Lorient, which was not worth more than 4,000,000. The struggle became so sharp and recriminations so numerous that Louis XVI. felt really anxious.

Calonne tried to battle against the storm. Thirty-two *lettres de cachet* were prepared for those Notables whose opposition was strongest, and complaints were lodged against some of his fellow-ministers. The King dismissed the Keeper of the Seals and replaced him by Lamoignon, the Chief Justice whose bold and unscrupulous nature seemed suited for the upholding of the Prime Minister's designs. But Calonne desired besides the discharge of a minister whom the Queen favoured. Marie-Antoinette took offence, and Calonne was himself dismissed. He had but just surrendered his portfolio when some more of his misappropriations were discovered. The *Cour des Monnaies*, in examining the accounts of the *Directeur des Monnaies* (Treasury-Director) at Strasbourg, who had just been declared bankrupt, found a letter from the Comptroller-General authorising the *Directeur* to debase the specie. In face of such a revelation, Louis XVI. found it necessary to resort to severe measures. Calonne, seated at a supper-party, received a *lettre de cachet* exiling him to Lorraine.

Thus deceived by a minister in whom he had placed confidence, Louis XVI. appeared to be terribly discouraged, and was even seen to shed tears. The public, who had received the news of Calonne's disgrace with joy, now loudly demanded the recall of Necker. The Notables and even the ministers desired it. But, instead of meeting the wishes of his people, the weak Monarch bestowed his choice on a man for whom he had no liking, but who was in high favour with the Queen. This was Brienne, Archbishop of Toulouse. Though his peer in immorality, he did not share his forerunner's talents, and was more at home in a gathering of women than at the helm of public affairs. For twenty years Brienne had aimed at becoming minister, and in the Assembly of Notables had only withstood Calonne in order to replace him. He was appointed Chief of the Council of Finance, and it was understood that the new Comptroller-General, Villedeuil, would rank as his head clerk.

The financial crisis was daily becoming more acute, and on all sides bankruptcies were declared. In order to supply the most crying needs, Brienne submitted to the Parliament an Edict creating a loan of 60,000,000 *livres*, and promising a reduction in the expenses of the King's household of 40,000,000 *livres* instead of the 20,000,000 that Calonne had pledged himself to obtain. Won over by his assurances, the Parliament registered the loan. The Notables, in the meanwhile, resumed the sessions that had been interrupted by the change in the Ministry. A statement of the condition of the finances, for which they had never ceased to clamour, was at last surrendered to them. Although this statement was neither complete nor accurate, it gave indications of a deficit of 140,000,000 *livres*. The Archbishop-Minister availed himself of this discovery to urge upon the Assembly the necessity of voting the territorial subsidy and the stamp-tax. For this he was reproached with forgetting in the Ministry the doctrines he had professed in committee, and with preaching, like Calonne, "taxation and submission." Not daring to assume the responsibility of weighting the country with fresh charges, the Notables refused to vote the taxes, and demanded a yearly statement of the receipts and expenditure, and the appointment to the Financial Council of capable men outside the ministerial circle to keep watch over the money transactions. Some of the committees demanded a revision of the civil and criminal laws, and the modification of Edicts relative to the Protestants. A member, who had played a brilliant part in the war of American Independence—by name La Fayette—ventured to propose that a request should be made to the King to convoke a National Assembly in five years' time, *i.e.* in 1792. " What, sir," said the Comte d'Artois, " you ask for " the convocation of the States-General !" "Yes, Monseigneur," replied La Fayette, "and even more than that."

On the 25th of May, the Notables separated. As regards the immediate results of their labour, they left things very much as they found them. But their deliberations had, nevertheless, a far-reaching effect. They completely changed the disposition of the public. Not that the mistrust of the Government was the lessened. On the contrary, it had been fomented. The people, seeing that the Ministry had paid no regard to the wishes of the Notables, began to question the utility of the Provincial Assemblies, which they had previously so much approved. They feared that these local bodies would, in their turn, be resolved into " blind or coerced agents of the will of the reigning power." At the spectacle of the opposition and patriotism of the Notables, France felt herself re-created, and it was not long before those who considered the convocation of this Assembly to be only the prelude of greater changes, had their presumptions fully verified.

The Debates of the Notables were succeeded by those of the Parliament. That body alone, by virtue of its legal character, could give the force of the law to the projects of the Government. One Edict instituting Provincial Assemblies, and another suppressing statute-labour, were registered without opposition. After this the Parliament was called upon to pass judgment upon the stamp Edict. Then the discussions began. Calonne was denounced, and complaints made of the expenses and dissipations of the Court. At last, after debates that resembled, it is said, those of the English Parliament, the magistrates did as the Notables had done—they demanded a statement of the financial condition of the country. The King refused to grant one, and alleged that the holding of examinations of that nature was not a function of Parliaments. The magistrates reiterated their request ; the King persisted in his refusal and insisted upon an immediate registration of the stamp-tax. After the King's first response, 25 voices had been in favour of demanding the States-General, and 27 had requested the simple withdrawal of the Edict. Upon this occasion 63 voices rejected the Edict and 60 voted for the convocation of the States. Upon this the Parliament drew up some *Remonstrances,* in which it entreated the King to withdraw the Edict, and expressed a wish " to see the Nation assembled as a preamble " to all fresh taxation."

The Parliament which, until then, had been justly blamed for its indolence and servility, recovered in a moment its former popularity. In order to modify some of its provisions, the King withdrew the stamp Edict, and, without expressing himself upon the question of the States-General, forwarded to the Parliament the scheme of the territorial subsidies, and gave orders that it was to be registered without delay. By a majority of 72 votes to 48, the Parliament resolved to maintain the principles it had adopted, and a Decree was formulated declaring that the Nation alone had the right to grant subsidies, when need of them had been clearly demonstrated It further resolved to send a deputation to the Monarch to *solicit the convocation of the States-General.*

It was the month of July, 1787, and the excitement in Paris was universal. At the *Palais Royal,* in the *cafés,* everywhere people spoke only of the grave events of the day. Everyone expected a *coup d'état.* In the provinces the agitation was just as great ; all the Parliaments evinced their resolve to follow the example of the Paris magistrates. The Court party, however, was determined to prevent the convocation of the States—understanding full well that the effect of such a proceeding would be to undo in an instant the centuries of continued labour that had been devoted to the extension and consolidation of the Royal Authority. Self-deceived in regard to its own power, and ignorant of the strength of public opinion, the Government decided to employ arbitrary measures. The Parliament was commanded to attend a "Bed of Justice" at Versailles. Immediately the magistrates protested in a Decree, in which they maintained that "the con-"stitutional principle of the French Monarchy was that all taxes "must be consented to by those who had to pay them." In adhering to the taxes levied during the last few years, the magistrates declared that they had consulted their zeal rather than their legal powers, and that the excuse for their conduct lay in the fact that they had been led astray by the misrepresentations of prevaricating ministers. On August 6th the stamp and territorial subsidy Edicts were registered at Versailles. On the 7th, the magistrates issued a Decree, by which they declared the registration to be null and void. An immense crowd in the interior and vicinity of the *Palais de Justice* applauded the announcement of the Decree. Thus was open war declared at last, not—as was thought at Court—between the Ministry and the Parliament, but between the Throne and the People.

It was expected that the Ministry would immediately quash the Decrees of the Parliament and fling forth *lettres de cachet* against the magistrates. The men about the Court urged the employment of severe measures, and the Baron de Besenval told the Queen that, "It was high time for the King to show the Nation who "was master. Unless he did so," the Baron affirmed, "he might "be obliged to lay down his crown never to put it on again." The Government was irresolute, and there was division in the Council. Malesherbes, who had formed part of it since the withdrawal of Calonne, objected to forcible measures, and voted for the Appeal to the States-General. Whilst the Ministry hesitated, the excitement of the people increased. In the midst of the agitation the Government had the stamp and territorial subsidy Edicts made public, and unscrupulously declared that these new taxes had been agreed to by the Notables. The Parliament protested against the publication as it had protested against the registration, and in a Decree, dated August 13th, declared it null and void.

This time the Government resolved to act. In the night, an officer of the Guards served each member of the Parliament with an order to betake himself to Troyes within twenty-four hours. On the following day threatening placards were posted throughout Paris and at Versailles. The King's two brothers had been instructed to register the Edicts at the *Chambre des Comptes* and the *Cour des Aides*. Both of these courts, however, followed the example set by the Parliament, and passed resolutions qualifying the registration as illegal, and demanding the recall of the magistrates and the convocation of the States. Outside an anxious crowd awaited the result of their deliberations. A rumour having spread that there were some dissentients among the members of the *Cour des Aides*, about sixty persons burst into the hall where the session was being held, and asked to see the registers. "Have "confidence in the Court," said one of the councillors to them, "and respect your King."

The *Cour des Monnaies* and the *Châtelet* intervened in their turn and sent deputations; the one to the King, the other to the Keeper of the Seals, to request the recall of the Parliament. In vain did the minister have cried in the streets a regulation suppressing a considerable number of offices in the households of the King and Queen. He succeeded only in annoying the members of the Court circle. The public, who looked upon the proclamation as a falsehood made up to impose upon their credulity, would not be conciliated. The populace trembled with excitement, and an "ir-"ruption from the *faubourgs*" was prophesied. The Government feared an uprising, and had already caused all the clubs, which it looked upon as "the resorts of malcontents and grumblers," to be shut up. Military precautions were now taken, and Paris was inundated with patrols. "A very imprudent move," wrote a contemporary, testifying "that harmony no longer reigns between "the Monarch and his subjects."

Yet in the presence of this tumult the only decisive step taken by Louis XVI. was the yielding up of his authority into the hands of Brienne. The popular indignation soon spread from the capital to all corners of the kingdom. A month before, all the principal Parliaments had passed resolutions demanding the recall of the Paris magistrates, the bringing of Calonne to justice, and the convocation of the States-General.

These requisitions, simultaneously launched in all parts of the country, were so many sparks to inflame the minds of the people. In order to put an end to the threatening "confedera-"tion," some of the ministers proposed to suppress all the Parliaments, to supplant them by Superior Councils, and to transfer the registration of laws, either to the Council of State, or to Provincial Assemblies presided over by men devoted to Court interests. Among the ministers, who most vehemently urged repressive measures, was Lamoignon, Keeper of the Seals, who divined the incapacity of Brienne and secretly aspired to play the *rôle* of Chancellor Maupeou. But Brienne, preoccupied with the events then taking place in Holland and apprehending a war with England, refused to augment these home difficulties. Besides, the thought of asserting his supremacy in the eyes of the people by pacifying the Nation's anxieties flattered his vanity. He entered into a treaty with the Parliament, whereby the latter consented to extend for two years longer the second twentieth that was to have expired in 1790, and the King agreed to withdraw his Edicts. Such was the price paid by the Parliament for its release from exile. On September 24th, the Government had a Declaration cried in the streets that revoked the two much-disputed Edicts, and in that act proclaimed its own shame. "What "are we to think," the people said, "of a Government that demands "an increase of over 100,000,000 *livres* in taxes, declares such in-"crease indispensable, deals one authoritative blow after another in "order to extort it, and, in less than six weeks, revokes all previous "actions, foregoes the resources, and contents itself with a slight "extension of a tax already established?"

The Parliament, on its return to Paris, was received by the

populace with every demonstration of delight. Yet its re-installation did not cause unqualified satisfaction. It had been hoped that the prolongation of the crisis would have obliged the Government to convoke the States-General. Some ardent spirits accused the magistrates of being false to their principles, and characterised their conduct as "cowardly." At bottom—in spite of the appearance of peace—the feeling of resentment was as strong as ever, and outrageous placards, threatening the King and Queen, were still posted. The Government too continued to take precautions. The numerous patrols that gave to Paris the aspect of a position fortified against the enemy were withdrawn, but all the officers of the Guards were forbidden to quit the metropolis, and the clubs remained closed. A Decree of the Parliament, ordering an inquiry into Calonne's administration, was quashed. Everything confirmed the belief that the reconciliation of the Court and Parliament was only a "patching-up"—a fictitious peace that must soon be followed by other conflicts.

By the month of November, all fears of a war with England subsided. At the same time the financial condition of the country was as serious as ever. The extension of the second twentieth gave promise of resources, but only at a distant period. The Archbishop, not being able to resort to taxation, resolved to try another loan. He conceived the idea of starting one of 420,000,000 *livres* to be consummated in five years by successive share calls. By this means he assured himself of five years' respite. With the view of commending this gigantic loan to the public, . Brienne was obliged to promise to assemble the States-General at the expiration of the stated period, reserving to himself the right of not holding to his promise when the time came. As he intended also to pass the law, so often clamoured for, according civil rights to Protestants, he made up his mind to present both Edicts in a Royal Session, in which, though not a "Bed of Justice," he would make use of the Royal presence to compel the assent of the Parliament. This scheme being decided upon, he endeavoured by bribery and by all his powers of persuasion to create a favourable majority in the Parliament. What wonder that at this time

Mirabeau said : " What we want is a Constitution; *France is ripe* "*for Revolution.*"

On November 19th, at 9 o'clock in the morning, Louis XVI. made his appearance quite unexpectedly in the midst of the Parliament, which, as the vacation was but just finished, was composed of comparatively few members. The preceding night private notices had been addressed to all the magistrates of whose suffrages the Ministry felt sure. The Keeper of the Seals read aloud the Loan Edict, and the discussion was then opened. Several magistrates spoke energetically against granting more than one year's loan, and demanded an earlier convocation of the States-General. " Why put it off till 1792?" cried one ; "are not "the finances in a sufficiently disordered condition? The truth is, "Sire, that your ministers wish to avoid the convocation of the "States-General, because they stand in fear of surveillance. But "their hope is vain. Two years hence, the necessities of the State "will force you to convoke them." For a moment Louis XVI. was moved. He would perhaps have yielded to such forcible representations if he had not been under the influence of his ministers. The debate was still progressing when the Keeper of the Seals drew near to the Monarch and spoke to him in lowered tones. Then, turning towards the magistrates, he declared the Decrees registered after the customary formula of " Beds of Justice." A prolonged murmur issued from the Assembly at this sudden transformation of a simple Royal Session, with its privilege of free discussion, into a " Bed of Justice." The Duc d'Orléans, who was present, declared that the registration appeared to him to be illegal. Louis XVI., visibly embarrassed, hurried on the reading of the Decree relating to the Protestants. After that he rose and retired, having been nine hours in session.

Immediately after the departure of the Monarch, the Parliament signified by a Decree that it had not been concerned in the registration of the Edict. The following day, a deputation was commanded to bring the registers to Versailles, in order that the King might himself see this Decree erased, and the Duc d'Orléans and two magistrates were sent into exile. These arbitrary proceedings following hard upon the forced and almost fraudulent registrations, greatly incensed the Parliament, and its resentment was fully shared by the public.

Two days after the Royal Session, the Parliament went in grand deputation to demand of Louis XVI. complete liberty for its members and the recall of the Duc d'Orléans. In some "Suppli-"cations," presented in regard to this subject, the magistrates, in the name of the law, declared that no citizen could be condemned without being heard, and thus, in the Duc d'Orléans' case, they pleaded that of all the French. The Monarch replied that they ought not to claim from his justice that which they should only expect of his goodwill. This contemptible response only aggravated the irritation of the magistrates, who retaliated in a Decree, in which they signified that no appeal to the King's goodwill was in question, for by a step so opposed to principles of public order, they would become the accomplices of despotism. They decided too that *Remonstrances* should be addressed to the King in regard to the use of *lettres de cachet*. This last decision nearly caused the storm to burst. Louis complained that he was tired of these agitations and wished to have done with them. It was resolved to make a raid on the Parliament, to put the more recalcitrant members in prison, and to banish others to Tours or Poitiers. The French guards received the order to hold themselves in readiness to march, and *lettres de cachet* were about to be issued, when, at the last moment, Brienne hesitated. After all, the Government contented itself with summoning the Parliament to Versailles, and the King removed the minute of the Decree from the registers. "I forbid you," he said, "to carry out this Decree "or to make any similar ones in the future."

Whilst these conflicts were taking place, the provincial Parliaments, bolder or more faithful to their principles than the Parliament of Paris, refused to register the prorogation of the second twentieth, to which the latter had consented, and persisted in demanding the convocation of the States-General as a preamble to all fresh taxation. Many opposed the establishment of Provincial Assemblies, and desired, in their place, the revival of the old States-Provincial, which not only possessed the power of voting taxes, but gave surer guarantees to the country than the new Assemblies were likely to do. From divers parts of the kingdom arrived *Remonstrances* in which the Parliaments protested, in the name of outraged justice, against the exile of the Duc d'Orléans and the two magistrates. The Keeper of the Seals, who received all these communications, sent them back, without reading them, and instructed the commanding-officers of the different provinces to enforce the registration of the disputed Edicts and threaten the rebel magistrates with punishment. These ill-advised ministers, who, whilst the tide of Revolution was rising on all sides, audaciously chose the path of violence, were, at heart, full of uncertainty and weakness. As if to accentuate the feebleness of the Government, Brienne included the Queen in all committees and gave her a preponderating voice in every decision. This action discredited the Ministry and intensified the people's hatred of Marie-Antoinette.

The year 1788 opened in the midst of these events. The crisis was appalling and the alarm general. The price of the Royal Bonds went down daily, and the payment of annuities fell off. In spite of all statements to the contrary, made by ministerial agents, the loan was not covered. The feeling against the Court was widespread—it was both hated and despised. The idea of the prompt convocation of the States General gained ground, and bills posted in various parts of Paris threatened a general revolt, if they were not summoned with the least possible delay. Other placards bore the words: "Kings have received their power from "the people only that they may protect the laws; they have no "authority to go beyond them." The spirit of revolt gained even the Court, and young nobles held the "most seditious" conversations in the King's ante-chamber. It was felt that the old *régime* was foundering, and a new one starting into existence. In January, 1788, the Parliament registered the Edict that restored to the Protestants their civil status. Granted in the midst of political reforms, this precious victory of the spirit of Tolerance, for which Philosophy had laboured throughout half a century, passed almost unperceived.

The Parliament had presented to the King *Remonstrances*—previously resolved upon—in which they formally demanded the abolition of *lettres de cachet.* "Sire," so ran these *Remonstrances*, "*Liberty is not a privilege, it is a right*; and the duty of "all Governments is to respect that right."

In the months of February and March, the one subject of conversation in the *cafés* and in all public places, was the coming *coup d'état.* All the ministers were at last agreed upon the necessity of overthrowing the magistracy. They did not see that behind the magistracy an oppressed Nation trembled. Yet, though the public mind was so greatly stirred, no one was very much alarmed. The people felt that they were on the eve of a great National Revolution, and were persuaded that, in spite of all its subterfuges, the Government would, in the end, be constrained to convoke the States-General, so that, even if the Parliaments were overturned, the States would be able "to raise a solid barrier "between the pretensions of the throne and the rights of the people." Mirabeau, writing to Montmorin, deplored "this terrible malady "of ministers of never being able to make up their minds to grant "to-day what would be infallibly snatched from them to-morrow." Though the subject of so many disturbances and alarms, the Parliament, far from giving way, displayed every day more firmness. To the *Remonstrances* which it presented to the King on the subject of the forced registration of the loan of 420,000,000 *livres,* Louis XVI. replied that, having assisted at the deliberations, it was not incumbent on him to take into account the actual number of suffrages. "If a majority in my courts could overrule my "will," he said, "the Monarchy would be only an *aristocracy of* "*magistrates.*" The Parliament defended itself with wisdom and dignity, "What a moment your ministers have chosen to bring "such an accusation against us! The one in which the Parliament, "enlightened by facts and retracing its former steps, is proving that "it is more attached to the rights of the Nation than to its own in-"terests, the moment in which, suddenly informed of the state of "the finances, it sees only one refuge for the Nation—the Nation it-"self, and therefore demands the States-General. Kings are but

" men and fallible ; and it is in order that the Nation shall not be
" abandoned to the baleful effects of sudden caprices, that the Con-
" stitution requires in the matter of laws the verification of the
" courts, and in the matter of subsidies, the previous consent of the
" States-General. The right of freely granting subsidies does not
" any more make of the States-General an aristocracy of citizens
" than the right of verification makes of the Parliaments an aris-
" tocracy of magistrates."

The agitated state of Paris and the provinces only served
to make the approach of some great stroke of policy more and
more believed in. Towards the end of April, it was known that
all the governors, commanding-officers, and intendants of provinces
had received orders to report themselves at their posts. Regi-
ments were mustered in all parts of the country, and the friends
of authority were uplifted with a sense of triumph. Councillors
of State, bearing ministerial instructions, started for all the large
towns, and twenty journeymen printers, summoned to Versailles,
worked night and day in the greatest secrecy, guarded by soldiers.
The King said aloud that he was tired of being in *bourgeois*
tutelage and meant to free himself from it. On May 3rd, he held
a review of all the troops assembled in Paris. This was looked
upon as another sign of the approaching stroke.

The same day, the Parliament passed a " fulminating " resolution, recounting the fundamental principles of the monarchial
constitution, and declaring that, in case the employment of force
should render it impossible for it to maintain those principles, it
delegated the sacred trust to the King, the States-General, and
every class—united or separate—that went to make up the
Nation.

On the morning of May 5th, the whole *Palais de Justice* was in
an uproar. The magistrates had just learnt that, on the preceding
night, an attempt had been made to carry off two of their colleagues.
Both of these had fled for refuge to the *Palais*. The Parliament
immediately sent off deputies to carry a complaint to the King, and
remained in session, during the whole day, awaiting their return.
Night came and nothing was seen of the deputies. Suddenly they

were informed that detachments of Swiss and French guards had invested the *Palais*. A captain of the guards presented himself to arrest the two members. Not knowing them, he asked to have them pointed out : "We are all Messieurs d'Esprémenil and Goislard !" replied the Assembly with one voice. The officer retired. At three o'clock in the morning, the deputies returned and announced that the Monarch had refused to receive them. This intelligence increased the anxiety. At last the officer re-appeared, provided with more urgent orders. The two then gave themselves up in the midst of general excitement, and the Parliament separated after a session of over 30 hours, stoutly protesting against the seizure of the two members, " violently torn " from the sanctuary of the laws."

On the 8th of May, the magistrates were summoned to a " Bed " of Justice" at Versailles. There, Louis XVI. announced to them his intention of restoring public tranquillity by converting that moment of crisis into a salutary epoch for France. Thereupon the Keeper of the Seals read aloud six Edicts that the King was about to promulgate. The *first* instituted, under the title of " Grand Bailiwicks," new courts of justice to deal with all minor civil and criminal affairs, and left to the Parliaments only the cognizance of civil actions having regard to sums over 20,000 *livres*, and criminal cases concerning the clergy and nobles alone. A *second* Edict—a sequel of the first—reduced the number of the magistrates of the different Parliaments, and retained of the Paris Parliament only the Grand Chamber and the Chamber of Enquiries (*chambre des enquêtes*). The *third* Edict, in which the King tried to cloak his attacks on the magistracy by certain reforms, suppressed all extraordinary tribunals : another abolished the *sellette*[1] and preliminary question.[1] By the *fifth* and most important of all, a single body was appointed to verify and register all laws of the kingdom. This body—called the Plenary Court—was to be composed of the Chancellor, of the Keeper of the Seals, of the Grand Chamber of the Paris Parliament (which included the

---

[1] Two antiquated methods of examining accused parties in Courts of Law. (*Translator's Note.*)

princes and peers), of the great officers of the Crown, the various dignitaries of the Church and Army, and a certain number of members chosen by the Council of State and the Parliaments of the provinces. The privilege of remonstrance was attributed to it, but the King reserved the right of dictating his orders in "Beds of Justice." The Monarch also retained the privilege of creating loans by his own authority without submitting them to any process of verification. "In the event," he was made to say, "of our being obliged to levy fresh taxes before the assembling "of the States-General, the registry of the said taxes by our Plenary "Court will have only a provisional effect until the assembling of " the said States, which we shall convoke, in order that these regis- "trations may, upon their deliberations, be definitely decreed by "us." Finally, a *sixth* Edict laid all the Parliaments under an inhibition of an indefinite nature, which forbade them, until fur- ther orders, to assemble for the transaction of any business, public or private.

Among all these reckless changes there was, at least, one wise alteration, that of entrusting a single court with the registration of the laws, and of separating it from the courts of justice. But, on account of its composition and limited powers, this court had, in fact, neither authority nor independence. France saw this clearly enough. She saw also that these Edicts of May 8th had but one object, that of leaving her disarmed against the onsets of absolute authority. The sole allusion made in these Edicts to the States-General betrayed the intention of the Ministry to evade its promises or to reduce that Assembly to a mere sham. The Govern- ment must have been blind indeed not to see that these new laws would create a general feeling of resistance. The opposition began at the " Bed of Justice " when the President protested against the despotic authority of the Crown, which, he said, the French Nation would never acknowledge. On coming away from the "Bed of "Justice," the members of the Grand Chamber wrote to the King to decline the functions conferred upon them by the Edicts. Con- voked upon the following day for the first session of the Plenary Court, they renewed their protestations. At this first session,

Louis XVI. asserted that he should persist in having his own way, but he did not dare to convoke the Grand Chamber a second time. The same day, all the other members of the Parliament returned to Paris and at once assembled to frame an Act of protestation. Finding the *Palais de Justice* occupied by soldiers, they retired to the houses of the senior members of the various Chambers, and each magistrate wrote individually to the Prime Minister, that he "ought not to and could not" give his adhesion to the Edicts that had just been promulgated.

The provincial Parliaments did not wait to have the laws presented to them, before they pronounced against them. On May 5th, 86 members of the Rouen Parliament pledged themselves by an oath not to lend themselves directly or indirectly to the execution of any Edicts or Declarations that attacked the *sacred principle of free* registration. The Parliament of Nancy passed a similar resolution. The protests that followed the promulgation of the Edicts were even more energetic. The Parliament of Grenoble rejected the new laws in the name of the rights of the Nation that were no less sacred than those of the Sovereign. In Brittany, the "States" joined their expostulations to those of the Rennes Parliament, and the nobility of Dauphiné passed a resolution by which they declared that if the Crown did not renounce its illegal proceedings, the province would revert to its right of self-government, and the son of the Sovereign cease to bear the title of Dauphin. At Toulouse, the Parliament had the temerity to make the following threatening declaration : "The people "having no longer any barrier between them and the King, *nothing* "*is left them but the consciousness of their strength.*"

In Paris the first feeling was one of despondency and consternation. Certain friends of liberty, indeed, were astonished to see the people so torpid. La Fayette wrote to Washington : "Dying "for liberty is not the custom on this side of the Atlantic." Soon, however, seditious remarks, threatening placards, and tumultuous gatherings showed that the people were warming up. The members of the legal profession solemnly burned a Decree of Council that had quashed the Parliamentary Resolution of May 3rd, and the new Edicts having deprived the *Châtelet* of its jurisdiction, that court refused to register them, but was at last constrained to do so at the point of the bayonet. Already the *Chambre des Comptes* and *Cour des Aides* had been suspended for rebelling against the Edicts. On the walls of the *Palais*, which had been transformed into barracks, placards were posted bearing the words: "*Palais* to "sell! Ministers to hang! A Crown to be given away!" Brochures poured forth on every side. At the *Comédie Française* the *parterre* had such a rage for political allusions, that it was impossible to decide upon a piece. Even at Court there was resistance. A letter of protest, signed by six peers of the realm, was presented to the Monarch. Not only was the abolition of the Parliaments followed by the interruption of the course of justice in Paris and the provinces, but the collection of taxes was everywhere stopped. The Royal Bonds were no longer saleable, and private individuals could not fulfil their engagements. Civil life seemed to be suspended.

The minister, however, did not draw back, but availed himself of every authoritative and intimidating measure that could be suggested to him. The new Edicts were cried aloud in the streets, and it was affirmed in the newspapers that they had the approbation of the country. The protests of the Parliament were quashed by a Decree of Council that was drawn up in the form of a manifesto and placarded throughout France. In this Decree the magistrates' resistance was stigmatised as an infringement of the laws. The public was inundated by an infinity of brochures that emanated from the office of the Keeper of the Seals. The police of the capital were all kept on duty, and frequent arrests were made. *Lettres de cachet* were issued against the provincial Parliaments, and troops mustered in all the towns where they assembled. Collisions took place and blood was spilt. Twelve gentlemen of Brittany, who came to Versailles to prefer some requests to the King, were thrown into the Bastille. But these measures of excessive severity only stirred up renewed resistance. At Pau the excited populace constrained the magistrates to resume their seats. At Grenoble a number of citizens of the three orders met in the

Town Hall and decided that the States of Dauphiné, which had been suppressed by the Crown for a century and a half, should spontaneously reconstitute themselves. On all sides the people were arming. Won over in their turn by the general excitement, defections took place among the troops. Private soldiers threw down their arms and officers sent in their resignations. In Paris still more serious disturbances were feared. Popular movements took place, not only in the suburbs, but in the heart of the city, and leaflets were distributed which bore the words: "Awake! "Frenchmen: it has come, the epoch of this Revolution that will "determine the regrets or the admiration of posterity, according to "whether we leave our sons slavery or liberty!" The placards, which increased in numbers every day, became every day more threatening. One placed on the front of the Queen's box at the Italian Opera was worded: "Tremble, tyrants; your reign is ending." The smallest incident sufficed to provoke an explosion.

Brienne had flattered himself that, at least, the Episcopate would support him with its assent and aid him with subsidies. On the very day of the "Bed of Justice," he convoked the clergy to a General Assembly and asked them for 8,000,000 *livres*. The bishops accorded him only a "free gift" payable in two years of 1,800,000 *livres*. Far from being disposed to make the sacrifices that he expected of them, they complained that his fiscal agents wished to levy the twentieth taxes on ecclesiastical possessions, and Louis XVI. was obliged to dispel their alarms by a Decree of Council that certified that the clergy were not subject to taxation.

But the bishops, in spite of the King's word, mistrusted the enterprises of an uncontrolled power and protested against the destruction of the Parliaments and the establishment of the Plenary Court. They declared, as emphatically as the sincerest lovers of liberty might have done, that "the people of France were "not taxable at will," and they demanded the convocation, with the least possible delay, of the States-General. No less blind than the Court had been, the clergy, thinking to safeguard their own interests, actually clamoured for the Revolution.

The Archbishop-Minister was overwhelmed by these remonstrances. He had exhausted all rigorous measures, and had not shrunk from the spilling of blood. Deserted by the clergy, disobeyed by the army, attacked by the Parliaments, and all the sovereign courts, and hated by the Nation, he understood at last, well enough, that he must yield. But he did not, at once, lay down his arms, hoping that some unforeseen event might yet save him. On July 5th he published a Decree of Council, that invited all Provincial Assemblies, Municipalities, Academies, and private individuals to communicate to the minister all the information they could discover in regard to the convocation, composition, and holding of States-Generals. Among certain sections of the public this invitation was looked upon as a sop to Cerberus; especially as no date was fixed for the assembling of the States. By turning people's minds to this subject, Brienne thought, no doubt, that he could create a diversion. But he succeeded only in plunging the country into a fresh state of ferment. In the meantime, on the 8th of August, the King, by Decree of Council, suspended the Plenary Court and convoked the States-General for May 1st, 1789.

The publication of this Decree filled the public mind with the most sanguine expectations. Nevertheless, no gratitude was felt towards the Government for the concession that only necessity or fear had succeeded in wringing from it. Yet, great as was the hatred already felt for him, Brienne was about to increase it. Deprived of the subsidies he had expected from the clergy, and nearly at the end of his resources, he drew upon the poor relief funds, and unscrupulously seized money intended for the hospitals. But, even these expedients failed him at last, and he was obliged to declare bankruptcy. On August 16th he issued a Decree of Council, by the terms of which the State payments were to be suspended for six weeks and were thereafter until December 30th, 1789, to be effected partly in specie and partly in paper. The maledictions of the public came down upon him "like a deluge." A portion of the Court circle abandoned him, and the Queen, with many tears, agreed to the necessity of dismissing her favourite.

On the 25th of August, Brienne at last tendered his resignation. At the news of it Paris underwent a sudden transition from a state of despair and rage to one of the intoxication of joy. The Archbishop was burned in effigy in the *Place Dauphine*, and the mob did not wait till Lamoignon, the Keeper of the Seals, had quitted the Ministry to inflict the same mark of infamy on him.

On the morrow of the departure of Brienne, Necker re-entered the Council, and at once purses that had been shut to the Archbishop were opened for the man of business, who generously gave his own fortune as a guarantee for the advances made to the State. One of Necker's earliest acts was to revoke the Decree of bankruptcy. Without taking any extraordinary measures, but simply by the effect of the confidence he inspired, he found means to provide for the more urgent necessities of the Treasury. Understanding what France expected of him, he recalled all the exiles, repealed the six Edicts promulgated on May 8th, and by a Declaration, dated September 23rd, restored to their seats the Parliaments and all the sovereign courts. The following day the members of the Paris Parliament presented themselves at the *Palais* to resume their interrupted sittings, and had great difficulty in squeezing their way in through the "prodigious multi-"tude" of men of all degrees, who came to salute and applaud them. At their first sitting, they proposed to bring an accusation against the Keeper of the Seals and the Prime Minister and demanded that the *responsibility of ministers* should thenceforward be an admitted principle of government. In the provinces, the return of the Parliaments was an occasion for still more striking demonstrations than those that had taken place in Paris. In the Declaration of September 23rd, the King not only reinstalled the sovereign courts, but advanced the date of the assembling of the States-General, fixing it for January 1st, 1789. The Declaration was registered by the Parliament on September 23rd, and cried in the streets of Paris on the 26th. This time the King's promise was believed, for the people had, as guarantee, the word of an honest man.

.   .   .   .

Thenceforward the drawing up of *cahiers*, the election of deputies, and discussions as to the best modes of representation, became the paramount interests of the country. During this period of intense anxiety Necker, by his wise financial administration, enabled France to live, and that achievement may be counted the chief glory of his second administration.

In the Declaration of September 23rd, Royalty avowed itself vanquished in its last combat. Condemned since the *coup d'état* of 1771, the Monarchy was then sentenced with death. This Declaration, which convoked the States-General and frustrated the attempts of May 8th, dealt a final blow at the old *régime*, and ushered in the Revolution; the Revolution that Louis XIV. prepared by his intolerance, Louis XV. fomented by the disorders and degradations of his reign, and Louis XVI. consummated by his weakness; the Revolution—born on the domain of Religion and transferred to that of Politics—that had, during a century or more, been the secret inspiration of the Philosophical Teachings. Upon several occasions—in 1754, 1757, and 1771—it had failed to break out, but it presented itself at last, dominant and irresistible, at the door opened to it by a self-dishonouring Power. The product of the thoughts and sufferings of several generations, the *cahiers* testified how—according to the words of Mirabeau—France was *ripe for Revolution*. They revealed, too, the profound abyss that yawned between the Nation and the Government that pretended to rule over it.

Some slight attempts were subsequently made to throw obstacles in the path of this victorious Revolution, but they were not put forth by the powerless and all but inanimate Royal Family. They originated entirely with the privileged classes, who sheltered themselves behind the Reigning House, as during long ages they had lived upon its life. These classes saw, with dismay, that they also were lost, and that a whole order of things that had nothing in common with the past was advancing swiftly. For seeming to support their cause, the Parliament suddenly lost its popularity. The Nation ungratefully forgot that it

N

was the Parliament that had demanded the States-General, and, in spite of errors and failings, the Parliament that had been during the entire century the buckler of France against the aggressive despotism of Church and King. The States-General left it no part to play. By the simple fact of their convocation, it was overthrown as a political institution, and, in its fall, it dragged down the ancient magistracy.

The Revolution replied to the last feeble adversaries confronting it by the mouthpiece of thousands of writers, who were the heralds of the new *régime*, and whose brochures succeeded each other with such rapidity that they became, in a few months, as numerous as those that the Bull Unigenitus had called forth. "You "are 200,000," cried the people on all sides to the privileged classes, "and we are 25,000,000. And you ask us what the French Nation "is without you! Look at our fields, our workshops, our counting-"houses, our ports, our fleets, our armies, our tribunals, our "academies, and tell us whether, without you, the people of France "are of any account!" The voice of Sièyes, who proclaimed that the third estate had been nothing in political life, while it ought to be everything, was the clarion call, at sound of which all that remained of the France of the past gave way.

Thenceforward, from behind the crumbling ruins of the Church, the wreck of the Throne, the battered walls of the Parliament, and the *débris* of Privilege, shone forth in full effulgence the light of the *Nation*,—the Light, that had been looked for since the morrow of the death of Louis XIV., but which, until this crisis, had been shadowed and obscured.

THE END.

Printed by Cowan & Co., Limited, Perth.

SOCIAL SCIENCE SERIES.

SCARLET CLOTH, EACH 2s. 6d.

SOCIAL SCIENCE SERIES—(Continued).

SOCIAL SCIENCE SERIES—*(Continued)*.

45. **Poverty : Its Genesis and Exodus.**   J. G. GODARD.
    " He states the problems with great force and clearness."—*N. B. Economist.*
46. **The Trade Policy of Imperial Federation.**   MAURICE H. HERVEY.
    " An interesting contribution to the discussion."—*Publishers' Circular.*
47. **The Dawn of Radicalism.**   J. BOWLES DALY, LL.D.
    "Forms an admirable picture of an epoch more pregnant, perhaps, with political
    instruction than any other in the world's history."—*Daily Telegraph.*
48. **The Destitute Alien in Great Britain.** ARNOLD WHITE.; MONTAGUE
    CRACKANTHORPE, Q.C. ; W. A. M'ARTHUR, M.P. ; W. H. WILKINS, &c.
    " Much valuable information concerning a burning question of the day."—*Times.*
49. **Illegitimacy and the Influence of Seasons on Conduct.**
                                                ALBERT LEFFINGWELL, M.D.
    " We have not often seen a work based on statistics which is more continuously
    interesting."—*Westminster Review.*
50. **Commercial Crises of the Nineteenth Century.**   H. M. HYNDMAN.
    " One of the best and most permanently useful volumes of the Series."—*Literary
    Opinion.*
51. **The State and Pensions in Old Age.** J. A SPENDER and ARTHUR ACLAND, M.P.
    " A careful and cautious examination of the question."—*Times.*
52. **The Fallacy of Saving.**   JOHN M. ROBERTSON.
    " A plea for the reorganisation of our social and industrial system."—*Speaker.*
53. **The Irish Peasant.**   ANON.
    " A real contribution to the Irish Problem by a close, patient and dispassionate
    investigator."—*Daily Chronicle.*
54. **The Effects of Machinery on Wages.**   Prof. J. S. NICHOLSON, D.Sc.
    " Ably reasoned, clearly stated, impartially written."—*Literary World.*
55. **The Social Horizon.**   ANON.
    " A really admirable little book, bright, clear, and unconventional."—*Daily
    Chronicle.*
56. **Socialism, Utopian and Scientific.**   FREDERICK ENGELS.
    " The body of the book is still fresh and striking."—*Daily Chronicle.*
57. **Land Nationalisation.**   A. R. WALLACE.
    " The most instructive and convincing of the popular works on the subject."—
    National Reformer.
58. **The Ethic of Usury and Interest.**   Rev. W. BLISSARD
    " The work is marked by genuine ability."—*North British Agriculturalist.*
59. **The Emancipation of Women.**   ADELE CREPAZ.
    " By far the most comprehensive, luminous, and penetrating work on this question
    that I have yet met with."—*Extract from Mr.* GLADSTONE's *Preface.*
60. **The Eight Hours' Question.**   JOHN M. ROBERTSON.
    " A very cogent and sustained argument on what is at present the unpopular
    side."—*Times.*
61. **Drunkenness.**   GEORGE R. WILSON, M.B.
    " Well written, carefully reasoned, free from cant, and full of sound sense."—
    National Observer.
62 **The New Reformation.**   RAMSDEN BALMFORTH.
    " A striking presentation of the nascent religion, how best to realize the personal
    and social ideal."—*Westminster Review.*
63. **The Agricultural Labourer.**   T. E. KEBBEL.
    " A short summary of his position, with appendices on wages, education, allot-
    ments, etc., etc."
64. **Ferdinand Lassalle as a Social Reformer.**   E. BERNSTEIN.
    " A worthy addition to the Social Science Series "—*North British Economist.*
65. **England's Foreign Trade in XIXth Century.**   A. L. BOWLEY.
    " Full of valuable information, carefully compiled."—*Times.*
66. **Theory and Policy of Labour Protection.**   Dr. SCHÄFFLE.
    " An attempt to systematize a conservative programme of reform."—*Man. Guard.*
67. **History of Rochdale Pioneers.**   G. J. HOLYOAKE.
    " Brought down from 1844 to the Rochdale Congress of 1892."—*Co-Op. News.*
68. **Rights of Women.**   M. OSTRAGORSKI.
    " An admirable storehouse of precedents, conveniently arranged."—*Daily Chron.*
69. **Dwellings of the People.**   LOCKE WORTHINGTON.
    " A valuable contribution to one of the most pressing problems of the day."—
    Daily Chronicle.

SOCIAL SCIENCE SERIES—(Continued).

SWAN SONNENSCHEIN & CO. LIM., LONDON
NEW YORK: CHARLES SCRIBNER'S SONS.

www.ingramcontent.com/pod-product-compliance
Lightning Source LLC
Chambersburg PA
CBHW030539040726
47497CB00008B/2513